FIGHTING QUIET

FIGHTING QUIET

Dana Hoff

ISBN 978-1-7334411-3-1 (E-book)
ISBN 978-1-7334411-4-8 (Paperback)
ISBN 978-1-7334411-5-5 (Hardback)

Front Cover Design by Pintado.
Developmental and Copy Editing by One Love Editing.
Interior Design by Pressbooks.

Printed by Ingram Spark in the United States of America.

First printing edition 2021.

Dana Hoff
Wentzville, Missouri

danahoffauthor.wixsite.com/books

To the quiet ones.

CHAPTER ONE

He was drunk again. His belligerent screams shook the house as he stomped across the kitchen looking for us. Looking for me. I shivered under my covers as something loud crashed downstairs. I prayed that it was Frank's head, smashing into something hard and lethal, and he wouldn't wake back up. *Ever.* But I knew it was the dinner I had left him before I went to bed. The pathetic assortment of stale chips and expired lunch meat. He hadn't gotten groceries in a few weeks, and it was all that was left besides the bottle of whiskey he nursed on the bad nights. Bad nights like tonight. Jason and I had eaten the moldy parts for ourselves, trying to leave the rest for him. But as I plated the chips and meat, I knew it wouldn't be enough. Nothing was ever enough. My stomach groaned loudly, aching and begging for food. I quickly tried to stifle the sounds with my blanket, but my body couldn't handle the last few weeks of blatant malnutrition. My eyes stung as I blinked away a stray tear. I was so hungry, and yet so nauseous I couldn't tell whether I wanted to eat or puke.

"*Where the fuck are you, you little bitch?*" His voice rattled up the staircase. My cue to hide. It was never good when he found us. Sometimes he was so drunk that he never made it up the stairs. But that was only sometimes. And the way his footsteps hammered across the floor, uncoordinated and lazy as they were, it would only be a matter of time before he'd find me and hurt me. My heart dropped as the distinct sound of the first step creaked, mixing with another loud groan from my stomach.

Come on. Get out of bed and hide!

"You better hope I don't find you..." he taunted in a slurred singsong as his heavy footfalls sounded on the second step. That was enough to get me going. I quickly slid out of bed and tiptoed to the closet, careful not to make a sound.

Quiet. *Be quiet.*

I could hear the sloshing of his whiskey hitting the hardwood as he climbed the stairs, inching closer. He was faster than normal, his steps more controlled and intentional as his heavy work boots hit each step. That meant he would hit harder, and his aim would be unfortunately accurate. I made it to my closet when a clammy hand closed around my wrist. Before I could scream, another hand found its way up to my mouth, clamping down. My back hit a hard chest as small steady breaths blew against my neck.

"It's just me, Maddie. It's okay."

Relief spilled over me as Jason's soft, soothing voice covered me. Protected me. Even as our foster father's drunken, hateful spews bounced off the walls outside my room, I felt safe. Jason was here now. He quickly pushed me into the closet and huddled in with me, closing the door, careful not to make any sounds.

We listened intently as his footsteps continued to ascend the stairs, but all I could hear was the pounding in my chest.

"I work all day..." he huffed, slowing as he neared the top of the stairs. "Just to feed you little shits, and *this is how you repay me?*" His voice boomed, and Jason pulled me under him, shielding me from the darkness that crept closer. Jason always knew how to keep me safe. On nights like these, he'd do everything he could to hide me before the inevitable beating would come. And when he'd find us, he always took the brunt of it, hoping to wear Frank out before he got to me. Jason was strong like that. So much stronger than any kid I'd ever met. He was only nine, just two years older than me, and rail thin like I was. But somehow, despite his age, his spirit could fill the entire room. Somehow, he made everything okay again even when the world around us was crumbling. I remember the first time I'd seen him the night I arrived at this godforsaken house. The overly happy social worker had knelt down and pointed at my new foster brother.

"And this is Jason!" she'd cooed, her high-pitched voice piercing my ears. I had just lost my parents a week ago from a car accident. They had run out to get groceries while I stayed with the neighbor. Groceries, and then gone, simple and tragic as that. And then it was just me. I sometimes figured that was why Frank seldom got groceries. Because he might be killed in a random crash like my parents. But I came to know better.

In that week alone, I had seen more faces than I ever cared to see again. A sea of strangers and strange places. Sleeping on beds that weren't mine, and wishing I could smell my mother's perfume, when all that smothered my senses anymore was the stench of other people's sweat and pity. Now, here I was in a new house, with a kid staring me down like he wanted to kill me. And I silently wished he would. I hated this new place, and these new smells. I hated this world without my parents and my house. I missed my before. Where Sundays were together, and the laundry was clean, and my parents were safe and alive. Certainly not here, with a strange musty stench coming from upstairs while a bizarre boy scowled at me like I was a piece of trash. Like I was unwanted. Jason's eyes had flashed dangerously at me, his lips twisting at the corners of his mouth like he wanted to tell her to take me somewhere else. At first, I thought he was actually going to tell her that, before he ran out the back door without a word. He hadn't even bothered to say "hi" or "fuck you."

"Looks like they'll just be two peas in a pod!" she'd laughed, turning her attention to my new dad.

"And this—" She'd gestured toward the tall, broad-shouldered man in front of me. "—is Frank."

Frank had politely extended his hand out to me, his green eyes bright and kind. I remember the way my hand had disappeared in his, and the way his callouses scraped against my palm. Just like my dad's. And for a second, I felt a sense of relief that maybe things could be like before. But I learned very quickly that there's only a before and an after. The pieces don't always fit back together when they break, especially if some of them are missing.

Jason's unwarranted hatred toward me had only lasted until my social worker had left. And by then I had escaped upstairs into my bedroom to begin the ultimate pity party. I had gotten well into my first round of sobs and had even begun plotting out my escape route when his shaggy head peeked in my room.

"Do you want to see my castle?" he had asked, his smile big and playful, like he hadn't just acted like a dang fool earlier. I wiped away the string of tears crawling down my cheek and frowned at him. Was he for real right now? I huffed, annoyed he was interrupting my escape plan and the fact he wasn't showing any signs of apologizing from earlier. I almost yelled at him to leave, but the way his face lit up intrigued me. He said there was a castle. And if there was even a chance of truth at that, I wanted in. His features were humble and maybe even guilty as he watched another tear fall.

"It's just outside, if you want to see it." He gestured toward the window where a tall tree stared back. My gaze darted from the window to him, his shoulders sagging like an apologetic dog. I suppose this was his peace offering. And right then, I think that was what I wanted most of all. Peace. I sniffed, pulling my shoulders back and headed over to the window, making sure I didn't get too close to him, and peered out at the yard. Disappointment flooded through me at the less than exciting scene below. Boring brown-yellowed grass lined with overgrown weeds scattered the lawn. There were no toys, no chairs, and certainly no castle.

"I don't see a castle," I sighed, doing my best to match the ugly scowl he'd given me earlier. But it clearly didn't do its job, because his face broke into an earth-shattering smile I simply wasn't prepared for. He shook his head, his black hair getting in his eyes.

"No, look again." He pointed insistently at the tree, his brown eyes sparkling and hopeful. I blinked at him, trying to see if maybe this was his way of distracting me while he did something mean. I couldn't read him, and I wasn't sure what to expect from all his mixed messages. One minute he was looking at me like I was the scum of the earth, and the next, his face was nearly glowing with reverence, as if I was an angel. *His* angel. I sucked on my bottom lip as I surveyed him, waiting for that terrifying scowl to come out again. For him to push me or scare me like some of the boys did at school. But he didn't; his smile just grew wider as he gestured toward the window again.

"Fine," I huffed as I pressed my nose to the glass, wishing hard that there was a castle. But no such luck as the tree continued to tower over us, unchanging.

"Oops, I forgot to sprinkle the magic dust." He shook his head and rolled his eyes as if he couldn't believe his forgetfulness. He reached into his pocket and pinched nothing but air in between his fingers. I watched unimpressed as he threw his "dust" against the window and stood back proudly, waving his hand as if it had worked.

"*Now* do you see it?"

I stared blankly at the tree, still as treelike as ever, no magical kingdom in sight. I turned back to confirm yet again that there was still no castle but stopped short as I caught his expression. It was pleading. No, *begging* for me to see what he saw. His smile was frozen and painted on as if one more denial would break him. And even though he had humiliated me earlier, and wasn't showing any signs of saying sorry, I wanted no part in breaking this boy in front of me.

I quickly nodded, breaking out my first attempt of a smile since my parents died. "Ah, I think I see it now…" I had said, pointing at the tree. His smile widened, relief crashing over his face in grateful waves. And I learned very quickly that I craved a little piece of fantasy in my own rocked-over world. Probably just like Jason had. We both needed that castle, and so there it was, tall and immaculate, standing where the tree stood moments before.

"Only those that are pure of heart can see it." His face fell and my heart constricted at the sadness behind his eyes. "Frank can't see it. So this is where we go when we want to be safe." His words were heavy and cryptic. I didn't understand them, and I didn't understand why my stomach sank as I replayed them over later that night in bed. But I didn't dwell too much on those things, because when your parents are gone and all you have left are the little moments, you focus on the good ones. I was ecstatic that Jason was willing to share his secret kingdom with me. And soon it became *ours*. We spent almost every summer night ruling our kingdom, dancing with the fireflies and making wishes under the moon. With Jason, I was strong and powerful. I could fight off trolls and tame dragons. I could entertain our guests at the royal ball and sing songs to heal the sick villagers. With Jason, I was a princess, and he was a prince. And for a little bit, I savored the happily ever after that followed my tragic before.

But the weeks went by, and the weather got colder, just like Frank's eyes. And I started to long for my before again. Though Jason and I had thrived in our magic, all good stories must come to an end. Frank's once kind smile seemed forced and faded whenever he was home, which was rare. So Jason and I were left alone to fend for ourselves. We washed the clothes, cleaned the house, and made sure that everything was taken care of before Frank came home. Jason was very particular about how things were to be folded and hung up. He would often refold the clothes I had done, his hands careful and precise. I'd never seen a kid so obsessive over household chores, but I also never saw kids do this much around the house to begin with.

"How come you always fold my clothes again?" I'd asked as I watched Jason redo one of the shirts I had just laid down. He froze and sucked on his cheek before he slowly shifted his gaze to meet mine. I flinched at the pain behind his eyes, the same pain I'd seen the first day we'd met after he explained that Frank couldn't see our castle.

"I've got to keep my princess safe," he'd whispered and dropped his eyes back to his work, more determined than ever with each crease and fold. Sometimes it felt like he spoke in another language that only he knew. Everything he said had a hidden meaning that I was too scared to decipher. I didn't understand how refolded laundry could keep me safe. Or how the Cheerios and water we'd been having every night was supposed to be enough for both of us. How could we fight off the dragon with empty stomachs? When Frank started to come home more often, I started to fit the pieces together. And when it was time for bed, Jason would take my hand and lead me upstairs, tuck me in, and kiss me on the forehead.

"Say your prayers and stay quiet, Maddie. We can't wake the dragon, okay?" he'd always warned before going to bed. I always thought that monsters only existed in our kingdom outside, and they stayed there for us to slay the next day. But fantasies sometimes twist with reality, and finally I understood what Jason had been trying to tell me.

I'll never forget the first time I heard the sound of Frank's fists pounding into Jason's flesh over the milk being left out. The milk that *I* had left out. I screamed the whole time as his hands flew, smashing into Jason's beautiful face. But Jason never made a sound. No crying or begging as I whimpered in the corner. Just silence. Instead, he'd just look at me, his dark eyes urgent for me to stay away and out of sight. And as Frank's evil green eyes practically glowed from the light of the moon, and his scaly hands hurt my prince, I learned that dragons don't just terrorize kingdoms. They can sleep down the hall in a musty old house too.

I jumped as the sound of glass breaking shattered outside my door, bringing me back to the nightmare I was living. *Glass.* Frank just finished the bottle of whiskey.

"You'd better tell me where you are, or—"

My stomach growled again betrayingly as I fought the urge to vomit up my disgusting excuse for a dinner. I squeezed my eyes shut, as if that would make the noises stop and I would be less hungry, less terrified. I felt Jason's body tense against me in defeat as a loud snarl of laughter ripped across my room. A series of footsteps pounded toward us, and Jason pulled me closer against him, bracing for the hurricane storm outside. A rush of air hit me as the closet door flew open, the stench of alcohol and cigarettes burning my nose. I refused to look at Frank; all I could do was stare at the back of Jason's neck as goose bumps formed at his hairline.

In a moment's time, Jason was plucked from me like a loose hair. An eerie chill replaced the warmth Jason provided as I watched Frank pull back his fist. Jason's head flung back with the first painful blow, and I smothered a sob as he fell to the floor. Quiet filled the room besides Frank's heavy breathing as my prince struggled back to his feet. Jason's eyes landed on me, pleading that I stay back. And for once I wished that he would just stay down and let Frank start with me. I started to run toward him, but his hardened gaze shot daggers at me as he wiped a stream of blood from his mouth.

Stay quiet, Maddie.

Or perhaps he wanted me to run, but there was no way in hell I would leave him alone. He never left me alone to fend against the fleet of dragons in our kingdom. And I sure as hell wouldn't leave him now as Frank eyed him like a piece of meat, ready for the slaughter. Frank wound back his fist again, and it crashed against Jason's nose. A sickening crack resonated across the room, and his body went limp and blood poured down his mouth onto the floor.

"*Stop it!*" I screamed, ignoring Jason's warning as I hurtled toward them. Before I could make it two steps, air rushed out of me as my back hit the ground. Rough hands gripped my throat, and darkness threatened to close in. I tried to suck in air, but there was none to take as his hands pressed deeper, scraping and stabbing. *Killing.* I clawed at his arms and tried to scream again, but nothing could escape me as I fought to breathe.

"I've had it with you, you little bitch," he sneered as sweat beaded above his brow. Light poured through the window, shadowing his features, disfiguring the beast before me. *The dragon.* His rotting breath clouded around me as he forced his body weight onto my neck. His once kind green eyes shone fiery and yellow as he watched my life slip between his fingers.

My prince. I needed to see Jason. I tried to turn my head, hoping that I could at least see one last beautiful thing before he killed me. He was nowhere to be found as blackness surrounded me, closing in fast. A weightlessness took hold as Frank's hands continued to squeeze around my neck. And suddenly I felt like I was floating. Drifting through the clouds above our magical kingdom where Jason and I had lived and loved. Where we had cherished each other and fought for each other.

Someone down below was yelling, but I couldn't understand what they were saying. Maybe they were telling me to fly free. Oh, how I wanted to listen and soar away under the whispering stars above, the moon leading the way. I'd be far from the hunger and the hurt. I'd finally be with my parents again. My angels. But a thought echoed over me that shrouded my peace. If I flew away, Jason would be alone. And suddenly the weight was lifted. My ears rang from the pressure, and I was finally able to heave in a gutted breath. One life-giving inhale. Commotion whirled off to the right, but I couldn't focus as black dots lined my vision. Voices and hushed whispers hissed all around me, but one spoke over the rest, loud and clear.

"Breathe! *Breathe!*"

I gasped for air, but my throat closed in, rejecting my will to live. A cough pushed air out, but only a small wheeze escaped. I felt a hand grip my wrist and pull, but I couldn't find my footing. The world started to spin, and I was quickly reminded how fragile I really was. A twig under the dragon's claw.

Larger, stronger hands gripped my shoulders, and once again I was floating. No, this time I was flying. I could hear the whoosh of air under my wings as I sailed on home. And then I couldn't hear anything.

Just quiet. And not even Jason could fight the quiet.

CHAPTER TWO

"Claire, honey, I'm sorry. I just can't afford to keep you here anymore," Carol sighed as she stuffed my clothes into a worn-out duffel bag. I blinked back at her, desperately trying to come up with another way to stay. I knew that this was coming. Carol had been giving me that look. Subtle hints of overstaying my welcome with random rental property ads and job searches. I had just turned eighteen last week, so I hoped and believed that Carol would keep me like she had for the last eleven years. If that's what you could call it anyway. It was more of a complicated dance of staying out of each other's way. It had worked well for the most part, and I suppose I should have been grateful. She had taken me in, the broken mess that I was, when no one else wanted to deal with all the hurt I carried. The girl who couldn't talk. The girl who lost her parents and had been nearly killed by her foster father. I was a lot. Trauma central in a not so delicately wrapped package. Yet Carol had taken the risk.

Looking back, I could see the appeal I must have had for her. Even though I was a hot mess on a stick, I was the perfect child. Only seen and never heard. A good little girl who kept her mouth shut. She kept me home for school, but I imagine it was so she could get her housework done while she raked in the measly checks from the state on my behalf. But she wasn't Frank, and she never saw me as someone with a disability like everyone else did. Perfectly capable to do all the chores, get groceries, and whatever else she needed. The closest thing she came to acknowledging my challenges was the time she brought home a stack of books on how to learn sign language. She never bothered to learn herself, but it had meant something. And finally, I had a hobby to pour my energy into that wasn't chores or self-pity. I was grateful she never saw me as less, but the fact she was sending me out on my own just a week into eighteen was perhaps a little too confident. And especially in this moment, I wished she would see me for what I really was. A scared kid that just needed a parent. I snatched my notebook and pen before she could toss it in the bag with the rest of my things and scrawled "Just give me one more day to find a job." I flipped the page toward her, my eyes wide and pleading.

I laughed internally at my pathetic bargain. I'd spent every day for the last three months applying for jobs with not a single lead. Fast-food restaurants, grocery stores, even places that didn't have a "now hiring" sign out front. I'd applied to all of them, hoping for a bite. But most places needed a lot of things that I didn't have. A driver's license, a car, a resume with at least two years' worth of experience. *A voice.* And now to top the cake, I no longer had an address.

She squinted at my desperate, barely legible handwriting, her frown deepening as she read.

"Claire, I'm sorry, I already have two kids coming tonight for an emergency placement. I need you out of here before they come, I just don't have any room for you anymore." She pulled my notepad and pen from my hands, knowing that I wouldn't be able to beg anymore. I wanted to scream, to cry, to shake her and hope that she could find her heart, wherever it was buried. But by the way she stuffed my worn-through books carelessly into my bag, I supposed that ship had sailed.

I grabbed her hand, and she gasped as if I had scorched her with fire.

"Please," I mouthed, but no sound came out. Just empty, voiceless air. Not even a whisper, just silence. Because Frank had taken my voice, among other things. Because it wasn't enough to just lose your parents. No, I had to lose my voice, my name, and what hurt the most, my prince. The doctors had tried to explain what happened when I finally came to after Frank's attack. What he had done to me. *To Jason.* But who could really *explain* a tragedy? They had tried to show me with X-rays and pictures what happened when Frank took his broken whiskey bottle and sliced it across my throat. How he cut through my vocal cords to the point where I could never speak again. Because strangling me just didn't send the message, I guess. They tried to explain that I now should be called Claire instead of Maddie. Just in case Frank got out of prison. And *then* I'd be safe. Protected.

And then they tried to tell me that Jason was dead.

They wouldn't tell me how, because that wouldn't be good for me. They wouldn't tell me when his funeral was or where he'd be laid to rest. They said that wouldn't be good for me either. Not appropriate or healthy for a seven-year-old girl. So I just sat in my quiet. The agony of trying to scream when you no longer could still stung so deeply. Because crying and screams were part of my happily ever before.

I blinked, a single tear falling as Carol thrust the duffel bag into my shaky grasp.

"Now you listen here, Claire. I know I haven't been the most...nurturing type," she admitted, her eyes glossing over. "But you're strong. You've been through a special kind of hell that most adults wouldn't be able to deal with." Her shoulders sagged slightly, as if she actually felt sorry for me, but then she pulled them back, her chin held high.

"I don't really know anyone else with a disability, but I imagine they wouldn't be able to handle it like you have. You know, maybe it was good that you lost your voice. You might not have been able to fight as hard if you hadn't." A crooked smile crossed her lips, but I didn't return it as I shifted my weight, gripping my bag tighter. I tried not to flinch at her words, as sincere as they probably were. I suddenly missed the times when Carol didn't speak to me at all.

She hacked out a cough that was likely meant to be a laugh, before she straightened up, her eyes falling to her hands. She hesitated, her fingers flexing like she was thinking about punching me. Instead, I watched with widened eyes as her hand dug into her pocket, pulling out a crisp twenty-dollar bill. She flicked it with her finger, making a satisfying snap before she slowly extended the money to me.

"Take it." She reached further, the bill tucked in between her slender fingers. I darted my gaze between her weathered face and the money, fighting the urge not to snatch it and run. Carol never gave handouts. There was always an endgame. Twenty dollars was a drop in the bucket for someone expecting to make it on their own, but to Carol, this was like donating her left kidney. I raised an eyebrow at her, not sure if I was ready to hear how she wanted me to earn it. Because everything was earned, never just given. Her smile returned as she recognized the question in my eyes.

What do you want?

She shook her head, coughing out another laugh. "I left home without a dime in my pocket when I was your age. A little money sure would have helped then, and I'm sure it will help you now. Just take it, and don't spend it all in one place." Her eyes flashed with warning before finally shoving the money in the front pocket of my hoodie. The sentiment was comical and ridiculous as I stared homelessness in its ugly eye. Twenty dollars might get me a bottled water and a few snacks from the gas station. It sure as hell wouldn't find me a place to live or keep the cold out. But Carol was right. It was at least something. If she was really sending me out on my ass, at least she wasn't sending me out empty-handed.

I stared at her, the silence between us suddenly uncomfortable. For me, silence was home. It was my calm and my normal, but now it hung in the room, crowding us with expectations and the unknown that lay ahead. Her gaze flitted to the door, her smile once again fading as she let out a cough that was actually meant to be a cough.

"The new kids will be here soon, so I think it's best if you leave." I stepped back, her words stinging as if she'd slapped me. The new kids. My replacements. Carol never took time to grieve her losses, whether I was one for her or not. To her, I suppose that was wasted time. Time better used working on her next chapter, and right now it had certainly reached the end of mine. I paused, giving her one last hurt look. The woman was getting older, her wrinkles lining every inch of her exposed skin. She had fed, clothed, and tolerated me, but that was the extent of it. If that was all I had known, then it might not have been so bad. But I had experienced a much greater love, the kind that every kid deserved. The distant memory of Sunday drives with the windows rolled down and laughter and music ached through me. Long hugs that held you the whole day and lullabies that carried you into the night. Gentle caresses of a thumb that brushed the tears away and kisses that cured all the hurt. Those were the things that cradled me when Carol's only daily interaction consisted of chores and grocery lists. She was no goddamned Frank, but I prayed that whoever these new kids were that she'd do better with them. But at least they would have each other. Just like I had my Jason.

I dropped my gaze to the floor, blinking back more tears. I refused to look at her again before I headed out the door, pulling it closed behind me. Without a second to spare, I heard the click of the lock turn.

I paused, letting my reality set in, the weight of it all crashing over me in agonizing waves. I was all alone now, as the quiet of the street mocked me. No uprising or offers to help from the passersby. Just that damned quiet.

Without wasting another second, I rushed toward the street, throwing my bag over my shoulder, and ran. And I kept on going, without any plans to stop. Running was the only thing that eased the constant pain. I could finally hear my heart pound in my chest, a kind reminder that it was still there. Still working, still pumping. As my feet hit the pavement, I stopped thinking. At Carol's house, all I did was think. Think about what I could have been if my parents hadn't died. What Jason would have become. If my parents and Jason could see me now, would they be proud? The list of thoughts I should be thinking were rushing at me too fast, and I wasn't ready for them.

Where was I supposed to go now? How was I going to make money? What the hell was I going to do with twenty dollars? I couldn't bring myself to deal with the questions because I didn't have any answers. I couldn't think anymore. I just wanted to exist. And so I kept running, putting off dealing with my reality for as long as I could. I ran for what seemed like miles, as the streets became less busy and the storefronts started to close. The streetlights buzzed on as the darkness started to settle. And by then, I couldn't run anymore. My sights set on a nearby bench, but I couldn't control my legs and collapsed against a wall, throwing my bag to the side. The temperature had dropped, but my lungs were on fire as I tried to catch my breath. Had I run a mile, or twenty? Where the hell was I?

Water. I needed water. I scanned the ever-darkening street, searching for a drinking fountain or even a store where I could ask to use their bathroom. I swallowed, my throat scraping with the movement as panic settled in. All the businesses were dark, no souls in sight. I couldn't remember when I last saw another human. I'd blocked out the entire run, shutting down my brain to conserve my energy. But what was the point if I was going to die of thirst. No part of this street seemed familiar. I had never been but a few miles from home, and nothing about the looks of the buildings or architecture suggested I was anywhere near it. But then I remembered I didn't have a home anymore. I fought the urge to cry, as tears started to well up again.

No, don't cry. I couldn't afford tears right now. I would just plummet myself into a dangerous game of dehydration, and I'd pass out. Or die. And another sinking thought filled me. If I did die tonight, who would miss me? Who would even know who I was? Did they have funerals for Jane Does? Who would even go? Who would *care*?

I jumped as something ricocheted against the street a few yards away. I froze, searching for the source of the movement, but darkness ensued, not a soul in sight. I slowed my breathing, trying to steady my racing heart so I could hear any more noise. After living most of my life in silence, I had gotten pretty good at taking in the world around me. I knew when to avoid Carol more than normal if she clicked her pen while she created the list of chores for the day. Or if she was in a good mood, she'd drum her fingers against the counter like rapid gunfire. I'd pick up on the little things over time that others might have missed because they were too busy thinking about what to say next.

I stared at the spot a few businesses down, where I was certain the noise came from. I squinted at something on the ground, a stream of light reflecting off it from a nearby streetlamp. It was a can. I licked my lips, the saltiness from my sweat sending my thirst into overdrive. I started to pray that the can would turn into a bottle of water when movement lurking in the shadows caught my eye. Whatever it was, it was big, with a hulking outline, too big to just be an animal.

I shook my head, wiping the sweat from my eyes. *God, you're delirious. Stay focused.* I froze as the unmistakable outline of a large man emerged from the darkness, his shoulders facing my direction. The hairs stood on the back of my neck as I watched a second man follow close behind, both of them seemingly staring back at me, though their features remained hidden. I prayed that they couldn't see me, but there's no way I remained unseen with all the ridiculous panting I'd done just moments before.

"She looks a little thirsty, doesn't she?" a muffled voice called out, followed by a menacing laugh.

Oh, *hell* to the no. I quickly stood when a wave of dizziness crashed over me. I took a step forward, but my legs were like Jell-O, heavy and off-balance. I stumbled as I heard the scraping of their feet approach behind me. I braved another step but slipped, hard cement scraping my knee as I fell to the ground.

"She looks a little tired too. Don't try too hard, baby!" Another laugh bounced off the walls, echoing around me. "We just want to have a little fun."

My blood ran cold as I thought about the kind of fun they wanted to have. Like Frank's hide-and-seek games where I ended up with my throat slashed at the end. I clawed my way to my bag before stumbling back up to my feet, their footsteps growing closer.

I managed to get my legs moving again, but I felt the sting of air on my knee as something wet trickled down my leg. I was bleeding. And I needed water so badly, as I sucked in a dry raspy breath. I felt like a baby deer learning how to walk for the first time as my legs started to cramp up, fighting any more movement.

I gasped as a large hand closed around my wrist and whirled me around effortlessly to face them. My eyes widened as they adjusted to the darkness towering over me. A giant of a man stood inches away, but what made my blood freeze over were the two white masks they both wore, with wide crooked smiles painted over their mouths. I stared up at the man clutching my wrist, my lungs forgetting to breathe. His grip tightened with his glare behind the white porcelain of his mask. His eyes gleamed with pleasure from my obvious pain, and I winced as his hand gripped my hip, pulling me closer.

"Why don't you get the girl a drink." His eyes flashed with his words as he continued to stare me down, the mask's wicked smile somehow growing wider. I braved a peek at the other man, his eyes nervously bouncing between me and my captor before reaching for a can from a box. He quickly popped the tab and held it out for me to take as bubbles fizzed over. Before I could stop myself, I grabbed the can with my free hand and sucked the contents of it down in a few seconds flat. I hated myself with every gulp, but I feared I would pass out right there if I didn't get some kind of hydration. I shuddered as the warmth of the liquid burned my throat, praying I didn't just pick my poison. The taste was tangy and bitter, but the distinct smell of alcohol furthered the unpleasant flavor. It must have been beer, though I had never had beer before. I had only smelled it on Frank's breath once upon a horror. I quickly tried to twist my wrist away from his grip, but he countered my move, pulling my body closer.

"Not so fast, baby. We did something for you, now you do something for us." He laughed that same bone-chilling laugh as his eyes dropped to my chest, his grip digging deeper.

"What is a pretty thing like you doing out at this time of night anyway? Don't you have parents that will wonder where you are?"

The sting of his words sliced me right open, but I couldn't worry about that now as his fingers started to dance around my zipper.

"A girl like you shouldn't be out this late. Somebody could come and hurt you." He feigned concern as his hand slid under my shirt. I cringed as his breath crashed against me, stale and rancid just like Frank's. And I wasn't about to play out that story again. I tried to pull away, but he yanked me back, his hand clamping down on my jaw, mashing my cheeks against my teeth. I felt the beer creep back up my throat as his lower region hardened against my leg. For a second, I thought that he was about to remove his mask, but he lifted it just above his mouth, his real smile even more frightening than the mask's. I froze as his lips brushed against my neck, his stubble scraping against my throat. He walked me back against the wall and pinned me, barely giving me enough room to breathe as he waited for the fight to leave me. I hardly had enough left in me anyway, and I wasn't ready to waste the last of it yet.

"We were waiting for something pretty like you to come along. And then you just fluttered right in like a songbird." His nose brushed against the sensitive skin near my scar. "And we can't wait to make you sing." That was enough to rage the last fight in me, but his hand quickly moved down to my throat, too close to my scar. The tender raised flesh burned under his touch, his smile widening as I writhed beneath him. I had learned enough from Frank that all men weren't loving and protective like Jason or my father. Some of them only knew how to break and take. But with these men, this was something new. Something scarier. I'd already been on the receiving end of a man that took too much. And by the way they looked at me, I knew they wanted more than I would ever be willing to give.

"This looks like it hurt, baby. Did someone already come and steal your song?" he taunted, his tongue darting out, licking the base of my scar. The beer threatened to come up again as his other hand reached under my hoodie, tracing toward my breasts. The fight in me roared again, and I had to take my last chance. My legs were liquid, but they were all I had. I let out a deep exhale and raised my knee up at his groin, knowing enough that this would give me back my bearings.

But he knew better. Before my knee met his inner thigh, his hands wrapped around my leg and twisted, sending a shooting pain up my shin. White-hot pain crashed across my cheek, and suddenly I was flying to the ground. Thick hands wrestled my hands above my head as my cheek throbbed with the pounding of my heart.

"Whoa, now. She's got a good fight in her." He let out a low, unsettling laugh as the world spun around me. "Now let's see if we can make this one sing after all. Not that there's anyone around to hear you try."

CHAPTER THREE

The weight of the bag gave and swung as I shot two more jabs to the center, my knuckles still bruised from last night's fight. Sweat dripped from every pore as I finished out my last rep. Because it was train hard or lose hard. And I had already lost too much. I grimaced as I rounded out the last punch with a kick, picturing his face, hearing the satisfying crunch of his nose. Watching his blood pour like he'd made hers.

"Nate, you need to calm the fuck down," Jesse laughed as he threw a towel over his shoulder. "You already won tonight's fight, and you're still undefeated. You need to get over yourself and just take the night off. Come with me to Jake's and get a drink? I'm taking your sister out, and I need someone to supervise me so I don't get her pregnant." His smile grew as I flipped him my middle finger. He knew I didn't drink when I trained. I rarely drank to begin with. I'd seen too much of what alcohol could do to a person. How it could cause someone to hurt and abuse. Lucky for Jesse he was a happy drinker.

"Naw, Jesse. Go take your girl out. But I swear to God if you knock her up." I whistled before throwing a few more hits and a groin kick to the bag. Jesse watched with an unimpressed smirk as I sent it swaying back and forth, the chain clanking on its hinges as it swung.

"You know you want little nieces and nephews that look like me. I mean, have you *seen* me? I look like fucking Zeus, baby!"

I glared at him as I unraveled my hand wraps. "Whatever you say, man. Now don't be late—you know how Samone gets when you make her wait for things." I pointed at my ring finger this time, reminding him what my sister really wanted. He clicked his tongue and shook his head playfully.

"I know, I know. You want me to put a ring on it just so I can be your brother in-law already. Just say it out loud so I can hear it. Go on, I'm waiting."

"You're already my brother, whether you like it or not, ya prick. And I mean it about the pregnant thing." I threw my own sweat-drenched towel at him as I headed toward the lights. "Now get out of here so I can lock up. I'm taking tonight's shift, so I'll see you tomorrow, alright?"

Jesse wiped away a fake tear before heading to the door. He tapped the bell hanging above the entrance, and I couldn't help but laugh as I watched him high-knee his way to his car, probably thrilled that he finally was getting a night alone with Samone. He'd been training his ass off for the last month for tonight's fight which of course he'd won. And tonight, Samone wanted to celebrate. Jesse had been dating my sister for the last few years, but they were pretty much exclusive since the day I moved into the neighborhood. He was the first kid brave enough to talk to me. I still didn't know why he did to be honest. I was an asshole as a kid, and even that was an understatement. I never smiled, I broke a lot of things, and I had an ugly scar above my eyebrow that screamed damaged and unapproachable. The place where a dragon had sliced it open after he stole away my princess.

Jesse didn't care about how he was supposed to feel about people, he just felt how he wanted to. And he'd always been like that as long as I knew him. Even the first day he found me, not a day after I had been adopted.

"What the hell is that on your face?" he'd asked as I threw rocks against our mailbox. I choked away a laugh as I caught the boy standing in front of me, completely unfazed by my go-fuck-yourself glare. He was a whole foot shorter than me, and he was swimming in a shirt a few sizes too big. That was Jesse, alright. He had grit, and he was fearless, even when he was a pint-sized pipsqueak. Or maybe he was just a little stupid, one of the two. He pointed above my eye where my scar was and adjusted his glasses, waiting patiently. Like he had asked about the weather, and not something loaded with loss and grief. I hadn't even gone into what happened to my face with my adoptive parents, although I was sure they knew. Most of the adults in my life knew. They'd even made me change my name before I was adopted. They said a name change would help me start over fresh. Fresh from the living hell that Jason had lived, I guess. But I wasn't ready to delve into my past with a complete stranger. Because stories like that made grown adults cry. And Jesse looked like the kind of kid that might faint if he saw blood.

"I fought a dragon so I could save a princess," I muttered, hoping that he would just leave me alone. Instead, his face split into a smile and he sat down next to me.

"Seriously?" He shoved his glasses up the bridge of his nose again, his eyes wide with wonder. "Well, where's the princess now?"

My heart nearly ripped out of my chest as I tried to grapple with what to say next. How could I possibly explain that I had failed to protect her. She was dead because of me. Because I didn't tell anyone what he was doing to us. If I had just told someone. Just one fucking person.

"She's sleeping in her castle," I'd whispered, praying that his questions would stop. And they did. Jesse always seemed to know when enough was enough. We spent the rest of that afternoon throwing rocks at my mailbox in silence. Side by side. And Jesse never really left after that day.

He thought it was cool that I was adopted. He always said that my family chose me instead of just having me. I never looked at it that way until Jesse said that out loud. He had that way about him, to bring perspective I never saw myself. He thought it was even cooler that my sister was deaf. Every time he would come over, he had a new sign he wanted to show me and Samone. She learned how to lip-read at a young age because our father was a fighter himself. Sometimes he wouldn't be able to use his hands to sign, too injured from his fights. But that didn't stop us from learning. I didn't know sign language before I was adopted, but both Samone and Jesse taught me many things that year. They helped mend the wounds that they couldn't see on the outside. They reminded me of the things I was capable of. They taught me what it meant to try again and succeed. Jesse and I poured our everything into learning sign language just so we could keep up with Samone. She was always way cooler than us, though we never told her that. But that never stopped anyone else.

Especially not the guys at the gym. Even when we started getting into mixed martial arts, she had all the fighters wrapped around her little finger. She volunteered to help mend cuts and wounds when we were younger, the daily job hazard for a fighter. And when Jesse shot up a few feet and replaced his glasses with contacts, Samone started showing up at the gym a little too much. Jesse and I both threw ourselves headfirst into training. For him, he loved the thrill of combat, the adrenaline of the dance to see who could overpower the other. But for me, every fight was another chance to save her. To protect the girl I'd failed. I thrived on the pain I caused because every opponent was Frank. The bastard who stole Maddie away from me. For me, fighting was the only way I could bring her back and to finally take him down.

My dad started letting me take over parts of the gym as I trained. He thought it gave me some sense of direction, and that much was true. Since I started fighting, I'd found a second family. And once I had family, there wasn't anything that could stop me from defending it. The guys at the gym looked out for each other. This place was everything to my dad. Everything to me. It became my second kingdom, and it nearly sent me into a tailspin after someone tried to fuck with it last month. We suffered two break-ins over the course of a week. Both times, thousands of dollars from the safe was stolen and the office had been wrecked. I'd already seen my castle taken under siege, and I wasn't going to let it happen again. I'd set up a cot in the back room, and Jesse and I had been taking turns guarding the place just in case someone broke in again. Because then, we would be ready.

I finished my rounds and shut off the last row of lights as I headed to the back room to lock up. I secured the lock to the safe as the sound of the bell above the door rang again.

"Jesse, what did I tell you about making Samone wait?" I called out from down the hall. But no answer. Only silence. A loud crash echoed from the main lobby, and instantly I was on my feet, heading out into the hall, to the dark gym.

"Jesse, you better fucking answer me if that's you." But no one responded as I stared into the black abyss.

Quick movements in the back corner pulled my attention to it. As my eyes adjusted to the darkness, they landed on a shadowy figure standing unmoving near the punching bags. They immediately froze as if they saw me too.

"The gym is closed, now I'm going to need you to leave."

I watched as they stood there, swaying nervously, mapping out their next move. They backed away, seemingly uninterested in leaving. Or getting closer to me. But they wouldn't get too far. Not in my castle.

"You picked the wrong fucking time to come into a gym that trains ultimate fighting champions. If you're looking for more money to steal, you'll have to find it somewhere else." My voice hardened as I rounded the punching bags, closing in on him.

He was listening now. I watched him slink his way toward a wall, avoiding me completely. Another loud crash boomed through the gym as he bumped into a cart filled with dirty towels. A painful thud followed when he hit the ground, tumbling over it.

Alright, I was done playing games. He wasn't going to mess up my second home again. Not this time. I brisked toward him, my knuckles cracking as I prepared to swing.

"Come on, get up and face me," I demanded as he scrambled back to his feet, wobbly and lazy with each step. The distinct smell of beer filled the air as I watched him scurry behind a punching bag. Just like the beer that Frank slammed before he pounded his fists into me and Maddie. That was enough to get my hands on him, to show him who he was dealing with.

My hands clutched the front of his sweatshirt before I shoved his back against the wall. He was much shorter than I anticipated, my chin clearing the top of his head easily as I pinned him. His frame was small and weak in my grasp, but all I could see was Frank as I pushed my weight against him.

"You got a weapon on you?" I demanded, searching with my free hand. My hand brushed past his hips and grazed his chest before stopping along the seam of his shirt. It was torn and wet, probably from drinking too much. I probed further until my hand was fully pressed against curvy, unexpected flesh.

Fuck me.

I was pinning a *woman*, and my hand was groping her bare breast.

A soft, terrified exhale fell from her lips as she stilled under my touch. I immediately backed away, and she slid to the ground, her body shaking uncontrollably. I quickly pulled out my phone and turned on the flashlight, the light flooding the room and the woman I'd just assaulted. The sight of her was like a punch to the gut. No, a straight kick in the jaw—at least that's what I deserved anyway. A dark cascade of waves fell over her face, her hands spread wide and pleading for me to stop. The sleeve of her sweatshirt fell past her shoulder, exposing bruises and scrapes that laced up to her neck. Jesus Christ, not only did I force my hands where they didn't belong, I *hurt* her.

"Whoa, hey. *Jesus.* Are you okay?" I wanted to punch myself for how stupid I sounded. *Of course she's not fucking okay. You just shoved her against the wall and molested her. You put bruises on her skin, for Christ's sake.* I took another step closer, and somehow, she curled herself into an even tighter ball, away from me. Her legs pulled up to her chest protectively as blood poured from an open wound on her knee. A wave of guilt rolled through me at the way I'd handled her. She was so small and fragile. Nearly broken in front of me. But I didn't see her—I only saw Frank. And for that, I lost sight of my own strength. I regretfully followed the bruises on her neck and shoulders. They ran deep against her skin, right down to the purple handprints around her wrists. But I didn't remember grabbing her arms. I reluctantly replayed the moment I pinned her and the places my hands had explored without consent. But I never touched her wrists. The welts were fresh though, as if someone put them there just moments before.

"Hey, easy. *Easy*," I coaxed, moving forward again and doing my best to ignore the way she shook with each step. "Let me just...take a look, okay?" She flinched as I reached for her hand but stilled as I smoothed my fingers over her knuckles.

Both of her wrists were swollen and raw, like she put up a fight worthy for the cage. The handprints were wide like mine, but I was more convinced as I traced the blisters that I didn't put those marks there. After years of fighting, I knew the stages of bruising on skin, and these marks couldn't have developed that quickly, even from the few times she'd fallen. I carefully examined her exposed shoulder, but my focus was pulled to her shirt. It was torn and ripped in the wrong places. Too deliberate, as if someone had intentionally tried to tear her shirt off. The fabric barely covered her heaving chest as a large tear ran down the middle. I knew I grabbed her shirt when I pinned her, but I never heard anything rip. I followed the shredded material down to her waist as anger started to replace my guilt. The button of her shorts was missing, and the zipper was broken and jagged. My gaze darted back to her wrists, and my jaw hardened as I put the pieces together, hoping I was miscalculating. But I swallowed as I accepted that I was likely her second unwanted male encounter of the night. Another ugly wave of guilt rolled through me as I reached for her face.

"Okay, let me see your face," I whispered as I cupped her chin. She jumped again but let me lift her toward me. Her hair fell like silk away from her face, and I held my breath as my fingers brushed against her bruised jaw. Time raced backward and stood still in the same moment as wide, honey-golden brown eyes met mine. Wild and terrified eyes that I knew from another time, from a distant kingdom. Her body tensed under my touch, as if she were bracing herself for yet another assault. But my hands didn't leave her. Instead, they squeezed tighter, an innate protectiveness seizing me as I pulled her closer. She stilled as my thumb followed the familiar curve of her lip, careful not to touch the swollen welt at the corner of her mouth. A deep ache pulled at my gut as my gaze fell to her throat, at the raised pink flesh at the base of her neck. It was a scar, separate from whatever assault she endured tonight. No, this was something that had marked her body for years. She started to pull away as my fingers drifted toward it, my head spinning with cloudy distant memories of a faraway land and a dragon. And a princess. But her body went rigid, her breath hanging in midair as my thumb trailed across her throat.

Her eyes, her scar, even her scent was Maddie's. *But Maddie was dead.* I'd watched her bleed out on the floor after Frank sliced her throat open. Just where this woman's scar lay. Another shaky breath pulled my focus back to her. Her eyes were squeezed shut as tears flowed freely down her bruised cheeks. She didn't want my hands on her. Of course she didn't want this. She'd already been brutalized. And here she was, her back against the wall in the dark, with a strange man invading her body again. Before my hands could explore further, they dropped to my sides, allowing her the space she deserved.

Her eyes snapped open, wondering where my hands were going to go next. I shook my head and lifted my arms to reassure her.

"I'm so sorry. I won't touch you anymore, okay?" Her body trembled with another silent sob, but she seemed to relax with my words.

"Please, will you let me take you to a hospital?"

Another painful surge shot through me as her mouth trembled like Maddie's did when she was scared. But this wasn't Maddie. This *couldn't* be Maddie. *Get it through your head, Nate.* She was dead. Murdered. And we didn't have time for ghosts right now.

"My name is Nate, alright? Nate Brooks." I tried to fight the shadows that fell over my face as I scanned her bruises. "Can you please tell me your name?"

Please say Maddie.

Instead, her lip trembled again. Just like Maddie's.

"That's okay, you don't have to say anything. You don't have to do anything you don't want to do, understand?"

She was too scared, too shocked to answer. Even in broad daylight in a crowded place, especially if I hadn't just attacked her, she would still probably be scared of me. Most people were, and I preferred it that way. But with her, I craved her trust. It was the most important thing in the world right now. I *needed* her to know that she was safe and I wasn't going to hurt her.

"Here, take this." I reached for the hem of my shirt and pulled it over my head, tossing it at her. Her eyes widened at my bare chest, fear still flashing behind them as she traced the tattoos that lined my arms. But her shoulders relaxed as she spotted the crumpled-up offering at her feet.

"You can put it on if you want. To...cover up." I took another step back to give her even more space.

Her watery eyes shifted from me to the shirt as if she were waiting for me to trick her. That innocent hopeful look, so familiar it hurt. I wanted to hold her and reassure her. To take her away to our castle and protect her like I used to. Instead, I turned away and stared at the opposite wall so she could dress in private.

After a few beats, the subtle rustling of her hands against my shirt filled the room. Until there was silence.

"You...good?" I called out, keeping my eyes trained on the wall.

Only the steady sound of her shaky breathing rattled in response.

"Hey...are you dressed?" I repeated, waiting for her to give the okay. Instead of answering, I heard a loud thud from behind me. Shit, she'd passed out. I whirled around ready to scoop her up, but she remained where she was. Still injured and scared, but still very conscious. A part of me was impressed she was still up. Half of the guys in the gym would be out cold if they'd gotten even a fraction of the hits she'd taken. I watched the light from the flashlight dance as a nearby punching bag swayed ever so slightly. She'd punched the bag. Samone did the same thing when she tried to get my attention. She'd hit something, whether it be a punching bag or me. So I took a risk and started signing, hoping that she would understand.

"Are you...deaf?"

Her eyes startled as she watched my hands move, but she stared back blankly, her eyebrows drawing together perplexed. Curious.

"Do you understand signs?"

She continued to stare, leaning forward, her honey eyes nearly glowing with each movement.

"Okay. You don't have to say anything to me, but I need to get you to a hospital."

She quickly shook her head, fear stretching across her tired, swollen face again. Before I could say anything more, she began to push herself off the ground, making her escape. But she immediately lost her footing, and she began to fall forward. She sucked in a breath as I caught her, her body stilling against my touch again.

"It's okay. If you don't want to go, I won't make you," I whispered, her soft breaths crashing against my bare chest as I held her steady. She bit her lip as she looked up at me, Maddie's face swirling through my head again.

"But you need to be looked at, do you understand?"

She shook her head again as exhaustion racked her body. The unexplainable need to protect her filled my every thought, every cell in my body. I wanted to shield this woman. To keep her safe. Before I could ask anything else, she fell forward, the fight slowly leaving her. I quickly wrapped my arms around her waist and hoisted her up. She relaxed into me, her head falling on my shoulder where it belonged.

It's okay, Maddie. You don't have to fight anymore. I've got you.

CHAPTER FOUR

A stream of silent tears fell as his hands tore at my shirt, the loud rip of the fabric pulling against my skin. My throat ached to scream, to say no. But I knew as his hands gripped my wrists, slamming them above my head, that he wouldn't listen even if I could.

"I think someone's coming," the other whispered as he stood above us, swaying back and forth nervously.

The man on top of me persisted, ignoring him as the unmistakable sound of a zipper ripped apart.

"I said, *someone is coming*, let's go," he repeated, his voice hardening as he took a step closer.

"Let them watch," he laughed, fumbling with his belt, while his free hand pushed into my throat.

I squirmed under him, searching for my apparent savior, but the street remained vacant. *There is no one else.* I stilled as his hand began to dip below my waistline when suddenly an unseen force yanked him off me. The sound of glass shattered against the street, his porcelain mask broken into a million pieces.

"Are you fucking kidding me?" a voice echoed against the walls. I didn't want to figure out who was talking and who wasn't, I just wanted to get the hell away.

I started to slide toward the wall when my hand hit my beer can, grating it against the pavement. A struggle broke out behind me as I tried to pull myself upright. Before I could gain traction, a strong grip circled around my arm, my back hitting the wall behind me again.

"No, you're not going anywhere, little songbird. We aren't done with you yet."

I couldn't tear my eyes away from his face, his mask no longer there to protect him. Long oily hair was slicked back behind his ears. His bright green eyes, far too much like Frank's, danced with amusement as I struggled under his grasp. His grin was evil and sickening as his hand slid back below my waistline, demanding and forceful. I started to fight him when his head knocked back from a deafening punch. A spray of blood spewed from his mouth from the blow, spattering across my cheek. I caught the recoil of my savior's hand and spotted a sharp tattoo peeking through the sleeve of his shirt.

A compass. And I prayed that it would lead me out of this hell. I peered up at the face of the man who defended me. But only the other masked man remained. Just him, me, and the bastard who helped himself to my body. I started to back away when my attacker regained his balance.

"You're done," he growled, wiping the blood from his mouth as he sneered at the masked man. "You have no idea what you've started. They'll be coming for you, and they'll tear you to pieces until you beg for them to kill you. But maybe I'll just make it easy on you. Maybe I'll just end you right here." He lunged at him, wrestling him to the ground as grunts and punches filled the street.

"Go!" the masked man bellowed as he threw two quick jabs to the other man's face. I started to run, but my legs were like lead, too heavy to move as the sounds of approaching footsteps closed in.

"Hey, it's okay! You're okay!" A distant voice cradled me as hands gripped my shoulders. My eyes flew open, the bitter taste of blood filling my nose and mouth. My hazy focus settled on a face that seemed strange yet familiar. Like home in a foreign land. His deep brown eyes heated with concern, his strong jawline tightening as my fight gave against his strength.

Nate.

His name was clear as I remembered my last encounter with him. When he'd pinned me against the wall and was nearly my second attack of the night. But instead, he'd shown me kindness and given me the shirt off his back. Heat flushed across my cheeks as I realized he was still shirtless. And we were still in the gym. I quickly peeked down to check on my own clothed status, relief filling me as I felt the damp fabric brush against my skin.

"Hey, look at me. You okay?" His hand tilted my chin back up to his face, his eyes searching mine. I had only gotten a rough glimpse of him in the stark light from his phone. But now, as the fluorescent light above captured him perfectly, he was breathtaking. *Terrifying.* His dark hair was out of sorts, but his face was powerful and sharp, like a weapon. His eyes were careful and kind, a far contrast to the dangerous scar hovering above his brow. I should have been intimidated, scared even as he watched me, his lips inches away from mine. But something about the way he looked at me, the way his scar fractured his face, he *calmed* me. I found likeness in that part of him. Proof that he'd experienced immeasurable pain just like I had.

Movement tore my focus to the corner of the room. A woman, her expression curious and cautious as she approached. Her dark hair was twisted into a loose braid that fell across her shoulder, elongating her tall frame even more. Nate followed my gaze and pulled his hands away. And before I could miss his warmth, he started to move his hands as he spoke. They were deliberate and firm with each word. He was *signing.* Just like he was doing before I lost consciousness.

"This is my sister, S-A-M-O-N-E." He spelled out the letters. *"She's studying to be a doctor, and she'd like to take a look at you if that's okay."*

She watched me carefully, measuring my reactions to his hands. Her beautiful hazel eyes widened as she surveyed my face, wincing at my swollen cheek.

"Nate says you're deaf. Do you understand signs?" Her hands moved gracefully, but slow enough for me to follow. I slowly raised my own hands, praying they wouldn't fail me.

"I'm not deaf. I just can't...speak." My signs were shaky and uncertain. I'd never actually communicated like this with a real person before. I'd only practiced alone at Carol's with books and videos. But it seemed I conveyed my message clear enough because her eyes dropped to my throat, tracing the ugly reminder of what Frank did to me. Her face flickered with sadness as if she knew my tragic story before I even told her.

"Can you please tell me your name?"

"C-L-A-I-R-E," I spelled out with my fingers like Nate did. I caught his mouth twitch as if my name offended him. Or maybe I wasn't signing correctly, and he didn't understand. She frowned at my nervous glance and stepped in front of Nate, flipping her braid so he couldn't see what she was saying.

"Claire, I would like to take a look at you, but it might get a little...personal. Would you like me to kick Nate out, or are you more comfortable with him here?"

I braved a peek over her shoulder at him to see if he was watching. Luckily, his eyes were fixed on my neck, his face seemingly somewhere far away from here. I usually hated it when people stared at that part of me. The worst part that forced me to remember the worst night of my life. But for some reason, when Nate's eyes traveled across my throat, it felt worshipped and respected.

Samone waved a hand in front of me, pulling me back to her.

I nodded and signed back. *"He can stay."*

Her face pinched as if she were considering how to ask her next question, but she raised her hands carefully, her face softening as she signed. I tilted my head at her movements, the gestures unfamiliar and strange. I glanced at Nate again, this time his eyes dead locked on mine. The gentle and tender man he'd been moments before had completely disappeared, and in his place stood a beast, his muscles rippling, his male presence storming the room.

I let out a quick breath, a chill sweeping through me from the change in him. Samone frowned at my reaction and repeated the signs, her movements less graceful and more direct.

"I don't understand. What are you saying?" I repeated the strange motions, shaking my head, confused.

Before she could respond, Nate stepped forward but kept his distance.

"She's asking if you...were raped." His voice was cautious and tender, but the sting of his words whipped through me like a punch to the gut. I swallowed, my throat suddenly constricted and tight as air seemed to dissipate in the room. To hear it was one thing, but to see it signed so blatantly, the movements so much more vulgar and hateful than the sound. I sucked in a breath horrified, shaking my head defiantly.

"No. I..." My hands were failing me as I tried to explain, my brain too foggy to answer. The bitter memory of his hands everywhere crowded me. On me. *Inside me.* The smell of his breath on my neck as he tore at my clothes. Tore at my body.

"He...tried. But..." I dropped my hands from the weight of the words and immediately regretted it as I caught Nate's expression.

His brown eyes blackened, crisping at the edges like he was being burned from within. For a moment I thought he might hit something, but he stayed rooted and statuesque, his fists clenching at his sides.

"Thank you, Claire. I know this is very difficult and scary," Samone jumped in, tapping Nate on the shoulder. *"Nate, would you please go get us some ice?"* His scorching glare shifted to Samone, but she held her ground, pointing toward my face.

"For her cheek?"

The fire within him died immediately as he peered up at me. After a few uncomfortable heartbeats of not being able to meet his gaze, he nodded and headed for the door.

"Oh, and for Christ's sake get a shirt on." She threw her hands around, exasperated, before he left. After he closed the door, she stared at me in silence for a moment, assessing the visible scrapes and bruises with a delicate eye. But then her focus dipped to the torn fabric from my shirt just barely peeking out from Nate's cover-up.

"Claire? I need to know if there are any injuries that I can't see right now. Is it...okay if I lift your shirt?"

I blinked back at her, just wishing to be left alone. But her face was reassuring, and for whatever reason, I trusted her.

"Okay." I nodded.

Her cool fingers brushed against my hip before a rush of cold air stung my back. I felt her tense at whatever she was seeing before she gently pulled my shirt back down.

"I'm going to need you to take off your shirt. I'll give you a towel to cover yourself, but you're bleeding, and the cut needs to be cleaned."

I bit my lip, trying to fight the tremble that came in waves.

"Go ahead and turn this way." She guided me in the opposite direction.

I twisted around, now facing the other wall, and dozens of pictures of strong, determined men stared back, huddled together near what looked like a cage. I strained my eyes to see what exactly it was before Samone helped me lift my arms. She carefully pulled the fabric over my head, wary not to hit any bruises. A towel was quickly draped over my shoulders, but the sting of air still hit my exposed skin.

"This might hurt a little, so if you need me to stop at any time, tap my shoulder."

I sucked in a breath as her fingers began coating my back with a cold cream. I nearly reached for her hand for her to stop when I heard the doorknob twist open. I heard his footsteps pause, and I hoped that he couldn't see whatever

Samone was cleaning. But based on the curse under his breath, he most certainly did. His footsteps quickened, rounding toward me.

"What happened to you?" He wasn't signing anymore though I imagined Samone was watching every word that fell from his lips.

I didn't know why, but I couldn't look at him. I never cared about what other people thought of me, especially random strangers. But for some reason I couldn't look him in the eye. I couldn't face him, and I sure as hell couldn't sign my way through what I'd experienced. I *wouldn't*. He slowly approached me, his left hand clutching the bag of ice while the other reached for me. I followed his movement, bracing myself for the impact. But I wasn't prepared for his gentleness; I could have melted into him as his fingers brushed against my jaw.

"Easy," he coaxed, cautiously edging the bag against my cheek. The coolness of his breath crashed against me. I couldn't resist looking at him anymore. I slowly shifted my gaze upward, and something about the way he peered down at me sliced me right open.

His eyes.

They felt so familiar. I could see light golden flecks splashed across the dark umber of his irises. Flecks I'd known before. They burned bright as he swept over the bruising along my neck, pain twisting at his beautiful features.

"Did you know the person who did this?" he whispered as he dropped the bag of ice to my neck, soothing another bruise above my collarbone. God, he was so close. *Too close.* I could feel his body heat against me as I replayed his question. This one I could answer.

I lifted my hands to respond, using the small gap between us.

"No, they...had masks on."

His already murky eyes blackened to a deep onyx as a vein popped in his temple.

"They?" he repeated, his voice dangerously low and threatening. Drops of water cascaded down my chest from the ice melting against the heat of his hand. I reached for the bag to pull it away from my skin, but my hand collided with his. Fire and ice crashing into each other. I flinched from the pressure, and he immediately pulled the bag away, water dripping across my shoulder.

"Sorry," he whispered, his face filled with guilt as he followed the trail of liquid down my throat. He let out a slow, even breath, as if he were calming himself, his eyes like knives as they darted back up to my face.

"Did you catch any names? Anything we could track them with?" His tone was hopeful but lethal. As if he were silently counting the ways he would end them once he found them. I remembered the compass tattoo from my dream. But I wasn't sure if it was a real memory or something my brain made up in the midst of the trauma. I blinked back at him, letting silence fall over us.

"I understand if you don't want to talk." He watched as another bead of water fell down my neck. "But we have a guy that trains here that works down at the station. I'd really like it if you would talk to him. Samone or I could translate for you."

Before I could answer, a quick knock rapped at the door.

Nate paused for a second, his jaw clenching as if he wanted to say more. He finally settled with silence and gently placed the bag of ice in my hand.

"I'll be right back."

He stood, his height taller than I remembered, and as he pulled open the door, my eyes locked with a much shorter, stockier man. He pulled back his lips in a grimace as his eyes settled on the place Samone was cleaning. Nate quickly blocked his view and closed the door, leaving us alone.

"*Who was that?*" I signed, pointing toward the door.

Samone peeked behind her, color creeping across her cheeks. "*That's Jesse, my boyfriend.*"

I recognized him from one of the pictures hanging on the wall, his smile wide as he lifted a large and shiny belt above his head. She, too, peered up at the picture and bit her lip with a grin.

"*That was the night Jesse asked me to be his girlfriend. Although, we'd technically been dating since we were kids. Jesse started coming around after Nate was adopted, and we've been really close since.*"

"*Adopted?*" I repeated. I knew that sign by heart. The gesture was so simple but held so much more meaning. As if someone were picking you up, just as you are. Damaged, broken, or cast aside, and taking you for theirs. I had often hoped that Carol would adopt me, hoping that she'd take me as I was, unconditionally. But I could only focus on one broken piece of me at a time. And that was one I refused to think about as I sat in a strange gym being mended from an attempted rape.

"*Yeah, I was eight when my parents adopted him.*"

"*Were you adopted too?*" I hated asking such intrusive questions, but I suppose we were beyond that as she moved to cleaning a scrape a few inches above my left breast.

"No, my parents said they always wanted to adopt. And I always wanted a brother, so I guess it worked out for everyone."

"I grew up in foster care." The admission felt strange as my fingers formed the words. I had never had to tell someone I grew up in foster care because everyone already knew. Mainly because I only really ever talked to Carol anyway.

Samone stared for a moment at my hands as I finished signing, her brows drawing together.

"How long have you been using sign language?"

I shrank in front of her, suddenly self-conscious.

"Not for long." That was an understatement. I had pored over those books every waking moment, dreaming about the day I'd finally be able to use them. But even in my wildest dreams, I never imagined it would be like this.

She stared openmouthed at me before her focus pulled back to my throat. I shrank even more in front of her as a fire ignited behind her stare. Like Nate's, but perhaps even scarier.

"Is that from foster care?"

A part of me wanted to crawl into a shell and hide as Samone started to crack away at the pieces I'd tried to glue together over the years. No one ever asked about my scar; they only stared and speculated. Most people never even spoke to me to begin with. But here in this room with her, I had no more walls to keep me safe. And another part of me clung to her, begging for her to truly *see* me. Not just the parts of me that she could see on the outside.

Her eyes glassed over from my silence. Because in the quiet, sometimes the answers are the loudest.

"Nate doesn't talk much about his life before us. He wouldn't actually talk at all until Jesse started hanging out with him." She wiped her hands with a towel before throwing it back on the table. *"All he really says is he survived, and I hate that for him. I hate that for the both of you..."*

Another quick knock rapped on the door before Nate peeked in.

"Jesse brought the clothes you asked for. I'll just leave them here, okay?" Nate dropped the large bag Jesse was holding moments before. He shot me one last lingering glance before closing the door again. And this time, I was the one blushing.

"Do you want help getting dressed, Claire?"

I shook my head as I reached for Nate's shirt. Samone quickly snatched it before I could pick it up and tossed it into a laundry basket on the floor .

"Not in that sweaty mess," she signed before heading to the bag Nate had delivered. Joy sprang across her face as she returned with it in tow, dropping it on the table next to us.

"You're a little shorter than me, but I think these will fit you just fine."

I started to shake my head, but Samone threw her hands on her hips, her face donning a mother hen glare.

"I want you to have them. Please." She unzipped the bag and pulled a black sweater and pants from the bag and placed them on the cot. *"They're really comfortable. Much better than Nate's UFC shirt."*

"U-F-C?" I repeated, spelling the letters awkwardly.

She paused at my question, her eyes narrowing at me like I had three heads.

"Do you know where you are right now?" she asked, pointing at the wall with all the pictures.

"No." I shrugged before I caught Nate's chiseled physique, his arm in midstrike above a cot in the corner of the room.

"You, my friend, stumbled your way into a UFC gym. Ultimate Fighting Championship. Nate and Jesse, they're fighters." Foggy memories of Nate saying those words before he pinned me echoed in my mind.

"Like...boxing?" I threw my fists with two short jabs in the air but winced as pain shot up my arm.

"Kind of. It gets a little more personal the way they fight." I felt her gaze bore into me as I scanned the rows of pictures. Men and even some women, their faces determined and focused as they danced around that strange cage.

"Why don't I give you some time to yourself. You can wear whatever you want, but these clothes are yours. I'll be back in a few."

"Thank you."

She nodded, her heavenly smile hugging me before she left the room. I'd never met strangers so generous before. Samone was the picture of lovely with her kindness and careful hands. And for a moment, I saw a glimpse of the future I might have had if someone had given me a chance the way Carol never could. The way Frank never even dreamed of. An education, the ability to communicate with the world without clinging to my notebook and pen. What it would have looked like if I had a *family*.

I dropped the towel in the basket in the corner, and for some reason I turned away from the picture on the wall where Nate stared back. His face pulled back dangerously as his fist lurched forward. Sweat dripping down his chest. *His tattoos.* I threw the sweatshirt Samone picked for me over my head, but I could still feel Nate's picture eyes on me. Those familiar haunting eyes. I climbed onto the cot, sitting underneath it to get a closer look, hoping no one would come in to find me drooling over his picture.

I slowly traced his face with my fingers, his eyes cutting right through to my soul. Even as he glared down at me, his sneer ferocious and delicious, he felt like a haven. Like home. Samone's words replayed in my head like a record. Nate was adopted. He was a *survivor*...like me. And maybe that's how I recognized him. He'd experienced trauma and heartbreaking change like I had. And that scar above his eye told me a story much like my own. And I suppose survivors recognize a part of themselves in each other. In that way, through all our pain, we connected.

The soft cushion from below felt cool and refreshing against my swollen skin. I laid my untouched cheek against the pillow and let out a breath as I focused on Nate's photo again. From here as I lay beneath him, his body tense and ready for the fight, I felt safer than I'd ever felt. Untouchable and protected. I let out a quiet laugh as my thoughts became more delirious again as exhaustion rolled through me. I pictured Nate, sword in hand, fending off the dragons much like Jason had once upon a happy time. But Nate didn't need swords. He'd do fine with just his hands. The way they moved when he spoke. I could only imagine what they did when they fought. What they did when he loved and touched...

Hushed voices whispered from the other side of the door, but they strung together like a chorus, lulling me to sleep. My eyelids fell heavy as Nate's voice carried the tune. I couldn't fight anymore as it swept over me and held me. And when the quiet came, I let it take me far, far away.

CHAPTER FIVE

"I'm calling Briggs. And he better find the fucks that—"

Samone clamped her hand around my forearm as I reached for my phone.

"She needs to be the one that reaches out to the police, Nate. You can't do that to her right now."

I felt the muscles in my jaw practically burst as I zeroed in on her.

"I'm sorry, were you in the same room with her? Someone beat the living shit out of her, Samone. She said they tried to rape her!"

She flinched at the vulgar gesture, and guilt swept over me as I caught Jesse's warning glare in the corner of my eye. I let out a breath, the breath I felt like I'd been holding since I first set eyes on Claire. She awakened something inside me. Something I kept away from everyone for a reason. The beast I only allowed out when I was in the cage. But as my eyes raked over her bruises and that goddamned scar, I couldn't hold on to the beast much longer.

"I'm sorry, okay? No woman deserves to be hurt like that. If that had been you in there..."

I couldn't finish the sentence as the beast threatened to break free again. She nodded, her eyes narrowing at me.

"Let her be the one to make that call, okay? You can't ambush her with the police right now. She's traumatized enough as it is."

"Samone's right. We shouldn't call the police just yet," Jesse agreed, but his face twisted into a sadistic smirk that only meant something amazing was about to come out of his mouth. "That just gives us some time to find the fuckers ourselves," he sneered, his eyes flashing with the vengeance I desperately craved.

"Are you serious?" Samone shoved Jesse back, but he barely budged, his eyes dancing with amusement as she pushed against him. She moved to push him again, but he caught her wrist, stilling her in his grasp.

"Look, I saw her for a second, Samone. Just a glimpse, enough to know that she was

wrecked. And Nate is right. God help us if someone hurt you like that..." His face grew even darker as he cupped her chin, pulling her closer. Samone's eyes widened as he placed a kiss on her forehead, gentle but possessive.

"*If someone tried to rape her, then we've got a rapist out on the street still. That's too close to this gym. Too close to you and all the other women that live around here.*"

"Make that more than one," I corrected through gritted teeth. Jesse's shoulders tensed as he met my gaze.

"Seriously?" he demanded, his face growing darker by the second. Samone nodded, dropping her eyes to the floor, her hands wringing nervously.

"*I'm calling your dad to come and stay with you until we get back.*" Before Samone could protest, Jesse pulled his phone out and walked into the hallway alone.

"*Where are you guys even going to go? She could have been attacked anywhere.*" Samone's eyes were tired and scared as she hugged herself.

My shoulders tensed as I remembered the uncoordinated shuffle of Claire's feet in the gym as she ran away from me. *Limped* away from me. Her leg was bleeding, and she was hurt and scared. She couldn't have made it far on that kind of injury.

"Just by the way she was limping, I imagine she wasn't attacked too far from here. And Briggs has been talking about some trouble they've been having a few blocks away near Carter's Street. I think it's worth starting there at least."

Jesse breezed out into the hallway, throwing his phone in his pocket.

"Your dad is three minutes out. Did you just say Carter's Street?"

Before I could answer, Samone stepped in front of him, her body shivering. "*Seriously, don't go down there. You guys are tough in the cage, but what if they have guns? You can't shoot them with your fists.*"

Jesse laughed as he slung an arm around her shoulder and kissed her hair.

"Samone. Have you *seen* these?" He flexed his arm in front of her proudly. "They're illegal in thirty-seven states and sixty-two countries—there's no way they'll survive these suckers."

Samone stared at him, her throat bobbing at Jesse's ridiculous confidence. Her eyes began to well and Jesse's smile disappeared as he drew her in closer.

"*We will be careful, okay? Your brother and I, we're stupid, but we're not that stupid. We don't take fights we know we can't win. If it's too dangerous, we're out of there, okay?*" He swiped away a tear and pressed his forehead to hers. And these were the moments that I was grateful Jesse was in our lives. He was my best friend, and he loved Samone. He would do anything for her, and he made it known with everything he did. Everything he said. A true gentleman, like most fighters.

Samone nodded and let him kiss her cheek before she pulled away, glaring at both of us. The death glare that could take us down faster than any of our opponents ever could.

"*You guys better not do anything stupid, okay?*" she demanded as headlights flooded the gym windows. Dad was here. And in just a few minutes, we'd be out there looking for the bastards who put their hands on Claire. I could almost taste their blood now...

Dad's urgent outline appeared at the door, and Jesse ran to open the door for him. As soon as the latch clicked, Dad shoved Jesse out of the way and lurched toward Samone.

"*Baby, you alright?*" He searched her reddened eyes and then turned to me, his nostrils flaring. "What the hell is going on?" he demanded, taking a step closer.

Dad was a ball of fury, and a hell of a fighter in his heyday. He'd taken down hundreds of powerful men in his career that they coined him "the Machine," programmed to defeat and conquer. The first few nights I'd stayed with him, I fully expected him to use his fists just like Frank had. I hated that Samone was there, just like I hated that Maddie was with Frank. I worried that he'd hurt her, and if he was going to hurt someone, I wanted it to be me. I even provoked him for a few months, breaking furniture, kicking in walls just to see if it would make him snap like Frank had. I even threw his championship trophy to the ground where it shattered into a million unfixable pieces. Just like me. He just stood there, his arms outstretched with love and patience. Something I never understood. Something new. And in the same breath, he'd wrapped his strong arms around me and cradled me. He'd let me fight him, but most of all, he let me cry. He taught me what was worth fighting for, and what it meant to fight.

He'd shown me videos of him sparring. I'd seen the broken, bloodied faces of his opponents after he was done with them. I'd seen the damage he could do, but he never put his hands on me or Samone. Not once. Instead, he played dolls with her and let her brush his hair and put makeup on his face. He treated her like the princess she was. And now as his baby girl stood before him with watery eyes and his son had specks of blood on his chest and hands from Claire's injuries, the fight behind his eyes roared. Something I respected and loved about him. Because to him, his family was everything just like it was to me. And right now, we were hurting.

"Nate, you better look at me," he warned, his shoulders rippling with his words.

"It's okay, Dad. No one hurt Samone. She's just nervous for us." I tried to shoot Samone a reassuring glance, but he stepped in front of her, blocking my view.

"And why would she be nervous for you?" he demanded, his eyes still trained on me.

"Because we're about to go have ourselves a fight." I could feel my muscles strain as I pictured the mess we were about to make. The hurt we were going to bring to anyone that harmed her.

"You know good and well, fights stay in the cage, Nate." This was rule number one at the gym. It had been the unwritten rule that I'd been raised on. So deeply rooted in everything we did, it was practically punishable by law. There was only one exception that would redeem a fight outside the cage. *To protect and defend.* And by God, that's what I was going to do.

"Dad, they tried to rape M—" I stopped myself as I nearly said Maddie's name. A name I hadn't said out loud since the day I found out she died. Even in the throes of my nightmares when I was back at Frank's and Dad would wake me up, saving me. Saving us both. I refused to say her name. My parents knew my past. They'd read the horrific story that the doctors and social workers had printed out before they agreed to invite me into their home, their family. I'd told Jesse one night when he got me drunk after a particularly gruesome takedown, what Frank had done to us. The fight always brought back the memories, the need to protect. The need to hurt. On that night, I couldn't swallow the pain anymore. Especially now as I nearly let her name slip, I wanted to tear something apart. Because she wasn't Maddie.

My dad's shoulders stiffened at my words, and he took another step closer.

"They tried to rape *who?*" he repeated, a muscle in his jaw jumping as the fire in his eyes blazed.

I tried to answer, but my voice was stuck in the raw anger that took hold of me. Images of them hurting her and clawing at her body rushed through me in disgusting waves.

Samone quickly came to my rescue and began signing the impossible explanation. I was grateful for her, as she covered all the things I couldn't vocalize. All the things I didn't want to repeat, for fear of allowing the beasts out before I got to the ones that hurt her. My dad's gaze shifted from my bloodied hands to the closed office door, his jaw tightening as Samone finished. He moved toward it, but this time, the fury my Dad came in with shot through me. My hand clasped around his wrist, my eyes shooting him with warning.

No one goes near her.

He flexed under my grasp, but his face softened as he caught my expression. My dad was a man to be reckoned with, but he had a heart of gold that was able to piece together the broken boy I was into the solid fighter I am today. And in the silence, he knew what I needed. What Claire needed. He dropped his chin in understanding, and I quickly let go.

"I'll stay with Samone, and I'll trust that my training didn't go to waste over all these years." A spark of excitement burst behind his eyes before it disappeared completely—a fair warning mixed with the thrill of the fight. Something we both clung to in the worst moments of our lives.

"*Be careful*," Samone signed, her hands circling and pleading. I squeezed her hand and kissed her knuckles, thanking her for what she did for us. What she did for Claire. But then the need to crush consumed me, and I quickly dropped her hand. I needed to get out of here before I let the beasts out too soon.

We weren't the ones she needed to be worried about.

The streets were bare as we drove through the night. In a way, I was grateful because there was no more prey for the bastards to take advantage of. The streetlights flickered as we neared Carter's Street. Parts of some of the buildings were missing, rooves torn apart, and walls splintered as if someone had rammed into them. I clenched my fists as I pictured Claire wandering alone anywhere near this hellhole, helpless and defenseless.

"What is that?" Jesse leaned toward the wheel, squinting at something sprawled against the edge of the curb. The tail of the headlights flashed over it as we got closer, and I prayed that it wasn't another hurt woman. I jumped out first, the truck barely into park as I rushed toward the motionless form. My hands clutched at cold fabric, my fingers brushing over uneven metal. A zipper. Relief swept over me as I rolled it over. It was just a duffel bag, stuffed to the brim with awkwardly shaped items.

"It's just a bag," I called out to Jesse as I started to unzip it. His footsteps cracked over the gravel a few feet away before he stopped.

"Nate."

I knew that tone. That was the same tone he used when he tried to tell me he was dating Samone. Or the time I'd shared my fucked-up past with him, and he wanted to talk about it the morning after.

I let the bag fall from my grasp as I stood and peered out into the black of the night. Jesse's phone was pointed at a hidden corner that the light from above didn't reach. A dark corner where bad things could happen. Where bad things did happen. My shoulders tensed as I saw it.

Blood. A splatter, gleaming from the light. Still wet. A pile of what looked like shattered glass lay a few feet away. I carefully stepped over the blood and reached for a particularly large and still-intact shard of glass. No, *porcelain*.

What the hell?

I picked up another large piece and placed the broken edges together. One gaping hole for an eye to see through stared back, the disturbing curve of a malicious grin painted on the lower half mockingly.

"What the fuck?" Jesse demanded, leaning over my shoulder to examine it.

"She said they were wearing masks, Jesse," I practically spat as I stared down at the disturbing piece of evidence in my hand. A shudder of anger rushed through me as I pictured her held down, staring back at this porcelain nightmare. Smiling and taunting as they tried to rape her.

Movement caught my eye in the unlit corners of the street. A figure cowering in the shadows.

"Who's there?" I shouted as Jesse flooded the light from his phone in their direction.

The quick blur of someone's shoes skittered in the light before escaping back into the darkness. Jesse and I took off toward the sound and quickly closed in on them, compared to their slow, uneven footsteps. Like Claire's was. Flashbacks of me shoving Claire against the wall in the gym burned through me. I'd forced myself on her and basically molested her after she'd been nearly raped. And she couldn't tell me to stop. She couldn't say *anything*. I couldn't make that mistake again. I quickly yanked on Jesse's shirt, and we slowed down until we were just a few feet away.

"Hey! We don't want to hurt you, okay?" I called out to the shadows.

The footsteps stopped, and loud, heavy breathing huffed in the darkness.

They were out of shape, and they weren't going to be able to run much further. So I took a step back, pulling Jesse with me.

"We just want to know if you saw a girl here. If you saw her get hurt." I hated the way I underplayed what happened to her. But if they knew something, I wanted them to talk, so best to keep it simple.

The footsteps shifted, and Jesse moved his phone to light the source of the sounds. Cold, gray eyes stared back, as wispy white hair fell every which way across his head and face. His clothes were dirty and ragged, his face worn and weathered from life and the cold.

"Did you see what happened?" I repeated, holding up the broken shards of the mask in my hand.

He lifted his hand, shielding the light from the phone, eyeing the both of us like he wanted something first. I quickly pulled out my wallet and held up a twenty-dollar bill, hoping that was enough.

"Here, take this." I stretched my hand out to him, softening my stance, raising the other gently. He quickly hobbled forward, snatching the bill from my grasp.

"They had her over there." He pointed where we'd just come from, the duffel bag still shining under the light.

"Who? Did you know any of them?"

The man shook his head, fear flashing behind his eyes.

"We don't mess with the Vex."

"The Vex?" Jesse repeated, taking a step closer. The man nodded, surveying Jesse up and down like he wanted him for dessert.

"They take women here sometimes..." His voice was weak and gravelly as he shot Jesse a toothless grin.

"And what do they do to them?" I took a step closer, tired of his games.

"They...*hurt* them." His eyes danced as he threw my word back at me.

"Where did they go?" I tried not to bark back, but I couldn't keep at this much longer. Not when we were talking about hurting *her*.

A squeaky laugh erupted in the darkness as the man held out his hand again. This time Jesse pulled some cash out of his pocket and slammed it into his palm.

"They fought. And she escaped, the lucky bitch. I've never seen one get away..." He hacked out another laugh. I tensed at his words, letting them replay. The bastard watched all of this go down. Every single rape. And he was laughing about it. I lunged forward, throwing my forearm into his neck, shoving him into the wall. He wasn't laughing anymore.

"Where did they go?" I hissed as the stench of alcohol fumed from his breath.

"One of 'em got away and headed down on Kendrick Court. The other was pretty messed up. He finally got up and turned down the corner there." He cocked his chin over where the duffel bag lay.

"What do you mean they fought?" Jesse asked, raising the flashlight higher, blinding him.

"Yeah, they got into it. He was about to take her when the other pushed him off. It was really somethin', the best show yet." His gray eyes glowed as he recounted the event like it was some fucked-up theatre spectacle.

"Tell us more about the Vex," I said, digging my arm further into his throat. Fear flashed behind his soulless eyes again, but he shook his head.

"I can't." His body started to shake as I pressed into him. "Whatever you want to do to me would be like heaven compared to what *they* would do. I've seen the shit they do to guys that talk."

I finally pushed off him, disgusted.

"You got a family? A wife? Girlfriend?" His toothless grin returned as he winked over at Jesse. "A boyfriend?"

"What the fuck do you care about my family?" Jesse was on him this time, before I could get to him. The toothless grin grew wider. More evil.

"Better hold tight, because they'll be coming for 'em. The Vex is on the lookout tonight, especially from the shit that went down over there." He looked around, his body shaking again. "You better leave, because they're probably watching us right now. And they don't take too kindly to strangers."

"Fuck off," Jesse yelled, pushing away from him. He quickly grabbed my arm and started pulling me to the truck. "Let's go get these bastards."

"I wouldn't if I were you," the man taunted in a raspy voice. "They'd have a lot of fun with the two of you." His maniacal laugh bounced off the walls as we headed toward the truck.

"Wait, I think this is hers." I quickly yanked free from Jesse's grip and snatched up the bag next to the blood.

We both piled back into the truck, and Jesse shifted into drive again, peeling out of Carter's Street, headed toward Kendrick Court. As we drove, something dug into my stomach from the bag sitting in my lap. A corner of a book peeking out of the bag. I started to push it back into the bag when the familiar raised edges of the title seemed to fly off the cover. One of my favorite sign language books that both Jesse and I had learned from when we were kids. I pulled the zipper down further until the book was fully visible, running my finger along the spine. I flipped through the pages, all of them worn through like someone had pored through it every day for years. I flipped back to the front page, the most worn of them all. And at the top, in a childlike scrawl, was a name, just barely legible in the dark.

Maddie C. Hampshire.

I punched the car light on as we sped down the street.

"Shit!" Jesse cursed, the light blinding us both.

Maddie C. Hampshire. The girl I couldn't save. The girl who possessed my every single waking thought. The thoughts that fueled my fight, kept me invincible in the cage. Undefeated. Because of Maddie C. Hampshire. But Maddie was dead. I'd seen her bleed out and take her last breath. They *told* me she'd died.

"Turn the car around." My voice was so low, just a whisper over the roar of Jesse's engine.

"What is that?" He pointed at the book, his eyes still glued to the road.

"Turn the car around," I repeated, my voice cracking and pathetic as I brushed my fingers over the impossible name.

Her scar. Her eyes, her *mouth.* They were all Maddie's. Claire was *Maddie.* I slammed my palm into my forehead, running my fingers through my hair. But he'd killed her. Sliced her throat open before she bled out as I just fucking watched. I threw a jab at the dashboard, my knuckles cracking against the surface.

"Fuck! Nate, what the hell?"

"It's *her,* Jesse." My throat closed up as I read her name again, over and over. I couldn't get enough of it.

"Who?" Jesse yelled back incredulously as he jerked the car into park.

"Claire. Jesse, Claire is *Maddie.*"

"Maddie? Like...your princess Maddie? But you—"

"Turn the car around, I need to get back to her. I need—"

"Nate. Calm down, alright? I'll take you back there, but let's think about this. She's been through a lot... Do you really want to bring her back to that night now?"

I pictured her face, terrified and bruised. Jesse was right—she'd had more than enough. She needed to rest, to heal. Bringing back the shitty past was the last thing she needed. I threw my hands through my hair again as I stared at her name, the only thing holding me together and shattering me at the same time.

"Look at you, man. You're losing it. You want to do that to her tonight? All of *this*?" He waved his hand at me as I pulled the book closer. "You sure that's even hers?"

It had to be. Everything about her seemed like Maddie. I rifled through the rest of the bag, tearing through the other books. All of them tokened with the same name. The same princess. I pulled a notepad out and flipped through the pages, the same sloppy chicken scratch filling each line. Random verses, poems, and unsettling comments filled each page. Requests, simple messages, and doodles. The last page cut right through my core, the writing more desperate and determined than the others.

Just give me one more day to find a job.

The words stung. The whole fucking notebook stung. And then it hit me. This was how she communicated. The stiff uncertain way she signed. At first, I thought it was the effects of shock, but it all started to make sense now. She had nothing but pen and paper to communicate for who knows how long. Fury washed over me as I put the pieces together. The way her bag was packed, and her plea for more time to find a job. She'd been kicked out.

Jesse shifted the car into drive, his knuckles white against the steering wheel as he too saw the fucked-up pieces fall together.

"Let's go get your princess."

CHAPTER SIX

My eyes fluttered open as hazy sunlight poured in the unfamiliar room. I lifted my hand to shield my eyes but winced from the pain, a sick reminder of the terrifying events from last night. Nate's protective stance caught midstrike above me in the photo eased my mind until I caught the broad outline of a man sitting in a chair next to the bed.

It was Nate. Relief spilled over me, his protective presence filling the room, but my stomach tightened from the tortured expression twisting at his face. Dark circles puffed under his deep, haunted eyes. His hair was even more out of sorts as if he'd been clawing through it all night, dark stubble lining his jaw.

"*You...okay?*" I signed nervously, scanning the room for Samone. I started to sit up, but he held up a hand, pleading I stay put.

"*Is this yours?*" he asked, pulling a bag sitting under his chair out into the sunlight. The familiar deep cobalt blue of the bag glittered in the light, but I frowned again at his face, as if the weight of the world was riding on my answer. I braved another scan of the room, suddenly wishing someone else was with us. His shoulders tensed as I swept the office, and I uneasily met his gaze again.

"*You know you're safe with me, right? I would never hurt you.*" Those familiar eyes ached for my understanding. But those eyes tugged at something deeper, buried under years of pain and silence. A boy and his castle shifted in and out of focus, like an involuntary reflex. A hammer to the heart. Jason's shaggy head peeking in my room after I'd been abandoned.

Do you see the castle now?

I blinked away the distant memory as Nate came back into focus, his eyes glassing over from my silence.

I slowly nodded, his shoulders relaxing slightly, though sadness crept across his face as if he didn't believe me. He unzipped the bag and carefully pulled out the notebook I'd used for years to communicate with Carol, filled with the short, unbecoming back-and-forth banter I held with her. He flipped to the last page and turned it toward me. I flinched at the pitiful plea I'd scribbled, its words mocking and taunting as I read them.

Just give me one more day to find a job.

"*Is this yours?*" he repeated, his eyes crisping at the edges again. I slowly lifted my chin, trying to regain the dignity that those words tore away from me. And then I nodded, fighting the tears that threatened at the corners of my eyes. I watched Nate's knuckles whiten from his grip, the pages wrinkling against his fingers. He slowly reached back into the bag and pulled out my favorite sign language book. His hands were careful with it, the spine barely held together from the years I'd sifted through its pages.

"*And this? Is this yours too?*"

I shrank at his question, humiliation flooding my cheeks at how pathetic I probably seemed. Between my pleading chicken scratch and my broken signs, I could feel him piece the truth together. Anger rolled through me as I sat up, ignoring his question.

"*Why did you go through my stuff?*" I demanded before pulling the degrading message I'd scrawled from his grasp. Guilt replaced the confusing emotions that were there before, but he stayed firm, his shoulders squaring as he held the book out to me again.

"Is this book yours?" he repeated, his jaw popping as if he were losing his patience. The man was damn near frightening even without being cornered in a room with him. But I focused on the way his body seemed controlled and careful. I appreciated the tender way he'd touched me last night after he realized I wasn't trying to steal from him. And though he seemed to watch me with an intensity that seemed far too personal, I believed that he would never intentionally hurt me.

"Yes." I finally surrendered, pulling the book from his grasp as well, tucking my belongings safely against my chest. I hated being so vulnerable when I had already been so weak and helpless last night. And in this moment, I craved to be in the safety of Carol's home again. There, I didn't have to face intrusive questions from strangers or feel the invading hands of men where they didn't belong.

Nate's eyes dropped to the floor, and I watched nervously as his arms flexed as if he were considering punching something. And I didn't want to wait around to see what it would be. I started to dip my feet to the floor, when he peered back up at me. His expression nearly stole my breath away. So much kindness, even love radiated from his face, and I couldn't keep up with his swinging emotions. The familiar roller-coaster ride I'd been on before so many years ago.

"Do you still need a job?" His voice was tender and judgment-free. He was genuinely asking, not just poking fun at my predicament. Not that Nate seemed to be the type of man who would make a woman squirm on purpose.

"Because if you do, I could really use some help around the gym." My heart stuttered with his words and the sincerity behind them. "Our front desk manager quit a few weeks ago, and we've been a mess without one. And I think you'd be perfect." He crossed his arms over his chest, his muscles bulging as he watched me. Waiting.

"What does a front desk manager do?" I shifted uneasily again, his gaze so intense it almost hurt.

"They welcome all the members as they come in to train, manage class schedules, and send out newsletters to our members. And...some laundry and cleaning here and there." Foggy memories of me tripping over carts of dirty towels from last night cut through me. He wasn't just being nice; he really did need someone. After years of managing Carol's household, I knew I could easily get this place back into shape with a vengeance. But the thought of welcoming guests without a voice made my stomach knot in all the wrong ways. Not to mention with disgusting bruises on my face.

I pointed to my throat and then to my face, shaking my head.

"Are you trying to say that you'd distract my fighters with your undeniable beauty?" And then he laughed. And I nearly melted at his playfulness. Nate was terrifying, but he was a straight up charmer that even I couldn't resist, even under these strange circumstances.

I looked down at my hands, blood pumping up my chest and my neck from his forward comment. No one had ever told me I was beautiful before.

"Hey, eyes up." His fingers cupped my chin, lifting my face toward him. I startled at his closeness, but his smile was reassuring, and I relaxed against his touch.

"First off, Samone hangs out here all the time and mends most of their injuries. They freaking love her, and some of them even know some sign language." He removed his hand, but his body was still close enough I could smell the cool mint on his breath. "Second, most of the fighters in our gym come here to train, not to talk. As long as you keep things organized and their equipment clean, you'll be just fine." He gently tugged the notepad and book out of my grip and placed them on the cot, stealing my makeshift shield.

"Third, if any fighters are too distracted by your undeniable beauty, you leave me to deal with them, understand?"

I shifted on the cot, fighting the smile that tugged at the corner of my mouth. This was too good to be true. Carol had instilled in me for years that there were no free handouts. And this seemed far too much like a free handout. My eyes drifted across his arms, his hands, wondering what he might want from me.

"It doesn't pay that great, but it's something to get you started and on your feet. We can start you part-time and then move you to full-time if you like it. What do you say we start with $15.00 an hour?"

I couldn't fight the shock that flooded my face this time. I quickly shook my head, dismissing the ridiculously generous offer. The most money I'd had in my entire life was the twenty dollars that Carol had given to me before she'd kicked me out.

"Okay...$16.00 an hour?" He leaned even closer, his hopeful gaze bearing into me.

"That's way too much. I can't accept."

He eyed me, his chin set as he considered my rejection. "Then let's talk about the other elephant in the room." He nudged the bag at his feet, filled with all my belongings.

"You don't have a place to stay, do you?" I could tell by the way his throat bobbed as he spoke that he hated asking me, but his gaze was hard and unrelenting, determined to get the truth out of me, and I was a terrible liar.

I nearly dropped my eyes to the floor again, but I didn't know if I'd be able to handle it if his hand touched my face one more time. Something about the way his hands lingered confused and terrified me, left me wanting more and yet made me feel more vulnerable than I knew what to do with.

"No," I finally admitted with a quick shake of my head.

He nodded, but his eyes remained unchanged as if he'd expected my answer. And for that I hated him. He seemed to be holding all the cards in a game I could never win.

"Jesse and I need help with rent. We have a spare bedroom that no one uses, and it would be perfect for you, if you wanted it that is. We'll start you at

$16.00 an hour, and you can pitch in with the rent and groceries. Eventually, if you like it here, we can talk about bumping your salary at a later date. You in?"

And finally, I felt like I was in the game and he'd dealt me a winning hand. The thought of sleeping in the same house as Nate scared me, but for all the wrong reasons. I wasn't worried that he would do something to me, but more so worried that I *wanted* him to do something to me. But he was playing as fair as he could, and I had no other prospects other than him. And I was glad I didn't.

"$8.00 an hour and we have a deal." I extended my hand out to him, meeting his focused and determined stare. His eyes flashed with relief as his hand swallowed mine whole.

"$16.00 it is. You can start whenever you're ready." His smile grew as he gripped my hand, refusing to let me pull out of the deal. Finally after a few beats he dropped my hand, his warmth trailing across my entire body.

"Would you like me to take you home?" I relished the word. *Home.* And yet, I somehow felt like I was already there. His eyes drifted south as if he were seeing if I was good to walk, but heat washed over me again as his gaze settled on my throat.

I nodded absentmindedly, and without a second to spare, his other hand pushed against my back.

"Alright, just lean against me and I'll push you up." I instinctively arched against the pressure of his hand, my chest pressing against his. Last night, I never thought I wanted another man to touch me again, but with the gentle way his hand splayed across my skin, I never wanted his hands to leave me. He moved me easily as if I weighed nothing, until my feet hit the ground.

He carefully pulled me up, but he didn't back away. Instead, his hand shifted to my hip, his careful gaze stealing another once-over.

"You okay?" he whispered, his deep brown eyes landing on my lips. I couldn't answer. His woodsy scent was everywhere. It seemed so familiar, like a brisk fall evening in front of a bonfire. Or a sweet summer night next to a tall oak tree where a prince and princess used to laugh and play.

I jumped as a gentle knock rapped on the door. Jesse's brilliant blue eyes shifted from Nate to me, his mouth curving in a mischievous grin.

"Hope I'm not interrupting anything..."

I started to pull away from Nate, but my feet were unsteady, and instead of giving me space, he moved closer, keeping his hand firmly planted on my hip.

"Jesse, meet our new roommate, and our new front desk manager." Nate beamed at me, as if he couldn't have been prouder.

"Fuck yeah!" Jesse's grin grew as he surveyed me approvingly. "When are you moving in?"

"Right now. We were just heading to the truck."

"Well…Briggs is here, and I told him that Claire wanted to speak to him." Jesse's grin disappeared as he shifted his gaze to me.

Briggs? Who was he, and why would I want to speak to him?

"Is Samone still here?" Nate asked, his body heat blanketing me. Jesse shook his head.

"She went home a few hours ago. She needed some rest."

Nate's jaw hardened as if he were in deep thought before he turned toward me, his tone softening.

"The police officer I mentioned last night is here. And I think it would be good if you would talk to him about what happened to you." I cringed at the thought of trying to sign my experience, my vocabulary already shaky and uncertain.

"You don't have to do anything you don't want, but it might help find the men who hurt you." Nate's hands slipped up to my shoulders, reassuring me. Unexplainable safety and protection covered me again. And those warm eyes that seemed to worship everything about me. He made me feel capable. Somehow, he seemed to make reliving it okay, as long as he'd be there.

Without thinking, I nodded again, my heart skipping a beat as his hand cradled my face, skimming my throat. And why oh why did I want to melt into him every time he touched me? He'd had me pinned against the wall, his hands exploring as he searched me just hours before. His movements had been rough and merciless. And yet now as he looked at me, he revered me like I was a queen. *His* queen. I felt like I knew his very soul. Like we'd met in a past life and we'd finally found each other again.

Relief seemed to overcome him from my answer as he turned to Jesse. A silent transaction passed between them, and then Jesse was gone. I paused at the way they so easily communicated without having to say anything. It was as if they could read each other's thoughts with just one look. One simple glance and there was mutual understanding. I had always craved that kind of relationship, especially since most of my communication was silent to begin with. But Carol never seemed to understand me, or she never tried anyway. The only thing I'd come close to was with Jason. How he knew when I was scared or hungry without me having to say anything. He always knew how to hold me and take care of me, even though I never asked him to.

"Let's have you sit back down, okay?" Nate gently pushed me back toward the mattress, his muscles hardening against my arms. I fought the blush that came hard, but he seemed not to notice. Instead, he leaned closer and whispered in my ear.

"Whenever you want to stop, just let me know okay?" His stubble grazed my ear, and my neck practically burst into flames from the heat of his breath. I couldn't nod, I couldn't do anything. I just stared, before a lean but very well-defined man peeked in. I eyed his pale skin, stark against a dark bruise along his right eye. His skin blanched even more as he surveyed me, wincing at the bruises on my neck.

"The fuck happened to your face, Briggs?" Nate demanded as he moved away from me and pulled a chair up for the man. "I thought you weren't fighting last night."

"Work," he muttered, the weight of the world seemingly crushing him as he sat down in front of me. I knew that look well, and whatever demons he was battling seemed to be winning. He eyed me for a moment longer, as if he were waiting for me to talk first. Uneasy silence filled the room as I stared back, unwilling to begin.

"I hear your name is Claire." His tone was soft and careful like Nate's. "My name is Peter, but most guys here call me Briggs. You, however, can call me whatever you want, okay?"

I nodded as his eyes shifted to my wrists, a flurry of emotions rushing over his face. Anger, pity, and a few others I couldn't quite read. "You want to tell me what happened to you?" I fought the urge to squirm as his focus drifted to my scar, the inevitable place where most eyes ventured.

"*It's okay*," Nate encouraged, signing as he spoke. Briggs watched Nate as he signed and then peered over at the notepad sitting next to me on the cot.

"Jesse says you can't speak. So if you prefer, you can write anything that comes to mind."

And suddenly I was grateful for him. Writing felt safe, and in the moment, safety seemed unobtainable.

"Why don't we start from where you were when this happened to you?"

I shifted uneasily, not sure how to answer that question. Was it hell? Because it definitely felt like hell.

I shook my head and shrugged, crossing my arms across my chest in hopes to create an invisible barrier.

"I found her bag off of Carter's Street. Next to a broken mask." A vein in Nate's temple popped out, his hands digging into his pockets, as if he refused to sign the disgusting truth. "She said there were two men wearing masks."

"Do you remember any identifiable traits? Smells, voices, personal descriptions, tattoos?" Briggs leaned forward, his proximity a little too close for comfort. I followed a bead of sweat drip from his forehead all the way down to his chin. The room was humid, but a distinct chill seemed to pass between us. I shivered involuntarily as unwanted foggy memories filled my mind. My attacker's face, his oily hair slicked back behind his ears. The way his breath smelled like cigarettes and that horrible beer they'd given me. Then the quick flash of the compass tattoo filled my thoughts, but I couldn't be for sure. At this point, I wasn't sure if any of it was real. It all felt like a horrible nightmare, and I couldn't grasp any concrete details.

"*I'm not sure.*" I shook my head, gripping my elbows tighter.

Briggs leaned back, silently surveying me again before turning to Nate.

"Did you find anything else while you were down near Carter's?"

Nate shifted as he glanced over at me uncomfortably. "Some asshole saw what happened. He said that some group called the Vex did this to her. That they've done this kind of thing before."

I stared at Nate, shocked. The man knowingly ventured into the street where I'd been attacked, looking for the dangerous men that hurt me. He even interrogated some stranger for me. Found my bag for me. And I'd been so angry at him for going through my things.

Briggs's shoulders stiffened and then sagged as if the weight of his burdens was finally burying him alive.

"We know all about the Vex. They're a dangerous organization we've been trying to take down for months." He eyed my bruises again, his gray eyes clouding over with each word. "They're brutal...and fatal, especially when it comes to women."

"Did you just say *months*? Why the hell am I just now finding out about them? They've been fucking around my gym for the last few *months*?" Nate seemed to grow three more feet as he towered over Briggs, his chest heaving with anger.

"Look, Nate. We've been trailing them for a while trying to nail every member and take them all down in one sweep. We've asked the media to keep it quiet so they don't think we're onto them yet." He glanced over at me and lowered his voice to a deadly whisper. "Clearly they don't give a fuck about human life, and they're not something to be messed with." He waved a hand at my face. I flinched at the example I was. The poster child for the ruthlessness of the Vex.

"So you didn't tell me there's a gang that brutalizes women *two blocks* from my gym? Just because you didn't want to own up to the fact your force hasn't done its job yet?" Nate took a step closer, his fists clenching. "You didn't think that our female fighters would want to know about the threat? That maybe my sister deserved to know so we could keep a lookout?" His shoulders rippled as he got daringly close to Briggs. "And maybe if we had been on the lookout, we could have protected Claire."

Briggs quickly stood, meeting Nate's gaze as if he'd finally found his fight again.

"As I said, the Vex is not a gang to be toyed with, Nate. The best fighters here wouldn't stand a chance against them. Not even you. And don't you dare tell me whether I'm doing my job or not. You don't know the half of the hell we've been through over them." Briggs rolled up his sleeve as if he were preparing to swing.

I felt the blood drain from my face all the way down to the floor as I caught sight of Briggs's arm. A sharp compass tattoo just visible enough to shatter me into a thousand pieces. The images of last night came flooding back in waves. As the masked man nervously watched another assault me. Break me. It wasn't a nightmare. It was a memory, plain as day. Betrayal filled me as I watched Briggs edge closer to Nate, his body tensing, preparing for the fight. His tattooed arm, strong and ready. Strong enough to protect if he wanted. But last night, he'd been too late. Briggs was here taking notes over my attack when he'd been a part of it the whole time. He was the same man that had torn my attacker off me. But he was the same man that had allowed him to assault me and mark my body. The same man that had offered me a drink and watched behind that goddamned mask as another man tortured me.

But *why?*

I let out a shaky breath, my body shivering from the chill that shifted in the room. Both of them turned toward me, but I couldn't take my eyes off his tattoo. The same tattoo that had led me out of that hell hole into an even deeper one.

"Claire?" Nate's voice was tender as he reached for me, but I pulled away.

I chopped my hand into my palm, signing "*stop,*" and he immediately retracted his hand, hurt and guilt crawling across his face.

My lip trembled as I lifted my gaze, daring to make eye contact with Briggs. To confirm the tale I so desperately wished wasn't true. Flashes of nervous glances behind the mask filled my mind. His voice echoing against the street as he demanded the other to get off me.

"Claire?" Briggs offered, taking a step closer, but he stopped as our eyes met. It was just for a moment. A blink of an eye before I tore my focus back on his tattoo. And the way that he swallowed, his chin lifting in acknowledgement, he knew. He knew what I knew.

CHAPTER SEVEN

The drive home was quiet after Claire ended the meeting with Briggs. She refused to talk to me, even after Briggs finally left the room. She wouldn't even look me in the eye. I hated myself with how crazy I had been, making the whole goddamned meeting about me and my gym, when it should have been about her. And she had already been so reluctant to talk in the first place.

"Claire, I can't begin to tell you how sorry I am," I whispered, peeking over at her. My heart nearly ripped in two as I caught her small frame balled against the passenger door, as far away from me as possible.

"I shouldn't have said anything. That was supposed to be your opportunity to talk, not mine." God, I needed someone to fucking knock the sense into me. She shifted in her seat but kept her eyes glued to her hands.

Maddie, please, please forgive me.

We finally rolled into the driveway, and for the first time she sat up, her eyes widening as the garage opened. A hint of a smile tugged at the corner of her mouth, and a selfish part of me was happy that she was happy. I couldn't stand to see her so upset. After she'd ended the meeting with Briggs, she was in even worse shape than before. As if she'd been attacked all over again. Of course she'd been scared. There were two professionally trained fighters at each other's throats when all she needed was a safe place to talk. To be protected.

I cut the engine and turned toward her.

"Claire, will you please look at me?"

The ghost of her smile quickly faded, but she shifted her focus to me, her eyes nervous as they met mine.

"Please know how sorry I am. I should have allowed you the space to talk. I—"

The coolness of her fingertips caught me off guard as they grazed across my jaw. Her honey eyes peered up at me, a guarded curiosity behind them. I let her hand explore as her stare moved above my brow toward my scar. The place where Frank had sliced my temple open after he'd killed Maddie. But Maddie was alive, and her mouth was inches from mine. A sudden sense of realization crossed her face, as if she'd just realized she was touching me, and she quickly withdrew her hand, color flushing her cheeks.

"Hey...it's okay," I whispered, reaching for her hand, craving for her touch again. She shook her head and bit her lip, mortified.

"*I'm sorry, I don't know why I did that,*" she signed, putting distance back between us.

Had she recognized me? Was this the time to tell her who I was? No. I couldn't see her in any more pain. I'd done enough of that for today. She needed more time to heal like Jesse said. Maddie deserved at least that much from me.

I needed to watch myself, *force* myself to use Claire instead of Maddie. The questions circled like hungry vultures above me. How did she survive? What happened after she was taken away? Why didn't she try to find me? And God help me, what had her life been like without me? Pain sliced deep as I remembered the pleading statement she'd written for more time to find a job. That she'd been communicating through pen and paper for who knows how long. My life had been filled with so many blessings, so many second chances. She deserved them so much more than I did.

And now I wanted nothing more than to give her back the semblance of the life she deserved.

"Do you want to see inside?" I asked, pointing toward the door. The trace of her smile reappeared, and I held on to it, never wanting to let it go.

"Okay, just let me help you." I quickly got out and rounded the front of the truck as she pushed her door open. I slowly extended my hand for her, careful to give her space. She took my hand in hers and slid to the edge of the seat, her eyes meeting mine again. Thoughtful but guarded. Golden like the sun.

"*I'm not mad at you.*" Her hand trembled in mine as she signed with the other.

Sweet relief spilled over me with her words. But her lip quivered, and I immediately wanted to sweep her up and carry her away, far away from any more pain.

"*Last night...*"

My thumb caught the tear before it fell across her cheek.

"Tell me, Claire. What's wrong?" I wanted so badly to steal her hurt, to hold her until it faded away.

Her shoulders sagged, her eyes dropping to her knees.

"Hey, keep your eyes up." I lifted her face, her body leaning into my touch again. I swiped her cheek, brushing another tear away as she peered up at me with those beautiful wide eyes.

"*Will you show me your house?*" Her smile returned, but deep hurt still flickered behind her gaze. She was going to tell me something important. I wanted to press for more, but I didn't want to push her away again.

"*Our* house," I corrected as I helped her to her feet. I carefully led her to the door and pushed it open for her. "After you."

She took a step inside, her smile widening as she swept over the kitchen. Jesse and I were successful fighters, and our earnings reflected that, but we kept our home modest enough. We'd just moved in last year, when we finally had enough money to pool together for a house.

"*It's like a* castle." Her words cut through me like a knife, and the way she peered over at me, the knife twisted deeper. Just like she used to as we danced around our tall oak tree.

She quickly helped herself to the fridge, peeking inside to see what we had. A girl after my own heart.

"Are you hungry?" A loud grumble of her stomach responded instead, and she threw a hand over her mouth to cover a silent giggle. God, I missed her laugh. The sweet memory of it echoed in my thoughts as we played under the moon.

"Ma—" I stopped dead in my tracks as I almost let her true name slip. Her breath hung in the room as she waited for me to continue.

"Maybe I can show you to your room, and you can rest a little while I make you some breakfast? Do you like pancakes?"

My heart ached at the way her eyes lit up like a beautiful morning sunrise. God, I wanted to pamper this woman, to show her what she deserved and to cherish her for the queen she was.

"Alright, take my hand."

She gently pressed her palm into mine, and I wrapped my fingers around hers, letting her warmth wash over me. I slowly walked her down the hall to the spare bedroom, the room with the most natural light. The morning sun flooded the walls, washing over the white bedspread and the sitting nook surrounded by some of Samone's favorite books. Sometimes Samone would sleep here, but she refused to stay long, insisting that Jesse marry her before living situations got serious. But now, Samone was even happier to share the space with someone who truly needed it. After Jesse and I got back from Carter's Street, I'd spilled my guts to her and my father. I'd always kept what happened to me and Maddie a dark secret with them, because I didn't want to awaken the pain that came with her death. The agony of not being able to save her. But now that she had been resurrected, and she was in my gym, it was finally time for me to come clean. Jesse, Samone, and my dad agreed that they would do anything to help her. To help me. So Samone spent the better part of the night making sure that this room was beautiful and peaceful for my Maddie in case she decided to stay.

"This is so beautiful!" She headed straight to the sitting nook, running her hand along the shelves. A long fulfilling sigh escaped her lips as she pulled a book from the highest row. A fairy-tale storybook, filled with castles, princesses, and dragons. Adventures she was all too familiar with.

God, I needed to get away before I blurted out everything. I couldn't stand lying to her anymore, even if it meant protecting her.

"I'll go get your bags. And...the bathroom is across the hall with lots of hot water if you wanted to take a shower."

Before she could respond, I left the room, closing the door behind her. It killed me to hide the truth, after all the years we'd been separated. The impossible circumstances we reunited under. It was too perfect, too ridiculously insane. She deserved the world, but most of all she deserved the truth. And I was going to give it to her.

I rushed to my room to think. To figure out what I'd say, how I'd tell her.

Would I just come out with it? Call her Maddie and see if she caught it? Tell her the truth and show her where I found her name in her book? The spring of bathwater sounded down the hall. Good. That would give me enough time to plan. But then darker thoughts started crowding the impossible ones. Maddie was in my house, taking a shower, and tonight her head would be resting just a bedroom away. How did I get so lucky? What had I done to deserve this gift? I wanted to show her the world. My world. To give her gifts, to wine and dine her...

Shit. *Breakfast.* My queen was hungry, and I needed to serve her. I headed to the kitchen and started on the pancakes and eggs. Slicing fruit and brewing coffee. Maddie was going to get a true feast fit for a royal, far from the fucked-up Cheerios and water we'd stomached years ago. After about twenty minutes of cooking, the sound of the water squeaked off and I tried to fight the images of her wet, soaking body out of my mind.

I grabbed two plates and started filling them as the sound of the doorknob turned behind me.

"Breakfast is almost ready," I called out as I plopped the pancakes onto each plate.

Quiet footsteps danced across the floor. But instead of heading down the hall toward her room, they were approaching me. A gentle hand rested on my shoulder, and it was enough for me to freeze as the sound of water dripped onto the floor. Was I prepared for whatever I was going to find if I turned around? God help me. I slowly turned to find a majestic—no, *immaculate*—view of Maddie's body, a towel modestly draped over her. Water droplets continued to cascade down her shoulders, her dark hair brushed back as the sweet smell of summer rain hung around us. I watched her carefully as her eyes nervously peered up at me, her teeth biting into her bottom lip.

"My bag?"

Shit. How could I have been so clueless? I forgot her clothes in the truck, leaving her naked and stranded in the bathroom. I'd been so obsessed with trying to figure out how to tell her the truth, I couldn't follow through with one simple task. I started to move toward the garage when she reached for my arm.

My eyes fell to her hand, over the deep bruises that marked her wrist. Her face. And I couldn't fight the anger that rolled through me again. Without another thought, my hand skimmed her shoulder, scoping out her bruising. They seemed to be healing, as a light purple-yellow halo surrounded her cheek and her wrists.

I was going to fucking tear the Vex in two. I wasn't sure how yet, but Briggs hadn't heard the last from me, and I knew Jesse would have my back no matter what I did.

I froze as her hand landed on my chest, and then the other, her brows drawing together again as if she were solving a puzzle. She peered up at me, her chin trembling as she lifted her hands off my chest to sign.

"Take off your shirt."

Fuck me.

What was happening right now? Was she coming on to me? After everything she'd been through? At this point, I didn't care, I just wanted to do as she asked. I quickly tore off my shirt and met her gaze again as it fell to the floor. She stared, her eyes sweeping across my shoulders, until they fixed on a place above my heart. Her hands shamelessly returned to my chest, her movements scared yet urgent. She leaned closer, the scent of summer rain washing over me again with her dangerous proximity.

Her perfect pink lips parted as they fixated on my heart-shaped birthmark. The same one that Maddie used to admire when we were kids.

"You wear your heart on your chest," she'd always laugh. And it couldn't have been more true. No matter how much pain it caused me, I loved her fiercely even as a child. I didn't want any harm to come to her then, and especially now.

A shaky breath crashed across my chest, her sweet eyes meeting mine as tears began to spill. I reached for her, but she shook her head in denial, clutching her towel tightly against her.

She knows.

"Maddie," I breathed, unable to hold back anymore. She froze, her bottom lip trembling as her gaze darted from my chest to my scar.

"It's just me, Maddie. It's okay." The words I'd whispered to her on the nights when Frank would come for us. The nights when he'd pound up the stairs, always to Maddie's room first, but I was there to take the first punch and pray that I took his last. I was there to keep him away from her for as long as I could. And now, I was here again, to make sure that she was taken care of and safe.

A series of emotions flickered across her face. And my heart broke for her, as our shitty childhood seemed to replay in her mind. But I wasn't going to let Frank take away this moment too.

I lurched forward, pulling her against me. She didn't fight me; instead, she fell into me, her head leaning against my chest as my arms wrapped around her waist. I longed to hear my name on her lips, even in the heat of a whisper. But Frank had taken so much from her. From *us*.

I clutched her face and lifted it toward me, her eyes brilliant with color. With life. She sucked in a breath as we looked at each other, her hands exploring my arms, my chest, my face. As if she couldn't believe it. And how could she?

She tensed as I leaned in closer, her mouth just a kiss away. Her eyes dropped to my lips, and she sucked in her lower lip, fighting the tremble that shook the rest of her body.

I needed to be gentle. I needed to back away, give her space. But the way she looked at me, the way her body moved with every touch, I didn't know if I could. I peered down at her mouth again, the bruise from last night's attack still purple and swollen near her jaw.

Back away, Nate. Let her breathe.

I dropped my hands and took a step back, her intoxicating scent still swimming all around me. "Maddie, I...wanted to tell you earlier, but it just didn't feel like the right time. I found your name written in your book. I couldn't believe it myself, but I knew it was you, even before I saw your name."

Her eyes flew open, and she lifted her head, giving herself enough space to sign.

"They told me you were dead. That he killed you."

And in that moment, I wanted nothing more than to be locked in a cage with Frank, to take away from him all the things he'd taken from her.

I shook my head, closing the distance between us again, clutching her shoulders tighter.

"After Frank...cut you, I fought him..." I held back a choked sob as the horrible image of her lifeless body filled my mind. Her blood pooling all around her. The sea of red that I saw as I charged at him with the baseball bat I kept under the bed.

"I nearly beat him to death. I thought I'd killed him, but I didn't. And I wanted to for what he did to you."

Her hands reached for my face, smoothing over my jaw and brushing back my hair. Sweet forgiving caresses that I wasn't worthy of.

"I couldn't save you, Maddie. I should have told someone what he was doing. I should have just told *someone*—"

"*Stop.*" She shook her head again, her eyes deep and glistening with warning. "*You were nine. Nine. We were just kids.*"

"I was just so selfish that day when you came to me. Like an angel in the middle of hell. You were so innocent and beautiful." The guilt I'd held on to for the last eleven years soared through me as I clutched at her body.

"I knew what Frank would do to you, just like he'd been doing to me. I hoped that he'd spare you, but I knew better. And I still didn't tell anyone, because I just wanted you..."

The guilt flooded out with the tears I'd held back for years. But I was in front of my queen now, and all I had was remorse for what hell I'd brought on to her. The shit life she'd been dealt because I'd kept silent. I'd been thriving with a loving family, a gym filled with friends and people that cared for me. And she'd been nothing but broken and abused and forced to live a life of quiet because of me.

She pulled away from me, her body tense as she took me in. I prepared myself for her to shove me, to slap me. To kick me and make me hurt the way I'd made her hurt. I *wanted* her to hit me, to finally give me back a piece of what I'd given her. Instead, her lips gently pressed into my cheek, chaste and forgiving. Loving. Her fingers combed through my hair as if each stroke reassured me that it was okay. But it wasn't okay.

I tore away from her, the guilt even worse than before. I didn't deserve her forgiveness.

"Why aren't you hitting me? I deserve a swift kick in the nuts for what I put you through. Fuck, I deserve to be knocked out. I should let you take me in the cage right now and have at me."

Her eyebrows raised, a surprising flicker of playfulness reaching at the corners of her mouth.

"You want me to hit you?"

I gawked at her as her smile widened. Was she seriously *smiling* right now?

"Are you seriously smiling right now?" I backed away from her as if she were crazy. After everything I'd just told her, after I'd kicked up the dust of all our past trauma. She was *smiling*. Her grin faltered slightly as I took another step away from her.

"Teach me." Her hands hung in midair, her face suddenly serious as she waited.

"Teach you?" I repeated, my voice lowering as if I misunderstood. She nodded, a determined focus replacing the playfulness that was there moments before.

"Teach me how to hit."

I followed the movements of her hands, the way the bruises on her wrists burned against her skin. If she had known even a few moves, she might have been able to protect herself, even if it were against two men. I traced her throat where Frank had sliced her, a sick reminder of the way I'd failed her. I owed her everything. But to train her was undoubtedly the easiest way I could make it up to her. I could protect her and teach her how to protect herself.

"Okay. I'll train you...but it's not going to be easy." That was an understatement. Learning how to defend yourself was a *mindfuck*. And if it didn't break your spirit, it would certainly break down your body. Hit by hit. I pictured her in the cage with me, like so many other fighters I'd trained and fought. Compared to them, she seemed so fragile. Breakable. And I'd already broken her too many times.

"*Good. I hoped it wouldn't be*," she retorted, her eyes devious and playful again. But maybe I had her all wrong. She'd survived Frank when all hope seemed lost. She'd survived the quiet she'd been forced to live with, and she somehow got away from the Vex when so many weren't as lucky. She was strong, and she had a fighter's spirit, if I'd ever seen one.

"*I'll start working tomorrow, and you will start training me tomorrow night*," she signed as if she weren't asking. She was *demanding*. Her body still needed to heal, and she was still sore from the hits she'd taken from the attack. I started to fight her, but her glare cut through me. A queen's reprimand.

"*Shake on it*." She extended her hand out to me, her eyes reproachful but excited. "*And no tricks this time*."

I slowly reached for her, her hand soft and cool in mine.

"Whatever you say, my queen."

CHAPTER EIGHT

My Jason was alive. *My prince.* I could hear his footsteps just outside the hall in the kitchen, getting ready for the day. The day I would start my first job. The day that Jason would train me how to fight and protect myself. The day I would see him again, after everything. We'd spent all day and night yesterday going through an inventory of our lives and the time we spent apart. He'd listened carefully with a permanent scowl on his face as I explained Carol and the events that transpired the night she kicked me out. I specifically kept out the fact that Briggs had been my other attacker. Pointing blame on Briggs felt wrong for some reason. Not that he wasn't wrong for watching another man attack me. But because I didn't want to plunge Jason any deeper into my life's drama.

He'd told me everything about his life, his family. And it was so beautiful, everything he deserved and more. It hurt that he felt guilty for having happiness. He couldn't understand that I was happy for him, that I was *proud* of him. I couldn't believe he actually wanted me to *hit* him because he'd made it in life. As if my punch would make any impact on his muscles of steel anyway. But today was the day that would change. I craved the ability to be strong for myself. To finally stand up for myself. Maybe this would help me find my voice again after all these years of silence.

I quickly shoved the covers off me and ran to the bag of clothes Samone had given me. I'd never had a job before, and I wasn't exactly sure what you were supposed to wear to work. I mean, it was a gym, not an office, so I guessed that I wasn't supposed to look too fancy. But I still wanted to look beautiful. To feel confident when everything about today made my stomach knot in a hundred different ways. I pulled a cream hoodie from the bag and some black leggings so I could cover my body. Cover the ugly bruises still marking my wrists and neck. Samone had even given me some makeup along with all of her clothes. I'd never worn makeup in my life, but I spotted a bottle labeled "concealer" and figured that was exactly what I needed. After a few minutes of attempting to cover the purple marks, they'd finally blended in well enough that I looked more like myself. And less like a victim of the Vex. A poster child of weakness and vulnerability.

Another set of footsteps headed down the hall. Jesse was up too.

Okay. You can do this. I slowly headed toward the kitchen, the room buzzing with warmth as Nate flipped an omelette over the stove. We'd both decided last night that we would remain our changed names, though he'd always be Jason to me deep down. Just like I'd always be his Maddie. But the chapter in our lives was new. And I almost felt like Nate fit him better. It seemed to suit the man he'd become. He wasn't a prince anymore; he was a king. *A warrior.* And I didn't feel like Maddie anymore either. Maddie was the girl from my past, an emblem of the life that was struck with disaster and tragedy. Though I wasn't sure exactly what it meant to be Claire either.

"Good morning!" Nate's eyes swept across my face and then fell to my ensemble. I froze as his eyes darkened and his jaw hardened. I was never able to read Jason as a child, but Nate was a stranger. A familiar stranger that I had to learn all over again. And the way his eyes raked down the length of my body, I wished I knew what he was thinking.

"Is this okay?" I pulled on my hoodie nervously, shifting my weight as Jesse eyed me with a grin.

"Yes, you're...perfect. You look beautiful." His voice was hard and strained. That tortured look shadowed his features again as he walked over to a nearby stool and patted it. "Now come and get some breakfast." His response was a little unsettling and didn't make me feel any better about my outfit, but I did as he instructed, taking a seat at the bar.

"I hear Nate's going to train you tonight, Claire?" Jesse's eyes shifted to Nate as he tore off a piece of toast.

"Just some basic moves so she can wreck any bastard that tries to touch her," Nate threw back, stacking some toast onto my plate.

"You sure you're ready?" Jesse ignored Nate's glare as I took a seat.

Hell no.

"I think so." I nodded as I took a bite of his omelette. If I could have moaned, I would have. Loud, and obnoxiously. *The man can cook.*

"Have you ever seen Nate fight before?" Jesse's grin seemed to grow wider as his eyes bounced between us. "Because you're about to learn from the best."

I lifted my gaze to Nate, his jaw clenching as he stared back. *Oh, I've seen him fight before.* The last time he fought was moments before I'd nearly lost my life. The sound of Jason's nose cracking under Frank's punches echoed in my mind. But he was just a boy then. I silently surveyed his muscles rippling against the thin fabric of his shirt. Nate had morphed into a killing machine since then. A weapon. His body was lean muscle, cut and defined, and I could only imagine the kind of damage he could do.

I shook my head and dropped my fork to sign. *"I'm ready to learn."*

His eyes softened as they fell on me, but he threw his arms across his chest as if he still didn't like the idea of training me.

This time Nate signed as he spoke. I found it interesting when he decided to sign. Sometimes he didn't bother, but in his most heated passionate moments, he felt compelled to speak with his hands. And now all I could think about was what else he could do with them.

"I'm not going to teach her to fight. I'm just teaching her how to protect herself." A muscle in his jaw flexed, and I felt his body heat all the way from where I sat. Or maybe that was still the aftershock from yesterday.

"What if I want to learn how to fight?" I signed back, lifting my chin. His eyes fell to my throat, and pain shot across his face.

"Why don't you watch a fight first? I've got one recorded, if you want to watch it now?" Jesse didn't wait for my answer as he practically skipped toward the TV.

"Jesse, not now. It's five in the freaking morning," Nate growled, but I placed a hand on his arm.

"I want to see you fight." I nervously met Nate's gaze as Jesse's burned a hole in the side of my face.

"Please?"

"Claire." I raised my eyebrow at the way he signed my name. Earlier, he'd spelled it out, but now, in this moment his hand formed a C and his hand hovered over his heart, just where his birthmark sat. Right next to my name.

"When I fight, I…destroy." The way he spoke, the way his arms moved with his signs made the hair on the back of my neck stand up. My eyes drifted across his chest again, his muscles hard and threatening.

"No, Claire. He fucking *slays*," Jesse corrected, confirming my suspicions. "They don't call him the Dragon Slayer for nothing."

Blood rushed up across my cheeks as I replayed his words.

The Dragon Slayer.

Nate dipped his head, lowering his eyes to the kitchen counter. They called my king the Dragon Slayer. Painful memories of Frank's evil yellow eyes flooded my mind. His calloused hand clawing at my throat, ripping and tearing.

"*Eyes up,*" I signed, pulling my shoulders back. Nate's throat bobbed as he looked at me, a quiet smile lifting his cheeks. God, I loved that smile. It was even more beautiful than the first day we met, when he showed me his castle in the yard.

"*I want to see you slay.*"

"I like a woman that knows what she wants." Jesse grinned and leaned back with pride as he popped on the TV. "This one was from two nights ago."

The night the Vex attacked me. I glanced over at Nate again. His skin was flawless, no wear and tear like I had. If there wasn't video proof of the date and time splashed across the bottom, I would have never believed he'd been in a fight. My eyes snapped back to the TV. That same strange cage filled the screen as a crowd roared and cheered. And then I saw him, a warrior on his battleground. Nate, the Dragon Slayer, looking more mean and threatening than I'd ever seen him. Goose bumps raised on my skin as he and his opponent danced around the ring. The other fighter looked just as tough, but Nate had a scathing sneer twisting at his face that was enough to scare the hell out of me. I could feel Nate's eyes on me as I watched, but I couldn't look back. I was too hypnotized by their dance.

And then he moved in.

His attack was merciless, his hands, just covered in small padded fingerless gloves smashed right into the other's face. And then another, his head knocking back with the force. Nate didn't wait for him to recover. He brought his leg up, kneeing him in the ribs, and shoved him to the ground like he weighed nothing. My eyes widened as he tackled him, throwing punches like he could go at it for days. Blood splattered across the floor until another man jumped in between them, practically pulling Nate off him. A horn rang out, ending the match.

"The most classic ground and pound I'd ever seen," Jesse snickered. "I've never seen someone get taken down that fast. Your boy is ruthless, Claire." After a few beats, his opponent came to and rose, blood gushing from his mouth and nose. I tensed as he approached Nate from behind, expecting him to throw another punch. But he slapped him on the back like they were good friends. Nate turned and grinned at him, throwing his bloodied arms around him, and they hugged. Nate had just beaten the living shitake mushrooms out of this guy, and now he was *hugging* him.

I blinked, suddenly realizing that both Nate and Jesse were staring at me, apparently waiting for me to say something. I glanced down at Nate's arms, still straining against the fabric of his shirt. I'd been at the mercy of his strength two nights ago. He'd flanked that full-grown man in nearly thirty seconds. A man who was trained to fight like he was. But with me, he could have killed me if he wanted with one punch.

He started toward me slowly until I could feel his breath against my neck.

"Claire, what did you think?" He was signing again. His face was hardened and stoic, but hopeful. And then I realized, he wanted my approval. He started to reach for me, his hand hesitating as it drew near my face. Something on my face seemed to tell him it was okay because then his hand grazed across my jaw, his thumb resting right in the middle of my scar. His hands were weapons and yet now, with me, they were soft and respectful. Loving. His brows drew together as I pulled away from him, but they relaxed when I began to sign.

"Teach me how to do that." I pointed to the screen, when that earth-shattering smile lifted his face.

"That? I think you can do better than that..."

The drive to the gym was quiet, the sun just barely peeking over the horizon as we pulled into the parking lot.

Nate's hand clasped around my arm as we headed to the back entrance.

"Don't push yourself too hard, okay? Take as many breaks as you need, and remember we don't have to start training tonight if you aren't feeling up to it after work." He peered over at Jesse as he unlocked the door and went inside. "This place can be...a lot, so take it one step at a time."

I nodded, though I had no intention of taking it easy today. Not when he was inviting me into his life, allowing me to stay under his roof and giving me my first job. This was my one chance to show him I wasn't broken after all.

Because even though every time he looked at me I felt revered and respected, I'd been nothing but vulnerable and weak in front of him. It was time to show him I was so much more than a victim. I was a survivor too, like him.

The gym looked so much more inviting in the daylight. It was clean modern lines, with masculine splashes of color. It was well designed with a comfortable flow of equipment that seemed more expensive than my own life. I could tell why he felt so protective over it. It felt like a kingdom all its own. Nate's castle to escape to. I couldn't help but stare at the corner where he'd pinned me against the wall. The cart of towels I'd tripped over shoved in the corner with damp and bloodied cloths splayed across the top. He followed my line of sight, and his face darkened as if he too were replaying that moment.

I inhaled as his hands gripped my shoulders and gently turned me, so I was looking toward the front entrance. A grand front desk stared back, warm and inviting, a perfect complement to the space. I smiled as sunlight poured in, hitting the desk as if it were calling me home.

"This is where you'll be. I'll show you how to manage our schedules later, but today, I think you could just get to know the place and our members. If anyone has any questions about training rates and hours, there's a poster right here you can direct them to." I stared at the large computer on the desk, a major upgrade from Carol's old PC she would let me use when she was in a good mood.

"We get a lot of emails and inquiries about hosting fights at the gym or coordinating with agents on what fighters will go where. Can you type?"

I nodded, relaxing at his question. I'd loved to use the computer to write out little stories about a little boy and a little girl playing in their kingdom. I would write all day if Carol had let me. And now, maybe I'd be able to write to Nate. Tell him how I really felt about everything so my voice could shine and not hide behind broken signs and mixed messages. My gaze shifted to a phone sitting on the corner of the desk, my heart sinking as I realized I couldn't fulfill everything he needed from me. He laughed as he bent under the desk, pulling the cord with him.

"Trust me, I don't even know why we have this thing. No one calls us anymore—they usually just show up in person or email us." He quickly swiped the phone from the desk and tucked it under his arm like it had offended him.

I refocused back to the workout stations, random towels strewn across the equipment. The barbells and weights were mismatched in the corner. Several mats were shoved in strange places in the middle of walkways. But the large cage-like ring in the middle stole the show with spatters of blood lining the stairs.

"When does the gym open?" I asked, forcing myself to look away from the mess. Carol would have had my neck if I'd left even a window undusted.

"In an hour." Nate shifted his weight, guilt washing over his beautiful face. I quickly nodded and rolled up my sleeves.

"If you don't mind, I'm going to get started. Do you need me at the desk the whole day?" I scanned the room again, already strategizing my next move.

"No, you're free to roam wherever your heart takes you. I'd love it if you could pace the floor every now and then to make sure everyone is doing alright. But we can work up to that. If you'd feel more comfortable cleaning and organizing, we can have that be your focus for the day." His hand skimmed my shoulder, and heat trailed across my skin all the way to my belly. "But please, don't push too hard, okay?"

I took a step back, shaking off the heat that shot across my cheeks.

"Where are the cleaning supplies? The laundry?" I asked, ignoring his request. His eyebrows drew together, worry shadowing his features, but he pointed toward the back corner.

"Thank you, Nate." I signed his name the same way he'd signed mine earlier this morning. My fingers crossed into an *N*, and I threw it over my heart. Before I captured too much of his reaction, I fled to the back on a mission.

I quickly gathered bleach and a few clean cloths and started wiping down each equipment piece. Cleaning and running were my happy places. Even though I'd been forced to manage Carol's household for years, I enjoyed the control I had over spaces. Otherwise, I would get trapped in all the things I didn't have control over. But here, in this gym, I could manage the safety and cleanliness of each spot. And each time I wiped a surface down, I felt like I was finally doing something for Nate. After he'd already done so much for me. After he'd protected me, put his faith in me that I could do something else besides be a victim.

I could feel his eyes trail me as I collected towels throughout the gym. I finally had most of the mess cleaned up as the first few people trickled in for the day.

"You're incredible." I jumped as Nate's voice laughed behind me. "I have never seen this place this clean before. And you literally did all of this in an hour?"

My jaw nearly hit the floor as I captured him up close and personal in his fighting gear. His broad shoulders shielded me from the sunlight as it glowed against his skin—his very shirtless skin. His hands were wrapped in the same fingerless gloves from the video, and I fought every fiber in my being to not look further south.

"*I'm not done—*" His hands reached for mine, cutting me off as I signed. His body was dangerously close as more members began to flood in. His smile faded as his eyes landed on my cheek, and I prayed that my makeup hadn't already rubbed off.

"Hey, Nate, you finally got some help around here?" A thick and burly man clapped Nate on the back before his eyes snapped to me. "Who's this beautiful creature?"

I stiffened as the man's gaze also rested on my cheek, his brows drawing together. Yup, my bruises were definitely showing.

"Art, this is Claire, our new front desk manager." Nate stepped back and nudged me forward. "Claire, Art is one of our trainers here. He's one of the best."

Art's kind eyes fell to my hand as I extended it toward him. His mammoth of a paw collapsed over mine, but not to shake—to analyze the handprint on my wrist.

"Someone messing with you?" His broad shoulders seemed to expand as he peered down at me.

"Don't worry, Art. We're taking care of it," Nate intervened, his jaw hardening. "Tonight, I'm going to teach her a few moves." The flames from his words nearly burned me alive.

"Good." Art dropped my hand and threw his arm around Nate's shoulder. "You're in good hands, Claire. And speaking of hands, are you the angel behind this miraculous cleaning?"

I grinned at him and nodded, finally able to breathe again as the topic turned to work.

"I've been here for seven years, and it's never looked this good." Art ripped out a hearty laugh, his rosy cheeks reddening as he slapped Nate on the back again.

"He speaks the truth." Nate's chin fell, a playful smirk crossing his face. "Now, this is her first day, so be easy on her."

Art's bearded grin widened as he gave me one last once-over. "I'm sure you'll fit in just fine here, Claire. Now wish me luck—I've got to get Jesse's butt into gear by the end of the month."

"Shut up, Art, and get your ass over here," Jesse yelled, bumping his fists together.

"Duty calls, Claire. Nice to meet you." He winked at me before hustling over to Jesse, who proceeded to throw him into some playful chokehold.

"How are you doing so far?" Nate's hand twitched as if he wanted to touch me, but he kept his hands to himself.

"I've still got a lot of laundry to do." I smiled up at him, hoping I could sneak away so he would stop staring at my bruises.

"Claire, you've already done—" This time I touched him, my hand planting on his chest.

"I'm okay, Nate. Now go and train so you can train me tonight." I lifted my chin, meeting his concerned gaze. His features darkened, his chest puffing out as if I'd turned on his beast mode. That's right, Dragon Slayer. Now let your princess work.

"Alright. But remember, take breaks, okay?"

I nodded up at him before turning on my heel and heading straight for the laundry room. I let out a deep breath and closed the door behind me, the smell of detergent and sweat filling the room. I smiled as I stared at the carts filled with towels. What in the hell had Nate done without a front desk manager? Cry?

I threw a heavy pile into the washer and started the load when the sound of the door opened and closed behind me.

Damn it, Nate. How was I supposed to convince him I was capable when he kept trailing me like I was about to break.

"*Nate, I*—" My hands froze as I swiveled around to find Briggs, his face pulled back in a determined grimace. I eyed the closed door behind him and then swept the room for any other exits. The supply closet was just a few feet away. If I could just distract him enough to escape inside.

"Claire, please just let me talk for a second, okay? I know you know where I was two nights ago. Just—"

I shoved a cart of towels toward him and lunged for the closet door. I managed to open it just an inch before Briggs's heavy hand slammed it shut, his body towering over mine. I quickly twisted away from him, but he countered my move, and suddenly I found myself with my back against the door, Briggs's arms blocking me in on both sides.

"Claire, please. I'm not going to hurt you. Just listen, *please.*"

I could barely hear his voice over the pounding of my heart. I tried to slow my breathing, but those same nervous eyes swept over me. The same eyes that had watched as that bastard tore at my clothes, thrust his hand in places it didn't belong. The same eyes that watched him hit me and throw me to the ground just because he could.

"I'm guessing you didn't tell Nate?" He shifted his weight but kept his arms locked in place, caging me in. "Because if you had, I probably wouldn't be breathing. So, for that, I'm grateful."

He actually thought I was keeping it a secret for *him.*

"Look, I just wanted to clear the air. That night, I was working undercover. I was babysitting that asshole, Arsen, trying to see if he'd come out with any more member names."

Did he just say Arsen? The bastard's name was *Arsen?*

"Arsen's one of the top brothers. I was trying to get him drunk so he could give me some more information on all the members. He'd been dropping leads the last few days, and that night was finally my in. I'd been at it for the last few months, trying to earn his trust. Just trying to get him to open up. And that night, he was finally getting somewhere until you came along." And then he had the audacity to glare at me like I had *inconvenienced* him.

"He was giving up names and addresses, and I was finally getting enough to bag a few of these guys. I wanted so badly to defeat these sons of bitches and...you were just a wild card."

So I was a welcome sacrifice for him so he could get some names? He was actually trying to tell me he was going to let him have his way, just so he could keep his friendship status?

I tried to push him away, but his arms pinned my shoulders back against the door.

"Claire, please. Look, I'm not trying to say that what I did was right or validate what happened. I'm actually here to warn you."

I fought back tears as his hands gripped my shoulders a little too hard. He caught my expression and relieved some of the pressure.

"Arsen was able to track you to the gym. They aren't very…keen on survivors and witnesses. If I were you, I'd head out of town. Maybe try to convince Nate to leave with you, because the Vex doesn't stop once they start. Do you understand?"

I couldn't nod, I couldn't blink. I couldn't even breathe. This was just too messed up. I'd finally been granted another chance with Nate, and then this happened?

Briggs removed his hands and backed away. "Look, just don't say I didn't warn you, okay? And don't worry, you won't hear from me again after today. I'm leaving tonight, and I suggest you do the same."

Briggs started to head for the door, when it opened, Nate appearing in the doorway. His shoulders tensed as his focus snapped from Briggs to the overturned cart of towels, to me, huddled against the door.

"What the fuck is this?" Nate growled, stepping in and closing the door behind him. The small room suddenly shrunk several square feet as Nate's presence crowded the entire space.

"Did you fucking *touch* her?" Nate demanded, backing Briggs against the wall.

"Nate, you need to get out of town, okay?" Briggs pleaded, his voice shaky as he lifted his hands in surrender.

"What the hell did you do to her?" Nate ignored him, shoving Briggs hard in the shoulder.

Without thinking, I threw myself in between them, my hands pressing against Nate's chest. My eyes searched his, begging that he'd back away.

"Answer me!" Nate shouted, veins popping out against his throat and temple as he towered over me as if I weren't there.

"The Vex is coming for you and Claire. They found out that she escaped to your gym, and they'll hurt her just as bad if not worse once they find her. You need to take her and get the hell out of here."

Nate's fury fell to me, and for a second, I was terrified, peeling my hands off him like I'd been burned. His face was flushed and contorted, his muscles flexing as he loomed over me. But I knew he would never hurt me.

"What did he do to you, Claire?"

I couldn't answer fast enough, anger flooding his face again.

"I swear to God, Briggs." Nate shook with anger, his voice terrifyingly low.

"Get the fuck out before I kill you." And I knew in my heart that Nate would do just that.

Briggs slowly lifted his hands and began to sidestep away from me. I quickly reached up to Nate's face, my hands smoothing against his neck, his chest.

Look at me.

Nate twitched as if he were contemplating ending Briggs as he neared the door. My grip tightened, more urgent as the doorknob twisted open.

And my lips crashed into Nate's as the sound of the door closed behind him.

CHAPTER NINE

Soft, gentle kisses trailed across my mouth, my jaw, my neck. Silent pleas I could have gotten lost in, if Briggs hadn't just cornered my queen in my kingdom. I tore away from her, searching her body, her face for any fresh marks.

"What did he do to you?" I demanded, my heart clenching at the way she avoided eye contact.

"*He...didn't hurt me, Nate. He just wanted to warn me.*" Her hands froze, as if she weren't sure how to continue, or she didn't want to. I watched her body language, my stomach sinking. She wasn't telling me everything.

"But why wouldn't he come to me first? Why would he get you alone, especially after you ended that interview with him—" My stomach sank even further as I caught her shoulders tighten at the mention of the interview. Just like they did when Frank came anywhere near her.

"Wait, does this have something to do with yesterday?"

Her eyes flickered with panic as I edged closer to the truth. "*Claire, please. I need to know what happened.*"

She shifted her weight between her feet like a caged animal, not sure what to do. But I wasn't going to let her loose until she explained what happened. Because if he laid one finger on her...

She finally stilled as her shaking hands began to sign.

"*Briggs was there that night.*" Her chest rose and fell with quick, nervous breaths. As if she were preparing herself for certain death.

"What do you mean? He was there when you were *attacked?*" She stepped away from me, as if she didn't like the truth spoken out loud. Her eyes started to bubble with fear or even regret as they peered over at the piles of unwashed towels. I took a step closer, blocking her view as the only reasonable explanation crashed over me in an angry red wave.

"Claire. Are you trying to tell me that Briggs was one of the men that attacked you?" I fought to keep my voice low and calm, but it came off clipped and harsh. Threatening.

"Claire." She jumped at the sound of her name, her eyes drifting to the towels again.

"*Will you please let me work? I—*" She tried to move around me, but I blocked her again, moving closer.

"No. You've already done enough, and by the looks of it, I think you need to take the rest of the night off. Let's make that the rest of the week. And training is canceled until you're fully healed." I couldn't believe I'd agreed to let her work so soon after she'd been nearly raped, much less train her in this condition.

Hurt swept across her face as if I'd slapped her. I nearly retreated, hating the pain I caused her, but this wasn't the time. Right now, I was going to push her, to get to the truth with Briggs whether she liked it or not.

"Now answer me. Are you saying...Briggs was one of the masked men?"

Her lip trembled even harder as a tear fell down her bruised cheek. She finally lifted her chin, meeting my furious gaze, and nodded.

Insurmountable rage flooded through me as I let the ugly truth set in. *Briggs* assaulted her. One of my own had tried to rape her. And he'd cornered her in my gym, after I'd asked her to speak to him about what *he* did to her.

And I'd just let him walk free. Roaring rushed through my ears as the dam broke loose. I needed to hit something. I needed to destroy, to *kill*.

I quickly moved toward the door but instead came nose to nose with Jesse.

"Nate, what the hell is going on?" Jesse demanded as he peered over at Claire, her shoulders shaking with quiet sobs. He quickly closed the door and stepped in front of her. As if *I* were the one threatening her.

"Briggs." That was all I could bark out, all I could muster as the sea of red thrashed around me, threatening to pull me under.

"Nate, look at me." Jesse took a step closer but kept his distance. He knew better than to get in my space when the beasts were out. "You need to walk whatever this is off. Look at her."

Jesse stepped back enough for me to catch a glimpse of my fallen queen. Guilt washed over me as I caught her face, a string of tears sliding down her beautiful battered face. She was scared, and she needed me. The need to end Briggs without mercy and to hold Claire and comfort her nearly ripped me in two. How could I have failed her so many times in just the few precious days I was gifted with her?

"Nate." Jesse took another step closer, dangerously close to me. "Let's walk it off."

Samone stormed in, her eyes blazing as she caught the sight of Claire cowering behind Jesse.

"*What the hell?*" Samone demanded as she headed toward her.

I hated how I couldn't console her. Jesse was right. She was scared, and it wasn't just because Briggs had hurt her. It was because I was livid, towering over her in the confines of a laundry room. Not only had I failed to protect her, I was terrifying her. Once upon a time, I was able to calm her and tuck her in at night. I kept the monsters away, and I kept her safe. But now, she hid behind Jesse as Samone comforted her. *From me.*

I shoved past Jesse and headed out to the gym to find him. To kill him. I could feel several pairs of eyes on me, watching as I marched past them. But none of them were Briggs. He'd left, the fucking coward.

"Let's go to the office, *now*," Jesse hissed in my ear as a few of the fighters stopped their sparring to watch. Jesse was right. I needed to think. Refocus and figure out what to do to defend Claire. I kept my head low as we made our way to the office. The buzzing in my ear lowered as Jesse closed the door and turned to me.

"Tell me what happened."

"Briggs was one of the masked men, Jesse." Heat blazed through me as I said the words out loud.

"Fuck," Jesse muttered under his breath, throwing a hand through his hair.

"And I just found him in the laundry room with her. She was...scared and—" My eyes landed on the cot she'd slept on after she'd been assaulted by the Vex. By *Briggs.* A smudge of blood still stained the sheet where she'd lain. Blood that Briggs had likely drawn...

"Did he say anything to you?"

My furious glare snapped to Jesse, and I backed down, trying to remember the desperate pleading Briggs had whined on about.

"He was blabbing about the Vex knowing who Claire is, and that we should hide low for a little while." I closed my eyes, trying to even out my breathing, my heart rate.

Calm the hell down, Nate. Focus for Claire.

"I don't know if he meant any of it, or if he was just trying to distract me from what he did to her."

Jesse blew out a breath, shaking his head. "I never fucking liked Briggs," Jesse growled, shaking his head. "What are we going to do?"

"I'm going to the station." I grabbed the keys from the desk and pulled the door open.

"Not without me, you're not," Jesse shot back as he fell in step next to me.

"You've got to train, Jesse."

"So do you."

But this was what we fought for. To protect and defend our families and our loved ones. This was the fight that lived in all of us. This was war.

As we drove to the station, I kept replaying the moment Jesse stepped in front of Claire. As if he thought I would actually hurt her. The way Samone looked at me as she rushed over to calm her down. The way *Claire* looked at me as I made her face the truth.

"Did you think I was going to hurt Claire?" I braced myself for his answer. Because if there was one thing I trusted Jesse for the most, it was his honesty.

"Hell no!" Jesse barely let me finish the sentence before he yelled at me. "I know you way better than that, Nate. I've seen you shove a guy for just looking at a woman wrong. And can we talk about that time you busted that guy's lip because he called that lady in the parking lot a bitch?"

I held back a snicker. I remembered the moment well. "In my defense, the woman was in her eighties. And she reminded me of your grandma Sally."

"God rest her soul, Nate."

"God rest her soul."

Jesse shook his head as he peeked over at me with a smirk. "I know just as well as you do that you would never lay your hands on a woman. Especially not Claire. But she was scared, and the last time she saw you, you were *nine*."

I let out a sigh as I pictured the sweet innocence we lost ourselves in when we were kids. Our castle, our escape. Our kingdom. Somehow, Jesse was always right. The last time she'd seen me, I was a thin little punk running off Cheerios and water. And now I was nothing but hard-trained muscle, designed to cause every pain imaginable. She only knew Jason, but how was I supposed to get her to trust *Nate*.

We finally pulled into the drive at the police station, and I threw the door open as soon as Jesse shifted into park. I'd start with seeking justice for what Briggs did.

"Stay civil, Nate," Jesse warned as I stalked toward the front door. I grunted in response, yanking the door open.

A young woman in uniform sat at the front desk, her eyes widening as Jesse and I both entered. And this was the first moment I considered the fact that both of us were still shirtless. And we both had fighting gloves on.

"May I help you?" she asked, her eyes shifting between us nervously.

"I'd like to speak to Peter Briggs' supervising officer, please." I did my best to stay polite, but instead I practically growled at her.

"And this is concerning...?" She narrowed her eyes at me, leaning forward as if I were about to dish out some serious tea.

"The fact that he is an asshole and needs to be terminated immediately," Jesse intervened with a wink. The woman stared back unimpressed but nodded curtly as she stood.

"Captain Marks should be back from lunch by now. I'll let him know you both would like to speak to him." I watched as she turned the corner before scanning the rest of the office. A few other men and women in uniform glanced our way, but most of them remained focused on their work. The tone in the room seemed tense, as many of the officers seemed anxious, even nervous. And deep down, it bothered me that two shirtless fighters at the station didn't seem to bother them in the slightest. They were dealing with something much more troubling. Like the Vex.

"Jesus," Jesse muttered as he surveyed the office. Jesus was right. Before I could respond, a tall graying man came from around the corner. The permanent lines between his brow deepened as he approached.

"Gentlemen, I understand you would like to speak with me about Officer Briggs?" His voice was gravelly and displeased as he offered his hand. "I'm Captain Marks."

His face was tired, large bags puffing underneath his eyes. I gripped his palm, his grasp tight and strong like a bull's. He reminded me of my father, a tough man with an even tougher face. But his body seemed to cave over from an unseen weight on his shoulders. A man who had seen too much and was inches away from an early retirement or an early death.

"Would you mind joining me down the hall in interview room two? I'd like to discuss whatever you have to say in private."

I nodded and we followed him down the hall past several officers, but none of them bothered to look our way. He waved us into an empty room and took a seat at the table, gesturing for us to follow suit. I had no interest in sitting down and having a conversation, but by the way he glared at us, this was the only way to bring justice for Claire. So Jesse and I sat across from him, all three of us staring each other down before I finally decided to speak.

"Briggs tried to rape my girlfriend." The sea of red crashed over me again as the words fell from my lips. I'd hardly had a moment to spare to consider the fact that I'd just called Claire my girlfriend.

"When and where was this?" Captain Marks demanded, his face growing three shades deeper with anger.

"On Carter's Street two nights ago. And he was just at my gym—"

"Where is your gym?" He leaned forward, his knuckles white as he balled his fists on the table.

"Just a few blocks down from Carter's on Maple Cove."

"Garrett, have them search the area." I followed Captain Marks's gaze as it fell behind us toward a large frosted mirror. Someone was watching us. Listening.

"Copy that, Captain," a voice filtered in through a hidden speaker.

"Go on." Captain Marks waved his hand, his mouth twitching as if he preferred I just shriveled up and died instead.

"Did you lose your officer, Captain?" Jesse taunted, crossing his arms as he reclined in his chair.

"I'm afraid Briggs has been missing in action since his last check-in two nights ago." Captain Marks sighed as he mirrored Jesse's confrontational tone. "So unfortunately, I am not particularly pleased with him right now either."

"Is it because he couldn't handle his work with the Vex?" I seethed, the beasts threatening to break free again.

Captain Marks stiffened, his chin lifting slightly as he turned toward me.

"What do you know about the Vex?"

"That they've been terrorizing and raping women on our blocks for the last few months." I stood, shoving my chair backward, and it scraped against the worn tile. Captain Marks watched me carefully, his eyes shifting between me and Jesse with a raised brow.

"Did Briggs tell you about them?" His voice was calm, but there was a fierceness behind it. The kind that could put you in your place within an instant. I glared at him as my breathing evened, forcing myself to remember that he was the key to getting justice for Claire.

"After she was assaulted, we went looking for the bastards. There was a guy on the streets who saw it all happen. He told us about the Vex, enough to where we knew there was something bigger going on. Briggs trains at my gym, so we thought it would be good that my girlfriend talked to him." Guilt swam through me as I pictured the way she'd shut down at the end of the meeting with Briggs. The way she'd frozen in horror as she looked at him, as if she recognized him. I'd been so caught up in the mess of the Vex, I hadn't seen her fear for what it really was.

"Just a few minutes ago, he cornered her again in my gym. He tried to tell her that they know who we are, and we need to lay low." I met Captain Marks's glare, my fists flexing as the memory of Briggs walking free flooded the red sea again. "With all due respect, Captain, this is your mess, and you need to clean it up. The hell we're laying low, and I'll be damned if the Vex hurts one more woman because you can't do your job," I snapped.

Captain Marks ran a hand over his jaw, his frown deepening as he took both of us in. "Do you think she would be willing to speak to us?"

I glared at him, not liking the idea of exposing her to yet another uncomfortable interview with the police. Because the first one had gone so well.

"She's been through a lot, Captain. I'm not sure if that's best."

He nodded, his eyes dropping to the table as if he were rethinking a thousand things, most particularly his career path.

"We will be sure to investigate Officer Briggs thoroughly once we locate him. And as far as your girlfriend, we would be interested in speaking with her. Because as of now...she would be their lone survivor."

I let his appalling words sink in. Claire had escaped yet another sure death.

"I'll tell you what, son. I will reach out to the media to get a press release going about the Vex to alert the community. I will do that right now, in fact, if you consider asking her to come and have a chat."

"I'll consider it." I seethed. And in the charged silence, we left.

****

A refreshing scent of lemons and bleach hit me as we walked through the front door of the gym. Fresh towels were restocked in the back, and all the weights were in the correct order, neatly tucked in the corner. I spotted the closed laundry door and started toward it when I spotted Samone, her arms crossed, sporting her infamous death glare that could take a fighter down faster than anything Jesse or I could do combined.

She marched over toward us, and I swore I saw Jesse cower in fear.

"I'm ordering you to leave Claire to do her work in peace. Just because you are technically her boss doesn't mean you get to boss her around."

Was that what Claire thought I was doing? *"I didn't—"*

"Don't you realize what she's trying to show you, Nate?" Samone's expression softened but only by a hair. She let out an exasperated sigh as she waved at the gym—the new and improved gym thanks to Claire.

"She's trying to show you that she is strong too. She isn't just a victim. She wants to prove to you that she survived like you did."

Before I could respond, the laundry door opened, and Claire emerged with a basket of fresh towels. Her eyes were cast downward, and a hint of a smile tugged at her mouth until she looked up at the three of us. She froze and my chest forgot how to breathe as her eyes widened in fear of me.

No...not fear. *Need.* Claire needed this. Samone was right, but maybe she didn't just need me to know she was capable. She wanted to know she was capable too. Samone turned to me, crossing her arms again to see if I would make the right decision.

"The gym looks beautiful, Claire," I signed stupidly, fighting on what to say next. Words were never my strength anyway. That was always Claire's. *Maddie's.* She would always give the formal announcements at our royal parties and entertain our villagers with poetry and stories. My eyes lowered to her hands, her knuckles white as she gripped the handles of the basket. And now she was forced into silence because of me.

I slowly took a step back, allowing her to continue walking. Her throat squeezed with a tight swallow, and she lowered her head as she walked past me.

I wanted to watch her as she stocked away the towels. Every movement of hers was graceful and precise. Like a fighter's. But that was what creepy guys did, and Samone was still glaring at me.

"If she wants to train tonight, I would suggest you follow through with what you promised her." Her eyes snapped to Jesse, and he flinched again.

"And you. I want to take a look at your wrist." She clutched at his arm and dragged him away before he could protest. As Jesse passed, he winked with a hungry grin on his face. Jesse loved it when Samone got bossy. *The freaks.*

I shot one last look at Claire. Her back was turned to me as she placed each towel gently in a cubby. And now she was bending over, the fabric from her leggings clinging to her skin in all the right ways. I tore my eyes away from her, only to meet Samone's judgmental glare again. Jesse was behind her, shooting me a devil's grin when Samone elbowed him in his ribs.

Okay, okay. I lifted my hands up at her and headed over to the punching bags, far away from the front desk and the laundry room. And I spent the day imagining that every mat, every punching bag, every obstacle was to defend my queen. To tear Briggs to pieces. Because now it wasn't just Frank. It was the whole goddamned Vex that would get to have a little taste of my poison.

The rest of the day had sailed by until it was time for closing. My heart stopped as Claire appeared from the back room. Her dark hair was pulled into a ponytail, her elegant shoulders straightened confidently as she approached. She'd changed into a tank top and shorts. *Training clothes.* I lifted an eyebrow as I caught the bold letters across her shirt, likely one of Samone's: *I can and I will.*

She wasn't going down without a fight. Something that excited me and terrified me at the same time.

"Claire, I—"

She quickly held up a hand, her blazing glare practically setting me on fire. Damn, she was just as bad as Samone.

"I'm ready to tell you what happened with Briggs."

I nodded, fighting the urge to wrap my arms around her and just hold her. But she was ready to use her voice, and I was willing to listen.

"I was telling you the truth earlier. He didn't hurt me—he actually saved me."

I cocked my head at her, confused. That creep on the street had tried to tell us that the two men fought as Claire escaped. But I caught the hurt behind her eyes and the still-fresh marks that lined her body.

"And what about all of this? Did he put his hands on you?"

She quickly shook her head, more hair falling loose around her face.

"So what, he just watched...? He waited until you'd been brutalized before he intervened?"

"I escaped because of Briggs, okay?" Her half-hearted defense made the sting

of the truth hurt even more. He'd saved her, but he'd allowed the attack to happen. He'd watched every forceful, unwanted touch. And for that, I prayed that Briggs knew better than to ever come back around here.

"The man that put these marks on me, his name is Arsen."

Rage boiled just under the surface, the beasts threatening their way out.

"His fucking name is *Arsen?* Did you get a last name?" My fists curled at my sides as I imagined the things I'd do to him.

She shook her head and straightened her spine, determination driving her every movement.

"Tonight, you're going to teach me how to protect myself." Her eyes gleamed with hope, her honey gaze pouring into me. *"If the Vex knows who I am, then later might be too late."*

She had me there. Though her body was still healing and she'd spent a full day working despite the fact I'd asked her not to, she was just as much a fighter as me.

"And kings don't break promises with their queens."

I let my eyes drift down the length of her body again, preparing myself to lose my first fight. Because with her, I'd finally met my match.

"You really want this?" I prayed she'd say no, but I knew it was just the selfish part inside me that wanted to protect her.

"Yes."

"Then get on that mat and let me work."

CHAPTER TEN

"Now first, we're going to set some ground rules." His eyes burned through me as he padded around the mat with his bare feet. "If at any time you want to stop, or you're in pain, you tap me. Hard. Do you understand?"

I nodded, but my "yes" must have not been reassuring enough because before I could blink, he was in my space, towering over me.

"Tap me." His voice was low and demanding, so forceful and serious it scared me and delighted me all at once. I patted his shoulder, but his jaw hardened as he glared at my hand like it had offended him.

"Claire, your body is on the mend. I'm about to teach you some moves that are going to push your limits and make you uncomfortable. You feel this?" He grabbed my hand and pressed it against his chest. My hand practically bounced off his muscle, but he trapped it in place, his heart racing against it. "Your tap needs to be sharp and serious to get through, because I'll be damned if I hurt you and you couldn't tell me."

He dropped my hand and cocked his chin at me. "Now tap me."

I lifted my hand and tapped harder, this time my palm smacking against his skin. I winced at the harsh contact, but his face softened with an approving nod.

"That will do." He crossed his arms over his chest and surveyed me. I could feel heat creep up my neck as he walked around me, taking in every angle.

"Are you a runner?"

All I could do was nod as my hands and my mind seemed to become sludge under his fiery gaze as he circled me with predatory ease, the hunter closing in on his prey.

"That's good. We can use that to your advantage."

He stopped, his shoulders squaring at me as his eyes crisped dangerously. "How did he attack you first?"

I tensed at his question, but I knew his intentions. He wanted to show me how I could have fought them off. "Did he come at you from behind or approach you from the front?"

I swallowed as I pointed at the nearby matted wall, but that was enough of an explanation for him. A fire blazed behind his molten glare, but he led me to the wall, careful and calm. Like the calm before the storm.

"He had you pinned?" He gently pushed my shoulders so my back was pressed against the wall. I couldn't help but remember the fury of being pinned by Nate too. But even in his strength, he held restraint. His movements had purpose as he searched me that night. He didn't revel in the pain he caused me like Arsen had.

I nodded again and slowly reached for his hands, placing one of them against my throat, the other on my hip. I peered up at him nervously, dropping my hands to my sides, waiting for his instruction. Anger tore across his face as he mirrored the same powerful stance Arsen had over me. But even as his strength pressed into me, his body crowding me, I felt completely safe. And after a few heartbeats of silence, he spoke, his voice soft and tender.

"I want you to think about the points of contact that are the weakest." His grip tightened around my throat just slightly. "You feel where my thumb is? That's your weak link. If you put force there, it will break." He reached for my hand and placed it on his wrist. "Push my hand away."

I pushed, but his strength overpowered me.

"The movement needs to be quick. Don't give me time to think about it, just break my grip."

This time I shoved his hand with all my strength, his hand flying off me.

"Again." His hand returned to my throat, his eyes narrowing with determination. I repeated the movement, my arm faster and stronger this time.

"Good. Now this time, I want you to pivot your weight away from me as you push." He motioned the movement before returning his hand around my neck. I repeated the move with ease, his smile peeking through as I practiced.

"Now when I break free, I want you to put me in a choke."

I stared at him stupidly.

"You'll probably get away if you break free, but why give him a chance to chase you when you could just take him out?"

He didn't wait for my answer and instead spotted Jesse as he locked up the front door.

"Jesse, come over here and help me show Claire what a good chokehold looks like."

"My fucking pleasure," Jesse practically squealed as he made his way over to the mat.

Jesse glanced at me, his smile widening as he caught my worried expression.

"*Prepare to be amazed*," Jesse warned as he signed. Nate grinned at Jesse as he shoved him against the wall in the familiar stance. Jesse cleared his grip with ease, throwing his arm around Nate's neck. "If your chokehold is strong enough, you can knock them out in just a few seconds flat." Nate quickly tapped on Jesse's grip and then moved toward me as if nothing happened.

"Your turn."

I glanced at Jesse before leaning against the wall. I preferred to just crawl into the fetal position and gradually fade away. He made it look so easy...

Nate moved me back against the wall with care and threw his hand on my throat as Jesse watched.

"I'm ready when you are," Nate prompted, and my knees buckled as his eyes dipped to my lips.

Okay...here goes nothing. I quickly shoved at his arm and twisted my weight like he'd instructed but paused when it came to the choke. My arm looped around Nate's neck awkwardly, and I wanted to hide away even more as Nate's head smothered into my chest.

"Here, let me show you." Jesse stepped in, adjusting my forearm so it was pressed into Nate's throat. "There we go. Now all you need is no mercy, and you have yourself a grade A guillotine choke."

Nate quickly eased out of my grip and peered down at me, his eyes shining with excitement.

"You want to try?"

"*Try...?*" I hoped he wasn't asking for me to actually choke him.

"I want you to actually choke me."

"Oh, God, yes. Claire, you've *got* to do it." Jesse practically jumped for joy as I blinked up at both of them.

"*No.*" I shook my head, taking a step back.

"Claire, you're not gonna hurt him. He was built for this. Hell, I'll do it for you if you want."

"No, Jesse. She's got to know what it feels like. She's got to know her own strength." Nate eyed me, patiently waiting for my answer.

"*You'll tap if it's too much?*" I tapped the wall, pointing at him nervously. Who was I kidding? He had to teach me how to *tap* him. My chokehold would do nothing.

Nate grinned dangerously as he moved closer. "Oh, I'll definitely tap. Are you ready?"

"I am," Jesse chimed in gleefully. Nate kept his eyes on me, that same predatory gaze cutting right through me.

"*Yes, I'm ready.*" I nodded.

Before I could think, his hand gripped my throat, his body moving in fast. I quickly rehearsed the moves and looped my arm around his neck, pushing my forearm against his throat with no mercy. Nate's girth and weight was heavy against my hold, but my arms didn't let up. After a few moments, Nate tapped my arm lightly, his face red as he came up for air.

"Fuck me," he muttered under his breath as he rubbed against his throat, red marks lining where my arms had held him. I stilled at his words, my stomach tightening at his request. And now my mind was wandering off to places I shouldn't let it. Unless...he was actually asking me to have sex with him. I shook off the ridiculous thought and took a step back. I glanced at Jesse, who started to clap at my performance, wiping away a few fake tears as he cheered.

"That was the most beautiful thing I have *ever* seen in my life." Jesse slapped Nate on the back, shaking his head. "Claire, do you know how many people would pay thousands of their hard-earned money to see you do that again? Hell, I think that's our next business endeavor. Claire against the Dragon Slayer. People would come for miles..." His eyes glossed over as if he could picture it now.

Nate patted Jesse on the shoulder dismissively, his eyes trained on me. Hungrily. "Thanks for your help, Jesse. You are no longer needed here."

Jesse's smile faded slightly as his eyes bounced between us.

"Yep, I'll just be in the back if you need me. Behave, Dragon Slayer," Jesse warned as he headed to the hallway.

I watched Jesse disappear before slowly meeting Nate's burning gaze again.

"You've got a grip on you, Claire. I mean, seriously, *fuck me.*"

Yeah, he totally just told me to fuck him. Again. I bit my lip nervously, not sure if I was misunderstanding him. I'd been out of this whole courtship dating scene basically my whole life, and my only source of relationships was from black-and-white movies. Was this how it was now? Did guys just come out and say it?

"Claire—"

I held up a hand, my palms starting to sweat over what I was about to ask him.

"*Did you just ask me to have sex with you?*" I cringed as I made the explicit gestures. His brows drew together, his eyes snapping between my hands to my face skeptically.

"I don't think you know what you're saying, Claire."

"*What...did I say?*" I asked, suddenly horrified, pressing further into the mat behind me.

"You just asked me to have sex with you." His jaw hardened, and this time his eyes were blazing with a new kind of heat that set my whole body on fire.

I couldn't respond. All I could do was breathe as he stared at me, those beautiful eyes growing hungrier by the second. His focus sank to my chest as my breathing quickened, his tongue darting out, wetting his lips.

"You didn't mean to ask me that...did you?" His eyes returned to mine, the masculine lines of his body somehow so much more defined as the light above cascaded over his shoulders. Like a warrior who had finally come home to his queen.

"Claire?"

I swallowed as sudden desire ached through me. The memory of his lips against mine, his taste. The way he might taste as his hips moved against mine.

"You know...I think that's enough for tonight," Nate grunted, taking a step away from me, putting distance between us. Disappointment replaced my desire as he took yet another step back.

"You did good. I'm just gonna go get my keys and...I'll take you home."

Before I could sign back, he took off, leaving me alone to wonder what the hell just happened. I slammed my hand against my forehead, clearly misreading the situation completely, but furious at the way he shut down. And now he was so cold as he practically stormed off. Classic Jason. He was always so hard to read, even as a child. A mask of emotions that I could never decipher.

A gentle hand fell on my shoulder, and I looked up, startled to find Samone. Her long hair was pulled over her shoulder, her face pinched together with concern.

"*Claire, you okay?*" I watched as she signed my name the way Nate signed it, her hand over her heart. And a sudden, unwelcome splinter of pain shot through me. A heaviness behind the sweet gesture.

I peered up at her and nodded, but I was no master at masking like Nate was. My confusion and pain were happily painted on, plain and readable on my face.

"*What do you say we have a girls' night?*" Her smile was kind and reassuring as she rubbed my shoulders.

"Hey, Claire, you ready?" I peeked over Samone's head at Nate as he stood near the hallway, waiting. His hard lines softened as he caught sight of me, a guilty wave moving over his face. And I was grateful that he could at least show a little remorse after being so cold with me. Samone turned and shook her head, blocking my view from him.

"*Claire is coming home with me tonight.*"

Nate glanced at me, his brows drawing together as he shook his head and signed.

"*You girls shouldn't be alone. The Vex knows who we are, and I'm not taking any chances with either of you.*" His jaw ticked as he threw his arms across his chest, unmoving. Stubborn and protective just like he'd always been. Samone tensed at his command, but her shoulders sagged with surrender.

"*Fine. But I'm still coming over, and there are no boys allowed in our room. Is that understood?*" She mimicked his alpha male stance, her shoulders pulled back with a ferocity I craved to have myself. Nate's hardened glare shot to me, but the ice melted away as he nodded.

"*Fine.*"

Samone laughed as she turned to me victoriously. "*And that's how it's done.*" She giggled and threw an arm around my shoulder as she led me to the back entrance.

"*Jesse, we're going home. The girls are staying over, so I think it's best if we watch over them instead of the gym.*"

Jesse peeked out of the back office, his face a little too hopeful. He quickly jumped in front of us, pinning Samone with a look that could only be compared to a puppy about to get his treat. "*Samone, you're staying the night?*"

She shot back a mischievous grin and shook her head teasingly. "*Only Claire gets to have me tonight. Isn't that right, Claire?*" I blushed as Jesse and Nate gawked back at us.

"You're a lucky lady, Claire," Jesse sighed as he eyed me with silent envy.

I peered over at Samone, her grin widening as she pulled me around Jesse toward the door. I could still feel Nate's eyes on me as we headed out to the parking lot. I started to head to the truck when Samone pulled me in the opposite direction.

Toward a motorcycle.

Nate was in front of us before I could figure out what was happening.

"Like hell you're putting her on that," Nate growled as he glared at her. Samone shoved at his chest, taking a step forward.

"*I think Claire is perfectly capable of deciding for herself what she wants.*"

I wanted to cheer as Samone defended me, but Nate's hurt gaze shifted to me. And it wasn't my intention to hurt him. I just wanted to know what caused him to pull away from me.

"*Claire...are you comfortable riding a motorcycle?*" Nate prodded gently. God, how I wanted to ride. To feel the sense of freedom I'd longed for ever since I was stowed away under Carol's watchful eye. I'd only seen people ride motorcycles in movies, but they always looked like they were having the time of their lives. As if rules didn't apply to them, and they could live however they wanted.

"*Yes.*" I nodded, admiring the curves of the bike, wondering what it would feel like between my legs.

Nate's face filled with worry as Samone grinned up at him with yet another victory under her belt.

"*Then I'll take her,*" Nate demanded, his arms flexing as he signed.

"*Why don't you ask Claire what she wants?*" Samone shot back, pointing at me. I bit my lip, fighting a smirk as Jesse randomly snacked on a bag of nuts while he watched our ridiculous exchange. *Where did those nuts come from?*

"Claire?" I startled as Nate moved closer, his woodsy scent surrounding me. "Will you ride with me?" His eyes danced with each word, his mixed messages swirling in my head again. I glanced at the bike, then Nate, and then back at Samone. And then she winked, nodding encouragingly.

I peered up at Nate, my eyes narrowing at him as I moved in closer, invading *his* space.

"*On one condition.*"

He raised his eyebrows, his eyes glittering dangerously as he waited.

"*You teach me more moves tomorrow.*" I let my eyes fall to his lips, just for a moment before they flickered back up to meet his gaze again. Our eyes did a push-and-pull tango, and suddenly I was craving his hands on me. Gentle and exploring. Careful and forceful. His chin raised, and he stepped away, pulling the door of the truck open. He reached inside and reemerged with a heavy leather jacket which he draped over my shoulders protectively.

"I was going to do that anyway." He grabbed the helmet hanging from the handle and fastened it safely under my chin, his fingers brushing against my neck carefully.

"I'll meet you two back at the house," he uttered as he threw a leg over and kicked up the ignition, the beast roaring against the quiet night. "Hop on."

I glanced over at Samone, her smile yet again victorious. Perhaps this was what she wanted the whole time. I slowly hiked my leg over the side, his warmth blanketing me as I scooted forward, his hard torso tucked in between my thighs.

"See you two soon," Jesse muttered as he threw his bag of nuts in his pocket, his lids growing heavy as they landed on Samone. Without a moment to spare, Nate peeled out, and my arms quickly wrapped around his waist, clinging to his wall of muscles.

The streets were mostly empty as we drove through town as the streetlights and stars lit the way. People always seemed to ride during the day in movies, but with Nate, as the moon hung up ahead guiding us home, night rides felt like the only right way to ride. His body moved with mine as we rounded each curve of the road. I loved the way he molded against me, my body fitting perfectly into his. I jumped as a flash of lightning flooded the sky above, followed closely with a loud rumble of thunder over the roar of the engine. Nate turned his head as if he were checking on me, before gripping the handles tighter and speeding up, hoping to beat the storm. Finally, we turned into the quiet corners of his subdivision. *Our* subdivision. I spotted the inviting porch lights from down the street as we weaved past a few parked cars toward his house.

Our house. He slowly rolled in and parked, kicking the stand up and helping me off first.

"You okay?" he asked as he helped me out of the jacket.

I shivered as a chilled breeze swept through the trees above, but Nate's hands found their way on me again, igniting the same flame from earlier. Desire and incredible need. But before I could melt under him, his hands quickly fell to his sides, an icy coolness replacing the places he'd touched.

"No." I shook my head, peering up at him as I unfastened my helmet and placed it back on the handle. The breeze picked up, my hair flying around me angrily as the storm finally caught up with us. Lightning flickered above, casting light over his beautiful, tortured face.

"What's wrong?"

I pulled away from him and started to move to the front door before I realized that it was still locked. Because I didn't have a key yet. Thunder rumbled overhead again as rain started to sprinkle across the yard and onto him. My eyes widened at the sight of him as water trickled down his face and dripped across his body, the fabric of his shirt pulling against him from the moisture.

"Claire, what's wrong?" His voice grew louder with the rain, and he showed no sign of trying to unlock the door.

"*I can't understand you!*" I signed, finishing it with a hard shove that came off as a barely noticeable nudge. *Stupid steel shoulders.*

"What do you mean?" he shouted as another clap of thunder shook the earth.

"*You're so hot and cold.*" I threw my hands in the air wildly.

A muscle in his jaw ticked as I signed, and guilt started pouring over his features with the rain. And I hated the way I wanted to kiss him as another flash of lightning flooded the sky above.

"*I thought you asked me to...*" I stopped, not wanting to sign the wrong thing like before. Because it ended up so well last time.

"You thought I asked you to what?" His low voice cut right through the downpour.

"*I thought you asked me to have sex with you,*" I finally caved, praying that he would understand this time. If not for my accuracy, perhaps he'd consider the context. My anger. God help me if he thought I was throwing myself at him again...even though I wanted to so badly. I wanted to feel his skin against mine. His breath against my neck, my name on his lips as he pushed his hips into me.

"*I asked you to have sex with me?*" he repeated, his head shaking back and forth vehemently, as if I had appalled him.

I dropped my jaw at his disgust, my desire for him dwindling with the hurt.

His eyes darkened as realization settled, before a royal hunger ran across his face.

"You mean from earlier when we were training?" Hurt trickled deeper as he let out a laugh. "It's an expression, Claire. I said that because I was...*impressed* with you tonight." He took a step closer, the rain bouncing off him as thunder shook beneath us. "And I would never command you to fuck me, Claire. A king doesn't command his queen." He took another step closer, his eyes burning into me. "Unless that's what his queen wanted."

I swallowed at the ferocity of his words, the danger and the carnal hunger behind them.

"How dare you think I don't want you. I'm just trying to protect you." His eyes wandered down my body slowly before that same guarded coldness came over him.

"*Protect me from what?*" I demanded, my chest heaving with need.

"*Myself. I don't want to hurt you. Not after what happened to you.*"

My hands fell on his chest, my fingers tracing every outline of his wet skin through his shirt. His muscles tightened under my touch as my hands crept closer to his waistline.

"Claire, please don't tempt me. I don't want to hurt you."

My hands paused, hovering over the places I wanted to explore. I peered up at him, pleading before removing my hands only to sign.

"*You would never hurt me, Nate.*"

Nate shielded my eyes as the flood of headlights fell over us. Jesse and Samone were here.

I watched them pull into the garage, when Nate's jaw brushed against my neck. The heat of his breath made my body arch against his, his tongue brushing over my wet skin next to my ear.

"I am a patient man, Claire. And believe me, if you want me, you *will* have me. I will claim every inch of your body the way my queen deserves." His hand gripped the back of my neck possessively. "But I want you to be ready. Because when I take you, I won't be holding back."

CHAPTER ELEVEN

I let the mesmerizing effect of Claire's body crash over me as I pictured her in my bed, her sweet scent lacing my sheets after I'd made love to her, worshipped her. She had retreated for the night with Samone, but I could still feel her hands trail down my waist, the way her lips parted after I told her I'd take her without holding back. And God, I'd wanted to take her right there like she had practically begged me to. But Claire deserved so much more than a clumsy fuck. I wanted to respect her body, to revere every inch of her.

"Nate, you alright?" I glanced over at Jesse as he took a swig of his beer. I was more than alright. All my thoughts were consumed by *her*. The way she felt against me, the way her body wrapped around mine as we rode through the night. The way I wanted to taste her as she writhed under me.

"I still can't believe she's here. How she walked into my gym after all these years." I blew out a breath, as the memory of her shaking on my gym floor tore at me.

"Nate, that's some destiny shit right there if I've ever seen it. Maybe it's a sign that she's your soul mate like Samone keeps saying." His mouth tipped upward as he took another long pull from his beer.

"Speaking of soul mates...I think I'm going to finally ask your sister to marry me."

I stared at him, hard, as lightning flashed across the room.

"Don't you play with my heart like that, Jesse Matthews." I laughed as a loud crack of thunder shook the house. "Are you serious?"

"Yeah, I'm serious." He sat back, his eyes sparkling like a lovesick psycho. "Does that mean I have your blessing? Because if we get married, I'm gonna get her pregnant. You know that, right?"

"You're an asshole." I laughed, chucking a pillow at him. He caught it with ease and threw it behind his head.

"I'll take that as a yes."

"Why now all of a sudden?" I narrowed my eyes at him as he took another drink. "Samone's been busting your ass about proposing all year."

"Your sister's special, Nate." His smile faded with each word. "She's going to be a *doctor*, you know?"

I nodded, not sure where he was going with that.

"I guess I just keep waiting until she realizes she can do better." His words cut deep as the truth came out. He didn't see himself as worthy of her.

"I don't know a lot about love, Jesse, but I know enough to say that she's fucking crazy about you. The girl practically glows around you. And you make each other better. Isn't that what it's supposed to be?"

"How do I make her better? I—"

"For starters, all the hits you take during your fights help her learn how to be a better doctor," I snickered. "You make her laugh when everyone else just pisses her off. She relaxes when you're around, and she feels safe around you. Jesse, she *adores* you."

"You really love her, don't you."

"Of course I love Samone. She—"

Jesse shook his head, cocking his chin toward the hallway. "No, I mean Claire."

I tensed at his words, heat shooting through me like white-hot lightning from the storm. I loved Claire so deeply it hurt. I'd loved her since the first day I saw her, scared and broken as she was. Like me. I wanted nothing but to make her feel better and to protect her from every pain.

Movement in the corner of the room stole our attention as light from the storm flashed against the walls. And there, shivering in the corner, was my queen. The woman I loved. I sat up, suddenly on high alert as I caught a glimpse of her face. Her cheeks were puffy like she'd been crying.

"Claire?"

I quickly stood and cleared the room in a few strides until my arms were around her. She was shaking, her small frame so fragile in my embrace. I cupped her chin, lifting her face toward me, searching her body.

"Are you hurt? What's wrong?" I slowly started to trail my fingers against her skin when her hands stilled them, her honey eyes fearful and nearly glowing in the dark.

"*Nightmare*," she signed, her lip trembling.

After I was adopted, I'd had nightmares for years. I relived the moment when Frank had sliced Maddie's throat open. When he'd tried to finish me too, but I'd used the baseball bat I put under her bed instead. The bat I was too scared to use, for fear he would take it and hurt her with it. But not that night. Because it was my last chance to save us, and it was all I could think of to protect my princess. I'd wake up in cold sweats after I'd beaten Frank's face to a pulp for the hundredth time. After I'd shaken Maddie's lifeless body as her blood pooled around her sweet innocent neck. My parents would soothe me and rock me back to sleep. They'd held me and let me cry. But did Claire have that? Had she ever been cradled when she was scared or reassured when the nightmares and the storms came?

Before I could ask her anything else, my phone vibrated against my leg. I caught the time from the bright digital clock on the stove. Two thirty in the morning. Who the hell would be calling now? I dug in my pocket and tensed as Dad flashed across the front.

"Dad?" I answered, pulling Claire closer against me.

"Nate, I think you better get down to the gym. We had some...company." His tone was calm, but the fury was rooted deep in every word.

I glanced over at Jesse as he stood. And with one look, even in the dark, he knew what had happened. We both knew.

"I'll be right there," I confirmed before hanging up. Claire peered up at me, those honey eyes pulling me in again. God, how I wanted to stay and comfort her. But if the Vex had anything to do with this, I wanted Claire to stay far away from it.

"I've got to go. I want you to stay here with Jesse and Samone. I promise I won't be long." I kissed her forehead, breathing in the summer rain from her hair. But Claire pushed away from me, shaking her head, that same intoxicating fire dancing behind her eyes.

No, I'm coming with you. Her hands were commanding as she signed. My little fighter, stubborn and headstrong like me. I loved her spirit, but I knew if she was anything like me, she'd do anything to protect the ones she loved. And I couldn't have her getting hurt because of me. Not again.

"No, I need you safe, Claire. Something's happened at the gym, and I don't want you near it." I glanced at Jesse, a nod passing between us as I pulled her closer, dropping my mouth next to her ear so only she could hear me.

"Why don't you keep my bed warm for me until I get back?" I felt the goose bumps form against her neck, my mouth hovering just inches away. I wanted to tell her how I felt, to tell her I loved her, but it was too soon, even if it was the truth. And my dad was alone at the gym. Her shoulders sagged as I pulled away, but she let me leave.

"I won't be long," I muttered to Jesse and headed to the door. I forced myself to close it and lock it, before getting in the truck.

Limbs and debris from the storm scattered the parking lot as I pulled in. I spotted Dad's truck parked near the entrance. But a fury boiled inside me at the state of the entrance, or what was left of it. The front doors had been busted through, and one of the doors was barely hanging on to its hinges as if someone had tried to rip it clean off. I scanned the parking lot as I got out and headed to the door.

"Dad?" I called into the darkness of the gym. Heavy footsteps crunched against broken glass inside, a dark, tall figure emerging from the wreckage.

"Nate?" my dad called back, his tired weathered face appearing at the door. Anger roared behind his gaze as he stepped through it, but his face softened when he saw me.

"You alone?" He swept the parking lot, searching for Jesse, when lightning flickered across the sky, shedding light into the gym. The light cast across the main floor, over what looked like more damage from the storm. Punching bags and barbells were strewn across the floor around crumbling drywall and broken glass. The wall of towels Claire had carefully washed and stocked from yesterday lay damp and yellow as the stench of piss hung in the air.

Something crashed in the distance, and both of us turned, our fists at the ready. A few pitted heartbeats passed when I noticed a small shard of a wall mirror swinging in the corner. It had fallen, the rest of its pieces shattered across the floor. I glanced around the gym, the looming threat of the Vex still hovering over me, over my father, my kingdom.

"You take the south side, I'll take the north?" I peered over at my dad, who nodded, his jaw set.

I headed back to the office, my heart pounding as I stopped in front of the office door. It had been busted through, like the entrance, lying in a cloud of drywall and dust on the floor. My shoulders tensed as I neared the safe, already knowing what I would find.

It was empty. Thousands of dollars gone. Hard-earned money from the years my father had poured into this gym.

My dad was a strong man, who'd managed to resurrect the ghost of a boy I'd been the day I arrived. A man who had devoted his life to his family. A man who had built this gym from the ground up along with every one of his fighters. Training them. Coaching them. Loving them. He was unbreakable, unyielding. But he'd already lost too much from the other break-ins. This was the last of his savings. *This* would tear him apart.

The Vex had destroyed my castle, violated my queen, and now they were going to break my father.

I started to head back to the main area when the lightning flashed again, illuminating the far wall. Large, messy words were tagged across it, the green spray paint still wet and dripping as if it had just been done.

I'LL MAKE THAT SONGBIRD SING.

"What the hell?" I muttered as I took a step closer, squinting at the brazen words.

"You have any idea what that means?"

I turned on my heel to face my father, to look him in the eye and tell him who destroyed his gym. Because of me. Because I wasn't here to protect it like I'd told him I would.

"Dad...I'm so sorry." I started toward the safe, but he grabbed my arm, shaking his head.

"Son, don't you dare apologize." His voice was hard, made of steel just like him. "God forbid you had been here when this happened."

"But the money—"

"You think I give a fuck about the money over your *life?*" He glared at me, his eyes somehow boring through to my soul. Just like they had the first day he'd laid eyes on me. "Nate, you bring a mean fight in that cage, but they would have killed you. And I can't lose you, do you understand?"

He didn't wait for my answer. Instead, he grunted at the cryptic message on the wall.

"I don't like the tone of that. You think that's got something to do with Claire?"

I read the words again as the threat sank in, the meaning crashing over me in sickening waves.

I'll make that songbird sing. The warning of what they still wanted to do to her was branded on my walls.

"Call the police. Tell them to get to my house, and you get home to Mom.

You hear me?" But I knew he did as I charged back out to the parking lot, praying I was wrong. Praying I hadn't let evil inside my home with my family. My queen. After leaving them to fend off the Vex alone.

I called Jesse, but the phone went straight to voicemail.

Fuck! Pick up the phone!

I tried again as I threw myself into the truck, turning the ignition. Straight to voicemail again. I slammed on the gas, dodging the broken limbs and trees scattering the street as I peeled out. Guilt rushed through me, my heart pounding with the staccato of the rain. I'd left Jesse alone with Claire and Samone. How stupid could I have been? The Vex destroyed my gym, but they'd *kill* them. But not before they had their fun. Rage pumped through my veins at what they would do to Claire and Samone.

I tried Jesse one last time, defeat and horror swimming through every cell in my body as Jesse's voicemail picked up again. I hadn't told Claire how I felt about her. I'd just left the three most important people in my life to face the Vex without me. Oh, God, please be wrong.

The rain had died down to a slow drizzle as I pulled onto my street. I cut the engine and shut off the lights before shifting into park several houses down. The police should be on their way, but the damage from the storm would slow them down. And there was no way in hell I was waiting until they got here.

Unsettling quiet filled the air as I cut to the back of the house. The quiet *after* the storm. The wake of blown-over fury after Mother Nature had her final say. Like the kind after Frank had thrown his fists into me and Maddie. The earth-shattering silence as I brushed away her tears and held her while he lay passed out on the floor, drunk and worn-out from beating on us. That quiet lives with you for the rest of your days. The promise that peace is only temporary. And the pain would come again no matter what you did to stop it.

I carefully moved up the stairs to the deck. It was dark, with only the light from the fireplace inside to guide me. I peered in the back window as my eyes adjusted to the dark when cold, hard metal pressed into the back of my neck.

"Open the door," a demanding, calculated voice instructed, pressing his gun deeper into my neck. I shifted my gaze to the reflection of the window, anger flooding me with the ridiculous mask he was wearing. The same kind we'd found near Claire's bag. *Fucking cowards.*

With just two quick movements, I could break his neck. Just—

The blood drained from my face at the sight of Jesse's body lying lifeless on the floor inside. He was surrounded by a sea of red pooling around his abdomen.

"I said *open the door*."

My throat closed at the sight of Samone. Another masked bastard was gripping her hair, her tank top torn at the sleeve, and blood dripped from her mouth. She was terrified and crying, but she was *alive*. I swept the room, searching for Claire, but only four masked men stared back, their guns pointed at her and a spot I couldn't see in the corner. Blunt force slammed into the back of my skull, sending me forward against the glass. I pulled back my elbow, shoving it deep into his rib cage. A gutted breath mixed with the cracking of his bones ripped through the air. I turned and threw him into a chokehold, thrusting my knee into the bridge of his nose. Another satisfying crack echoed against the tree line as I pulled the gun from his grip. His body went limp, falling forward down the stairs. I quickly aimed the gun at the glass. Three men now had their guns trained on me. But the fourth had his placed directly on Samone's temple. And the fifth...

My heart stopped as I saw her. Her wide, terrified eyes meeting mine. Her captor had his gun pressed against her bare breasts. They'd torn her shirt off her back, and now his forearm was digging into her throat.

"Put the gun down, or we will shoot them," his muffled voice called out.

I raised the gun, slowly bending down and placing it on the floor of the deck.

"Now come inside, slowly. We just want to talk." His cheeks lifted as if he were smiling behind his mask.

I slowly turned the doorknob and stepped inside, keeping my eyes trained on Samone and Claire.

"*It's okay, I'll take care of you*," I signed.

"What the fuck did you just say?" another demanded, stepping forward aggressively, his gun moving up toward my face.

"Search him," Claire's captor instructed, his voice callous and bored as he glared at me, his eyes like knives behind that ridiculous mask. The other men froze, glancing at each other like they didn't know what to do. Fucking idiots.

"*I said search him*."

One of the taller ones stepped forward, his eyes suddenly wary as he put his hands on me. I fought the urge to ruin him. I needed to pace this, or they'd have their way with Samone and Claire with no one to stop them.

"You showed up just in time for the show," Claire's captor snickered as he dropped his hold, and she crumpled to the floor at his feet. Guns cocked back as I took a step toward him.

"Before we begin, I wanted to ask you something." He let out a chilling laugh as his gun dragged down her jawline. "You like the quiet ones, don't you? I mean, everyone has their *thing*, right?" He paused, his gun hovering just above Claire's breasts. "I suppose I can't blame you. It's always the quiet ones that sing the loudest, ain't that right, little songbird?"

I let out a laugh, but it felt distant and cold as it echoed in the room.

"You guys must be joking, right? Hiding in the shadows with your masks and your guns, raping women. You ever thought of actually being gentlemen? You know, treating them with respect, complimenting them, taking them on a date once in a while? You'd be surprised what women do willingly when they feel loved and cherished."

One of the men tilted his head like he was actually considering it for the first time. *Jesus Christ.*

"Listen, why don't you and your creepy rape brigade leave these girls alone and fight me. No guns. Just hand to hand. I'll take all of you at once, but I can't promise I'll let you live after I'm through with you." I cracked my neck, so ready to break, to *kill*, that it hurt.

His hand caressed her cheek, and then he turned to me. His eyes shone bright and evil, just like Frank's.

"Ah, that's right. You're a *fighter*, aren't you? I'm guessing you saw the fun we had at your gym?" He dropped his hand from her face as he squared his shoulders at me.

Good, get the fuck away from her and keep your eyes on me.

"I think I'll respectfully decline a fight. I think we'd have more fun just making you watch—"

Claire slapped the hardwood, and all eyes landed on her as she started to sign.

"*Then fight* me."

"What did she say?" one of the cronies demanded again, his gun pointing at me nervously. Samone whimpered, her captor's gun pushing further into her jaw.

Claire's gestures simplified for the idiots as she pointed up at the ringleader. Her fists raised at the ready, and then her thumbs planted on her chest.

You. Fight. Me.

No, Claire. Jesus, be *quiet.*

"Is she…is she asking what I think she's asking?" The asshole cackled as he knelt down, his face inches from hers. "Does my little songbird want to *fight* me?" Before she could respond, his hand gripped her throat and slammed her against the wall.

Oh *fuck* no.

I lunged forward when pain rippled through my side as the others tackled me. Guns pushed into my face, their bodies pinning me as my queen was trapped in the dragon's grip.

"Stay down. You don't want to end up like your buddy, do you?" He waved toward Jesse's lifeless form, still sprawled across the floor.

His gun traced her neck and fell in between Claire's breasts. "You know, now that I think about it, that might actually be fun. What do you think?" He turned to the rest, his face lifting in a pretentious smirk behind his mask. "All of us against the sweet perky songbird."

Stupid snickers trickled through the room as his gun moved back to her cheek. He paused, his brain practically clanking out loud as it thought. "You know, they had that big cage in the gym. Just perfect for a captured little bird to sing." He dropped his hand from her throat, and Claire wheezed in a deep breath.

"Now you're talking," I taunted, begging him to come closer, away from Claire. "I'll let you use the cage, but only if you're fighting me. They stay out of it. Hell, I'll broadcast it for you—"

"Shut up." He thrust his gun at me, pulling away from her. "I'll decide the terms. This isn't a negotiation."

Where the hell are the police?

"We'll fight you in the cage, as long as she's in there with us." His eyes glittered with evil as he lowered his gun. "Broadcasting it live seems enticing enough. Instead of making you watch, we make the world watch. They need to see what we're capable of." He turned his attention back to Claire, his gun drifting below her belly button.

"When we win, I take her, and we kill you. Live. For everyone to see."

He froze as sirens wailed in the distance.

His hand cupped her chin, forcing her to look at him. "Tell you what. I'll bring you to my own cage...and then the real show begins."

"You won't be wearing a mask when you fight. Show me your face so I know it's you," I called out, demanding his attention away from Claire again.

He froze, my demand taking him by surprise. His sharp dragon eyes widened just like Frank's did after I swung the bat against his face.

He slowly dropped his hand from Claire's face and lifted his mask. His smile was ridiculous, toothy and evil, just like a dragon ready for a good slay.

"I'll remember you, *Arsen*," I growled, knowing this was the man who'd attacked Claire. Who'd marked her body and sprayed the threat across my castle walls. His brows drew together, now knowing that I had something on him, even if it was just his ridiculous name.

"You better." He quickly refastened his mask, and they slowly backed out, one by one, until all that was left was the quiet.

CHAPTER TWELVE

I watched Samone board the ambulance after they'd carted Jesse's still-lifeless body inside the van. Her vacant eyes shifted my way before they closed the door. No, not vacant. *Blaming* eyes. Numbing guilt sliced right through me as they drove away. As Nate's whole world was crumbling because of me. I'd brought this on them, and Samone would never forgive me if Jesse didn't pull through. They'd hurt her too, *touched* her. Because I'd run myself back into Jason's life after all these years. I'd nearly killed all of us tonight just because I had survived what the Vex did. But was surviving worth it, if others' lives were lost because of me? I could be a target for the Vex, but not while I pulled Nate and his family under with me.

I pulled the blanket the medics had given me tighter around my shoulders, blocking out the dead chill in the night air. Nate was talking to a police officer out on the front lawn. He was furious, his muscles tense as he spoke in clipped tones. The guilt sliced deeper as our eyes locked, his gaze darker than the stormy night sky before it cut back to the officer. I traced every one of his hard lines, hating that this was the way I was going to remember him. His face was so beautiful even in the thick of his fury. Like Poseidon in the middle of a hurricane. I gave him one last lingering look before I slipped inside the house, preparing myself to end this cruel cycle. Because sometimes a queen has to fall to give her king new reign.

I ran back to my room and quickly threw my clothes back into the duffel bag. It was mostly packed anyway. I'd left it packed expecting the inevitable pain that came with getting too close. It was too good to be true, and good things were always temporary for me, never permanent. I pulled a sweater on, threw the bag over my shoulder, and nearly walked straight into a hard, strong wall blocking the door.

"What the hell are you doing?" His eyes were dark and menacing, his voice deep and strangled, gutted with all the pain I wanted so badly to take away.

Instead, all I could do was stare back, my hands going numb from how hard I was gripping the bag.

"You really think this is the answer? *Leaving?*" His eyes crisped at the edges, agony reaching every tortured line of his face. "Claire, I will never force you to stay with me, so if this is really what you want, I won't stop you. But I can tell you right now, you leaving won't stop them. They'll still find you, and they'll—"

His voice choked at the unfinished words. I let out my own silent sob, swallowing the lump in my throat. But not for what they'd do to me. What I was doing to Nate.

"Claire, you're strong. You're a survivor—this is just another thing you're going to survive." His eyes fell to the bag in my hand which I quickly threw down so I could sign, to try and explain with my unsteady hands why I couldn't stay.

"*But Jesse and Samone... Nate, they* hurt *her, and Jesse*—" His hands collapsed over mine, swallowing them whole.

"Jesse would have done *anything* to protect you two, no matter what happened to him. And they'll pay for what they did to you and Samone, but *this.*" He threw a panicked hand toward me and my bag.

"*This can't be the way.*" His nostrils flared with every passionate movement. "*Don't you see what you did tonight?*"

Crushing guilt came over me again as I nodded. "*I brought pain back into your life.*" *I probably killed your best friend and brought a horde of serial rapists into your home where your sister slept to be specific.*

And then he laughed. Nate had the actual audacity to throw his head back and *laugh.* All I could do was gawk at him as I silently added making him insane to the list of things I'd done.

"*You don't think my life wasn't painful before? Claire, I'm a professional fighter. I* live *for pain.*" I narrowed my eyes at him, not sure how that made any of this better. I tensed as he gripped my shoulders, his closeness intoxicating and mind-numbing.

"And you didn't bring any of this on us. The Vex did that. You *saved* us. You used your voice, Claire, and they *listened.* You bought us more time until the police came. Running away only lets them get away with everything they've done. You can't fight the Vex with silence, Claire. Staying quiet doesn't stop the hurt."

More echoes of pain crossed his face as his eyes settled on my scar, the memories of his own silence from our childhood burning an unwanted trail through his point.

"If this is really how our story ends, then it's on you. But I have a better version that I want to write together." He offered his hand, his face that same desperate pleading expression from when we were kids. Nate was a wall of solid muscle, and his body was practically made of steel. But Nate was still breakable. And I didn't want to break this beautiful man any more than I wanted to break Jason once upon a time.

"This isn't a fairy tale. It never was, Nate. We don't get a happily ever after." I sagged with each word, hopelessness caving in on me. His jaw hardened, but a surprising quirk at the corner of his mouth tipped it upward.

"I didn't say it would be a happily ever after. It's the kind of story where the prince and princess find strength in each other." His fingers grazed the sensitive skin on my neck, his forehead pressed against mine. "We can't end the story yet, Claire. It's only just begun." His lips pressed against my hair, heat trailing every place he touched. I loved and hated how even in this moment he could kiss away my fears. How his touch could erase every one of my worries.

"Ahem." A gravelly throat clearing made me jump as an older graying man peered over Nate's shoulder—the same officer Nate had been talking to earlier. "May I have a word?"

Nate's jaw flexed, but his eyes stayed locked on me. "Captain Marks, have you met my girlfriend, Claire, yet?" An overwhelming wave of heat blistered up my chest and neck. *Girlfriend.* Nate just called me his girlfriend.

"I don't believe I have." The man quickly removed his hat and might have offered to shake my hand if Nate hadn't been standing in the way. Though it seemed he was blocking me from him on purpose. "It's an unfortunate circumstance that we're meeting under, but the pleasure is mine all the same." The man smiled, laugh lines forming at the corners of his eyes. They weren't nearly as deep as the "what the hell" line between his brows, but they framed his face nicely.

I shot him a quiet smile before Nate finally turned to him. "With all due respect, Captain Marks, I believe I've said everything I need to. Right now, I have some matters to take care of—"

"Nate, I was actually hoping to talk to *you both.*"

Nate's whole body went rigid, and instinctively he stepped in front of me, blocking Captain Marks's view of me completely. "I think she's been through enough the last few days, or maybe I wasn't clear enough. She needs to rest."

"Nate, I understand, and your concerns are very valid. I'm putting protective detail on you both indefinitely. I've scheduled a few on-duty officers to patrol your neighborhood and keep watch, but I need to make sure that we're all on the same page. I have something I need to discuss with you." Silence passed between them for what seemed like forever when finally, I placed my hand on Nate's back.

It's okay, Nate.

Finally, he stepped to the side, his eyes piercing into Captain Marks's, a warning glare to be gentle.

"Would you like to have a seat?" He gestured to the chair in the corner next to the books. Sunlight began to peek through the trees, a happy reminder that the storm had passed and the clouds were going away. I nodded and took a seat as Nate stood at my side.

"Your boyfriend has told me a great deal about the trauma you've suffered under the Vex's hands." His eyes moved over my face, taking in the ugly bruises, but all I could focus on was the fact he just called Nate my boyfriend. "He says you were assaulted by two masked men, one of whom is a reporting officer of the police department. Peter Briggs."

I winced at his words, spoken so bluntly from a complete stranger. I shook my head, peering up at Nate, hoping he could translate for me.

"Briggs didn't assault me. He just...watched." My hands clasped tightly together after I finished for fear I might start wringing them. Captain Marks frowned at my signs and looked at Nate expectantly.

"Briggs watched her get assaulted," Nate grunted as if it took everything in him to repeat it. Captain Marks's "what the hell" line deepened as his gaze bounced between us.

"Nate reported that you were sexually assaulted by Officer Briggs physically. Is that not true?"

"He cornered her yesterday in my gym. I was furious...and I didn't wait to hear her side of the story before I reported it to you," Nate admitted, glancing over at me nervously.

"I understand this has been very traumatic for you both. We *will* get to the bottom of what happened with Briggs as soon as we locate him, and we will complete a full and thorough investigation. Would you like to talk about that now with me?"

I quickly shook my head. I just wanted it all behind me. Rehashing those moments didn't seem to do anything but make me relive them again and again, when we needed to focus on the Vex.

Captain Marks waited a beat until he finally accepted I was choosing to remain silent.

"I do hope you trust us enough to talk to us when you're ready, Claire. Because when you are, I'll be here to listen." I slowly nodded as he threw his arms across his chest.

"Now, if you're okay with it, I'd like to focus on the Vex and what happened to you tonight. You see, to me, you hold some playing cards I think could finally take these guys down." Nate shifted next to me, his hand sliding on the back of my chair as if to cover me from whatever he was going to say next.

"As Nate tells me, the Vex left on the premise that they were going to fight you. Is that correct?"

I blinked up at him, the stupidity of it all suddenly hitting me as he said it out loud. I couldn't believe I'd actually tried to pick a fight with five armed men. Maybe it was the fact that Nate was there and I felt invincible. Or maybe it was the fact I was so fed up with everything they'd done that I'd lost my good sense.

I nodded, my own "what the hell" line creasing as he spoke. How could I have been so reckless?

"Well, what are your thoughts on following through with the fight?"

I let his impossible words sink in as Nate's body heat covered me.

"Are you fucking serious?" Nate growled, his knuckles cracking as he moved in front of me. "I think we're done here."

"Now hold on, you didn't let me finish. I finally reached out to the media like I promised you. They wanted to do a special on all the victims of the Vex. The women that no longer have a voice. I'd originally turned them down, for fear that bringing attention to them would terrorize the community further."

Different lines moved across his face, the sad kind that develop after years of pondering senseless killings and rapes.

"As much as we want to bring light to the victims, I think what our community needs the most right now is to hear from its lone survivor. They need to hear from someone who's escaped them. *Twice.*" His eyes glittered with a hint of victory that I wasn't sure how to share. Nothing about tonight felt like a win. "People need to know that these guys are serious, but they're not invincible."

"What are you talking about?" Nate demanded, still hovering over me, waiting for Captain Marks to say one more wrong thing.

"If there's one thing we've learned after the months of trailing these monsters, it's this. They are *power hungry.* Reputation is everything to them. You don't know how many times we've pleaded with the media to keep their shit out of the mainstream so they wouldn't escalate the way we've seen in the past. And if the first time they're being mentioned is from a survivor that's beaten them twice, and now picking a public fight with them? We'll round them up by end of day because every one of them would show to something like that. Every. Single. One."

Live television? I couldn't even talk about it with Nate in front of me…much less in front of a live audience. And was he forgetting the fact that I couldn't speak? The mere thought of attempting to sign my way through like a hellish charades game made me want to hit the ground running again, far away from here. I pointed at my throat, which all of a sudden started to close up as blood rushed to my ears. Nate didn't have to translate that for me.

"You don't have to be able to speak to have a voice, Claire." The noise stopped with his words, so simple and challenging as they were. "And I imagine you've got a pretty strong one too. Strong enough to take down an entire gang."

I just blinked back up at him. This was all too much. *First the Vex, and now he wants me on live TV?*

"If she's going to do this for you—" Nate snarled.

"And for all the other victims," Captain Marks added, and guilt shot through me.

"How are you going to keep her safe? You've already failed her too many times."

"As I mentioned, you both are under protective detail. I'll have an officer posted at your house, your gym, and another one to escort you to wherever you need to go. We will keep eyes on her at all times." There was something behind Captain Marks's gaze that I trusted. Maybe it was the kindness behind them, or perhaps there was something familiar behind those faded laugh lines.

"*Can I think about it?*" I asked nervously, looking to Nate for help.

"She wants to think about it." It seemed like it took everything out of him to relay my request. Captain Marks nodded and pulled a small piece of paper from his shirt pocket.

"Here is my card. Just get ahold of me whenever you're ready." I stood as he finally extended his hand to me, clasping mine firmly with the shake.

"Thank you, my dear." He released his grip and eyed Nate one last time. "Take care of this one." He cocked his head toward me and let himself out of the room, closing the door behind him. Strange groggy memories filtered in my mind's eye from his words. A cold hospital room. A strange visitor.

I turned to tell Nate that I thought I recognized him but froze at his haunting expression, a beautiful tangled mess of Jason and Nate mixed into one tortured man.

"Claire, please don't leave. Don't do this thing with the media. Just stay with me. *Please?*"

My heart shattered at the way he begged. I felt like he was moments away from falling to his knees in front of me. Leaving him hurt too much—I never wanted to, I just felt like I had to.

"You've already left me before..." His voice broke as he threw his hand in his hair.

I reached for him, his skin like fire under my touch. "*I never wanted to, not then, not now.*"

His eyes lowered to my hands and then to my mouth...desire lingering in the air so much, I could taste it. All of that fell away immediately as Nate's lips pressed against my neck.

"Claire." A heated whisper as his hand slid down my back. His mouth moved gentle and calm at first until my hands found their way to his hips, pulling him closer. An invitation for what I needed most from him, to take away the grime that the Vex had left on me. To baptize me with his love and affection in the wake of Arsen's punishing hands. His mouth moved to mine, his tongue glided over my lips, and I parted them, allowing him in. A low, demanding moan rumbled in his throat as he pulled me from the chair, our bodies colliding into each other. His movements were quick and generous, his hands roaming over my waist as desire pooled deep within me. I needed this just as badly as he did. Before I could let my own hands explore, he pulled away, his breathing heavy as his mouth fell next to my ear.

"Claire, I can't lose you again." He lifted his head, his pleading eyes reaching mine. His eyes were practically on fire as they bared into my soul, the flames licking at all the places I needed them to.

"I love you."

I tried to inhale, but my lungs wouldn't cooperate as his words washed over me. The last time I'd heard those words was clouded in a dream from another life. The echoes of my happily ever before when my parents would tuck me in and groceries weren't a death sentence. They'd whispered those words as they brushed my hair back, I was certain of it. But Carol had never uttered them to me. Not once. I wasn't sure what they even meant anymore, but I knew as Nate looked at me with an intensity I craved, I felt the same way.

"You don't have to say anything back...I just needed to tell you that's how I feel. I've...always loved you, ever since—"

"*I love you too.*"

Nate's eyes lowered hungrily as he caught my simple gesture. The sign I had hoped and prayed I could share with someone else and mean it. Just like I did now. Nate had offered me his home, a job, his world. And now he was offering me his heart. But this was the only thing I could offer him, and I wanted him to have it more than anything else. My hand felt light and natural as it formed the sign. I swallowed, my throat tight with need as I peered up at him nervously. Nate made all things possible. I never thought I'd hear those words directed toward me again. I never thought I'd sign with another human or tell someone that I loved them. But here I was doing both at the same time, to a man who had stolen my heart eleven years ago. Two damaged people who could still find it in each other to love, after everything they'd been through. Nate lifted his gaze slowly, his hand gently covered my still very firm "I love you" as if to cradle it and cherish my offering. He pulled my hand to his lips, and he gently kissed my knuckles, like he was kissing the very words I'd said.

"I love you, Claire. Just like I loved Maddie." His voice was a whisper, his breath heating my hand and covering me. "I'm going to train you like I mean it, Claire. I want you prepared for—" He stopped, his eyes blazing with anger at the unsaid.

I gently pulled my hand from his grasp. "*But Jesse—*"

He shook his head, his jaw tightening. "My parents are with Samone and

Jesse at the hospital, and I don't want all of us in one place at the same time. Not now, anyway. I just need to take care of a few things at the gym before I train you." The blaze behind his eyes grew even more heated, I could have melted.

"*What happened at the gym?*" I knew by the way his eyes flickered with pain that it wasn't good.

"The Vex had a lot of fun tonight." My stomach sank, imagining the worst.

"*Take me there.*"

His body tensed, and I could already hear the "no" fall from his perfect lips. But I was done with letting the Vex terrorize my king and his castle. It was time to take it back. I grabbed the scruff of his shirt and pulled him toward me, lifting onto my tiptoes, and caught his lips with mine. This time, I pushed my tongue against his as he let out another deep moan. Our tongues danced, my kiss commanding and forceful. *Your queen isn't asking.*

I pulled away, just for a moment, as I let the taste of him settle on my tongue.

"Oh, so we're playing dirty now, are we?" His voice was low and careful as he nuzzled at my neck. I arched against him in reply, letting him feel my own need for vengeance. "Fine, your request is my command. I'll tell the officers outside to escort us to the gym. Stay here, I'll be right back."

A whirlwind of a million different emotions flooded through me as Nate left the room. I was loved. *Wanted.* And so was he. But the Vex knew how to destroy and take. I couldn't let them ruin this, ruin Nate's kingdom. I glanced outside the window as a few of the patrol cars pulled away. The red-and-blue flash of light faded as they cut their lights and drove off. But the familiar sense that someone was watching prickled at the back of my neck. My gaze locked with Captain Marks as he sat in his car, those familiar laugh lines creasing at the corners of his face. He tipped his hat, and something passed between us, something that I'd experienced before. I took a step closer, the kindness of his eyes reaching back into the depths of that same cryptic memory I had locked away for years.

A cold hospital room, the quiet beeping of my heart rate as a much younger version of him sat next to my bed. His eyes had settled on the fresh scar that Frank had torn across my throat.

"You're going to be okay, kid," he'd said as he threw another blanket over me. "I've seen a lot of really scary things as a police officer. But I've also seen a lot of good things too. I've seen people overcome and grow into superheroes. Superheroes like you."

I remember how the words had stung. Because Jason had been my superhero.

"And don't worry. You will find your voice again."

The doctors had been very specific. I would never speak again. Never sing, never yell, never even whisper. And I had learned quickly that I couldn't even sob. I was voiceless. Mute. I wanted to laugh at the stupid category I had now fallen under. Like God had somehow had enough of my voice, he decided to put me on mute. Like I was an annoying television program. Yet here this strange man was, telling me I'd be able to speak again.

"Lost things are meant to be found."

I'd stared at him, soaking up his lies like they were rainwater in the desert. Because I was seven, and I wanted to believe that my superhero and my voice would come back to me. A nurse peeked in to check on me, but Captain Marks sent him a silent wave.

"She's alright, she's just resting. I'll leave as soon as she's asleep, but you better take care of this one. She's special, I can just feel it." I'd slowly drifted off to sleep as he sat with me, the dream of singing and laughing with my prince calming me as I fell into oblivion.

Another slam of a police car door shut outside, and I stepped closer to the window, closer to the man who had brought me hope when there was none. I pressed my hands against the glass, his laugh lines deepening as he pulled out into the street. He lifted his hand in a wave, but something behind those eyes recognized me. He knew who I was and what had happened to me. Maybe he even knew what happened to both of us.

CHAPTER THIRTEEN

The day they took me to my new house, Samone had a cut on her arm, just above her elbow. She was quiet, just like Maddie. Just like I told her to be when Frank was around. To anyone else, it probably looked like an insignificant injury, taped over with a Hello Kitty bandage. But Frank had just sliced my princess's throat open. And he'd given me fifteen stitches above my eye. To me, that cut only meant one thing. Her quiet only meant one thing.

The house was much different than Frank's. It smelled fresh and clean like soap and cinnamon. But adults were good at playing games and tricks, hiding the beasts until no one else was around. I hovered over Samone as her mother cooked dinner, eyeing her parents, waiting for them to grow their dragon claws. Samone never said anything to me; she just blinked at me like I was a puzzle she couldn't figure out. Her parents had tried to explain that I was safe, and that I wouldn't ever have to deal with Frank again. But I didn't like the way that her father's muscles bulged against his clothes. They were much bigger than Frank's had been. Much more damaging. They also tried to explain that Samone couldn't hear us. That she used signals to talk, and that maybe I could learn them one day. But I didn't believe them at the time. It took a long time for me to believe anything an adult said. Finally, after dinner was ready, her mother sat us around a table with spaghetti and meatballs. The same meal that Frank had cooked Maddie the day she arrived.

"Do you not like spaghetti?" her mother had asked, frowning as I shoved the meatballs around the plate. I frowned back, not sure how to handle a mother. I'd never really had one, and I didn't understand this new strange dynamic. She was beautiful. Her brown eyes were soft and careful, and her nose pinched upward like Samone's did. But hurtful things can come from kind-eyed people. Frank had been charming and knew when to put on a smile. Maybe she was the same way.

"Honey, you don't have to eat it if you don't want. I can make you something else." She shifted in her chair uncomfortably.

"Samone, why don't you show him how to twirl it on your fork?" Samone's father's voice was deep and raspy. But what confused me the most was his hands as they moved while he spoke. The strange signals they'd mentioned earlier. *The elaborate lie.*

My eyes widened as her hands moved back and forth in surprising response. And I started to wonder if perhaps they'd been telling me the truth when her hand knocked her fork over, covered in sauce and noodles. She sucked in a breath as it fell, splattering all over the floor and wall. The kind of tragic mess that would have sent Frank's fists flying. I threw my chair back and stood in front of her, preparing myself for the beating. But they'd just stared back painfully. Her mother froze midchew as her gaze bounced from me to Samone. Her father's jaw hardened as he gently placed his fork on his plate. I tensed as he stood, his chair scraping against the hardwood before he towered over all of us. I backed against Samone, her body small like Maddie's behind me. His footsteps were slow but heavy as he rounded the table toward us. I glared up at him, ready for whatever he was going to give. A prince before a giant. But he knelt down at my feet and slowly picked up the fallen fork. He wiped the sauce clean and smiled up at me. A playful exchange I couldn't understand.

"It's just some noodles on the floor. Nothing to worry about. We're all safe here." I waited for the beating. I knew it would come, but he'd gotten another fork for Samone and placed it next to her. And then he returned back to his chair and continued eating as if nothing happened. My stomach sank at what this might mean.

Sometimes, Frank wouldn't react immediately. Sometimes he'd let it air out for a little before he would punish us later. Perhaps it was the thrill of letting us squirm. Wondering when he'd pounce again. Safety was always an illusion with him. He was careful to never leave marks on our bodies until the very end. And by then it was too late.

Later that night, I'd wandered down to the kitchen while everyone else was asleep. There was a tall cabinet filled with porcelain plates and glasses. Breakable things. This time I wasn't going to let the beasts hide like Frank hid his. I would command them out, because I was tired of playing games.

My hand grazed the biggest plate. It filled the length of the cabinet, and it would make a lot of noise when it crashed across the floor. I slowly lifted it, Maddie's terrified face flooding my memories. Her strangled whimpers as he cut into her precious skin. I couldn't let that happen to Samone. The cool surface of the plate slipped between my fingers, and I watched it fall, the pieces shattering into a hundred pieces across the floor.

Silence breaks.

It doesn't just stop like the noise. Noise *stops*. But silence *breaks*. Like the plate I smashed all over the kitchen. Just like Frank's face after I beat it with a baseball bat. Like me as I watched Maddie take her last gutted breath. If I had just broken the silence and said something so Maddie could have been safe. If I'd—

I froze as a soft figure appeared in the doorway. Samone's mother, her wavy hair falling over her shoulders, her face obscured by the darkness.

"Jason?" Her voice was a whisper. Soft and delicate. Disappointed. And for a second, I felt guilty. I hadn't just broken the silence, I'd broken something of hers. She was much smaller than Samone's father. Her beating wouldn't hurt nearly as bad, but at least I'd see what kind of demons lived in this house. My body went stiff as she crunched over the broken pieces with her slippers, her blue robe gliding gracefully under the pale moon shining through the curtains. Her face was finally visible now against the light as she tucked her hair behind her ear. I couldn't read her expression though. Sadness? Anger? I'd memorized every twitch of Frank's face, each subtle quirk meaning something different, a warning of the pain we'd face or the mood he was in. But I couldn't read her, and that felt more dangerous than anything Frank could do.

"So this is how we begin?" she'd asked, her dark eyes meeting mine. I couldn't answer her. She was using words instead of her hands. This was unmarked territory.

"Fair enough," she sighed as she pulled another plate from the cabinet. "You know these were my grandmother's. They are very special to me, but maybe not in the way you might think." She lifted the plate and inspected it carefully, scraping an unseen speck of dirt from the rim with her nail. "My grandmother was a nice woman. But she always kept these plates safely tucked away for no one to use. I never understood why, considering they seemed to be perfectly good plates." She tossed it in the air and let it spin before she caught it, her mouth widening into a mischievous smile. "She just stored them away, only to look but never touch. And while these beauties sat perfectly displayed for everyone to see, we ate on plastic or paper plates." She laughed, shaking her head. "Silly, don't you think? I mean, why not use them if you have them?"

She leaned in closer, and I fought the urge to flinch.

"You know what the first thing I did when I inherited these?" She eyed me, waiting patiently for my answer. I had none, so she nodded and continued.

"We finally ate with them. We got out all the pieces, the formalwear. The whole nine yards. And then I quickly learned why she never used them. They're *breakable*, as you can see." She waved her hand across the floor at all the pieces still scattered shamelessly. "Samone, being a toddler, pulled one of the plates to the floor, and it smashed everywhere. Formal chinaware with a toddler—I mean, what was I *thinking*?" She laughed, her smile meeting her eyes. More guilt started to pour in as I liked the way she broke the silence. With laughter, instead of shattered dishes.

"I was of course mortified. And Samone started crying at the mess. She probably saw my face, and the rest was history...so... I broke one too."

I did a double take as I replayed her last sentence. *She broke one too?*

Her eyes danced as she watched me process her words.

"I see what you're trying to do, Jason. I have this superpower where I can read people's hearts from a mile away. And yours is beautiful and terrified." I watched nervously as she dangled the plate between her grasp as she talked.

"You see here in this house, things break and we pick up the pieces where they lay ." She tossed the plate in her hand, and it scattered across the floor like mine had. Silence breaks again. "Messes happen. Mistakes happen. And all we can do is hold each other when everything falls apart."

A large hulking figure crowded the doorway, and if she wasn't going to release her beasts, then he surely would. Samone's father emerged from the darkness, his dangerous face set as he surveyed the mess.

"You breaking dishes again?" he grunted. Something behind his eyes was reverent, like the way I looked at Maddie. A king approaching his queen.

"Yep," she laughed, pulling a cup from the cabinet and handing it to him. "Wanna break the cup? I just broke its matching plate, so it's only fair."

He shook his head and tossed it in with the rest of the mess, and another loud shattering exploded across the room.

These fuckers are crazy.

"Now go to bed, and we'll clean this up. You've got a big day tomorrow. We'll be taking you to school to meet your teachers." And I did as she told me, tiptoeing around the pieces without another word. I'd continued to break more things for the next couple of months. Furniture. Walls. But they never let their beasts out. It took Frank months to finally release them with Maddie. And I had stupidly hoped and prayed that he changed for her sake. But he hadn't.

But with my new family, everything was much different than Frank's. Their touches were kind, not punishing. They made me feel loved, a notion that I struggled to grapple with for years. They protected Samone. They protected *me*.

After a year, I finally considered the fact that maybe they just weren't like Frank. Maybe Frank was just a beast all his own. And eventually Samone's mom and dad became *my* mom and dad. And they did just as they said they would do on that first night. They held me and loved me when I broke. They always picked up the pieces where they lay. Every. Single. Time .

The rubble from the gym was even more devastating in the light of day. The police patrolled the gym parking lot as Claire and I wandered through the remains. The pieces of my kingdom, broken and scattered like my mother's formal chinaware.

Claire's hand smoothed over my shoulders as she scanned the damage.

"I'm so sorry, Claire. You worked so hard yesterday and—"

"This isn't the end. We're not done yet." I watched openmouthed as she stomped over to the front desk and started pulling out all the stops with the cracked computer. A hopeless situation branded by the Vex. Until the cracked computer screen lit up as it rebooted.

"Okay, witch vixen, what did you do with my queen?" I laughed when my phone buzzed against my leg. Dread shot through me as I saw Dad flash across the screen again. He'd be calling me with news about Jesse.

"Dad?" I answered, eyeing Claire as she clacked away at the keyboard.

"Hey," he uttered on the other end.

"Tell me Jesse's okay?" I fought the sinking sensation that shot through me from his displaced tone. Distant and furious all at once.

"It's not good, son." Pain shot through me as I braced myself for the news. "He..."

A feminine sob echoed in the distance. It was Samone's.

"Jesus, Dad, what happened?" I demanded, my throat closing up, my world spinning in twelve different directions.

"He's going to be your brother-in-law. The damn kid proposed to Samone after he got out of surgery, and for some reason she said yes." Another loud sob sounded on the other end. "But he didn't have a ring, so I'll believe it when he puts that rock on her finger."

"Mr. Brooks, I'm on my damn death bed. I promise the ring is at my house," Jesse's muffled, choked-out voice shot back.

"Dad," I snickered, running a hand through my hair, "I'm going to kick your ass."

My dad loved the hell out of Jesse. He'd taken him under his wing just like he did with me and showed us what it meant to be men, how to pick fights that were worth it. And especially how to treat women. Jesse had been trained not only how to fight like hell in the cage, but how to be a man of honor and strength in any relationship we pursued. In reality, Jesse had been trained on how to be Samone's husband since day one, whether he wanted to admit it or not.

"Oh, uh, your mom wants to talk to you." Dad's voice straightened up like it always did when Mom gave him that look. My dad was a mean son of a bitch that could tear any man a new one, but when my mom was around, she ran the rodeo. He waited on her hand and foot, not because she demanded it, but because she was *his* queen. A rustle of motion filled with static as the phone was exchanged. My mom's soft whimpering cries replaced the noise, and my heart broke. She never cried. She was a strong woman, who put up with the strong man my dad was. A woman who'd poured all of her energy and resources into making sure Samone's needs were met. And for some unknown reason, she'd agreed to invite me into her home.

"Honey, are you okay? Samone told me what happened—" Her cries trailed off as Samone joined in with her.

"We're okay. We're at the gym now trying to pick up the broken pieces where they lay." I knew my mom caught the deeper meaning behind my words.

"Claire's with you? Is she okay? When can we meet her?" I peered over at her as she continued to type at the keyboard, her face focused with determination. *God, she's beautiful.*

"She's safe, and I want you to meet her, but right now might not be the safest to get everyone together. The police advised we stay separated for now, to avoid putting everyone in danger. He put us on protective detail, but I'm not taking any chances."

Quiet sniffles filled the other end. "I'm really proud of you, Nate. You've always been my little fighter."

I groaned at her nickname but loved it all the same. "I love you too, Mom."

She laughed when another wave of silent sobs racked the line. "Be careful, okay?"

"Yes, ma'am. You raised me right. I'll take good care of myself." I glanced over at Claire as she headed to the cleaning supply closet.

"That's right, I did. Now if you don't mind, I'm going to get off the phone and plan a hell of a wedding with your sister. Take care of your princess, okay?" She hung up before I could respond. I let her last words settle like dust in the sun.

Claire emerged from the closet, toting several cleaning supplies and a broom. But she stopped, her cheeks reddening from my apparent stare. I brisked across the room and took the heavy supplies from her arms, relief filling her face.

"Jesse's okay. Better than okay, actually. He proposed to Samone."

Her eyes widened, her lips parting with a gasp. *"Did she say yes?"*

"Yeah, my parents are pretty excited. They also said...they want to meet you." I held back a grin as her cheeks turned three shades darker. She wiped her hands on her pants and scanned the gym.

"Are they here?" Her brows screwed together as she peered up at me, those eyes wild and nervous, though for what I couldn't possibly understand. She was perfect. They would love her.

"No, but we'll meet soon, whenever you're ready for that."

Heavy footsteps crunched over broken glass near the back entrance.

"Nate?"

Art's familiar bellow blasted across the gym. He glanced at me and then at her before his face broke out into a ridiculous grin.

"Art, I'm sorry, but—"

Art held up a hand and shook his head. "No need to explain. The email said it all." He turned his attention back to Claire, ignoring my confused stare.

"Claire, my lady. I'm here at your service. Where do you need me to start?"

Claire returned the smile as she lugged a mop and bucket toward him.

"Art, what email?" I demanded as he took the mop.

They both glanced at each other until Art pulled out his phone. "I guess we'll get started without you while you read. You should give her a raise, Dragon Slayer."

The email read:

Your kingdom has come under attack. A myriad of storms plagued our castle last night, causing an unfortunate amount of damage to the building and equipment. We need your help to restore its good name. All handy men and women, please bring your work boots and let's get to work!

The following crews will be needed:

Drywall repair, cleaning crews, painters, equipment repair, mirror installment, door replacement, and electricians.

Come defend your kingdom!

Claire Jennings

I could hear her voice, strong with conviction in every sentence. Claire used the word *myriad*. I didn't even know that was a word. Her writing was like prose, and I would have done anything to hear the soft feminine trill of her voice say those lines to me now, reciting a fucking work email like poetry to my ears. Claire had rallied her troops to defend their castle. *Our* castle. And she'd used her voice to do it.

The email was sent five minutes ago, and yet Art had come ready. And another trickle of members flooded in the broken entrance, a few of them carrying work gloves instead of fighting gloves. A familiar buzz of justice and vengeance floating in the air as Claire offered a broom to John, the Knockout King. John wore a permanent scowl wherever he went and had one of the best reported knockout stats in the gym. And there he was, grinning at Claire as she showed him what areas to start sweeping first.

Something deep and primal cut through me as I watched her. A hungry need to claim her as mine as the other fighters gathered around her. And she would be claimed to be mine and no one else's. But I was going to take my time with her. Train her, let her body get to know mine before I took her as my own.

Our eyes locked from across the room, and another mix of pleasure and pain shot through me. I couldn't lose her again. Tonight I wasn't holding back with training. If the Vex was going to be trailing her, she needed to be ready to defend herself.

Because I couldn't bear to pick up the pieces where they lay without her.

CHAPTER FOURTEEN

Nate said that my voice was loud enough for the whole world to hear. He couldn't stop bragging to everyone who came to help that I'd coordinated all of this on my own. And then he kept using the word *myriad* randomly as he worked and cleaned.

"This place looks a *myriad* times better," or "I can't believe the *myriad* of volunteers that showed up ." Art finally shut him down with, "I could tell you a *myriad* of ways to shut the hell up."

But by God, Nate was right. Hundreds of people came out to help. They just kept coming too, bringing tools and trucks of their own. I had hoped that maybe four or five would come, but Nate had a fierce following. The community and his fighters loved him, loved his family, and they loved their gym.

By closing time, there had been hundreds of volunteers that came out. Some of them had never even been to the gym before, they just wanted to help a local business. And by late afternoon, they had restored the integrity of the space and then some. People had not only donated their time and their handy skills, but they donated equipment and training gear, towels and snacks, everything that we needed.

"You ready to train?" Nate's chin nuzzled against my neck as I restocked a few freshly cleaned towels. I blushed at his touch and scanned the gym. There were still several members left sparring although it was ten minutes past closing.

"*Don't you want to wait until everyone leaves?*" I cringed thinking about learning to fight in front of people, especially professionally trained ones. I could barely get my head around learning to fight in front of *Nate*.

His grin widened as he shook his head. "They won't be leaving anytime soon. Dad decided to keep this place open twenty-four hours to keep it protected. You should have seen their faces when they knew they'd be able to have more hours to train." He moved closer, his fingers brushing against my neck and curling into my hair.

I felt several pairs of eyes on us. And for a moment, I didn't care. More eyes meant a safe kingdom.

"*Okay, I'm ready.*" I nodded, bracing myself to be close to Nate again. His hands touching me, his body against mine. Pinning me...*on top of me.*

"Why don't you take a few minutes and I'll meet you on the mat." And just when I swore he was about to kiss me, he jogged off, leaving me in a pool of desire. I wanted to know the *myriad* of ways his hands would move over me tonight.

I threw my hair back in a ponytail and plucked a water bottle leftover from the volunteer bin before joining Nate. He had already removed his shirt, and my stomach twirled eighty-seven different ways at the way he watched me step on the mat. As soon as my feet touched the surface, I was *his*. That same predatory regard captured me as he circled around me.

"Tonight, I want to teach you a move, but it's going to get a little *intimate*. You remember what I said about tapping?"

I nodded, his words setting my body on fire.

"Well, this move, you might not be able to tap me. You'll need to open and close your hand or wave." His eyes lowered to a spot next to my feet on the mat.

"I want you to lie on your back."

And now I was completely engulfed in flames. I stared at him, my heart literally stopping as I considered all the things that might happen when I did.

"Claire, I want to take this at your pace, but what the Vex did today. What they could have done..." His eyes became pools of molten lava as he played out the unspeakable. He was right. We didn't have time for games.

I slowly lowered to the ground until my back was flat against the mat, my knees bent upward. His eyes flickered dangerously as he knelt next to me.

The calm Nate provided was unsettling. Each of his movements was careful and planned, and mine were jerky and nervous as my heart raced and pounded against my chest. My gaze trailed down his arms at the lines of tattoos covering every inch of his skin. I'd never gotten a tattoo, but I imagined they were painful to get. And he had hundreds lining his skin, shoulder to wrist, like sleeves from a sweatshirt. He was no stranger to pain. Neither was I, but Nate seemed to crave it like medicine. Or poison. And as he planted both of his hands on either side of my head on the mat, I prepared myself for whatever he was going to give me. That dangerous part of me, that scarred, broken part, craved it just like he did.

"I'm going to do what we call a 'mount.' I'm going to get on top of you, and we're going to address a few different maneuvers you can do to get out of it." He waited, his eyes watching expectantly for my permission. After a beat, I relaxed. I lifted my chin and nodded, our eyes locking as he climbed on top of me. His knees posted on either side of my waist as he sat on top of my hips. He leaned forward and pulled at my wrists, pinning them both above my head.

"This is a position of power. From here, I can pin you, choke you, and strike you." He left out the part where he could slice my throat open like Frank did in this very position. "You have a major disadvantage from where you are. You're strong, Claire, but strength won't get you anywhere here. What's going to get you out is using your body to maneuver you through. Finding those weak links will be your key to escape."

He sidled up closer, his knees tightening against my waist. "Okay. The trick here is to fight your panic and go against instinct. If someone's on top of you, you're going to want to fight and struggle. All that will do is wear you out, and you won't win."

I blinked up at him, my eyes wide as he hovered over me. I wondered what all of his opponents thought when they were in the ring with him. Did they worry for their safety? Or did they welcome his advances like I was about to?

"Alright, what you're going to do is lift your hips up toward me and pull your arms down. Remember, you're going against instinct here. If the Vex had you in this position, you'd probably want to avoid getting closer, but closeness is your ticket out. The closer you are, the more control you have." His eyes flashed again dangerously, his lips pulling back into a wicked sneer. "With the push of your hips and the pull of your arms, you'll send me forward." He fell forward, showing me the motion.

"From here, you'll grab my waist, lock my arm in place, and roll me over." He peeked down at me to see if I was following, but I couldn't. His scent, his closeness, it was all too powerful.

"Claire, are you with me?"

I shook my head, and he quickly got off me. "Let's switch roles. *You* mount *me.*"

Oh my God.

He rolled onto his back and smacked his thighs, his dark eyes practically glittering with anticipation. I turned over and timidly approached him. I fought the urge to look around the gym, knowing full well there were eyes on us. I hated the way color started to creep up my neck as I hiked a knee over and settled over his hips. His body underneath me felt like rock-hard machinery designed for every possible pain and pleasure.

"Alright, now pin me." He threw his arms up over his head, ready for the taking.

Jesus. Can he not?

I gripped his wrists and just wanted to die. *Just tap and call it quits.*

I didn't. Instead, I nodded, bracing myself for whatever he wanted to do to me. Without a chance to rethink my decision, the world blurred as he thrust his hips forward. He yanked my arms down as gently as he could and rolled me onto my back.

Now I was under him again, his hips pressed forward between my legs.

"Did you get that?" His eyes bored into me, his body showing no signs of relieving the delicious pressure between us. I bit my lip and nodded, though I had no idea why. I hadn't the slightest clue what the hell happened besides the fact that Nate had me on my back. My legs wrapped around his waist.

"Good. Your turn." I wanted to protest when he moved away, but it was only for a second before he mounted me and pinned my wrists again.

I swallowed. *Okay, here we go.*

With surprising ease, I repeated the first few motions but got caught up a little in the rolling part. He guided my hands, our bodies tangled in every perfect way until I was safely on top of him.

"You're a natural." He laughed, like music floating around the room. Jason had only laughed a few times when we were kids. He was mostly stoic and nervous, like any bump in the night was a source of danger for us. And it usually was. But now, his laugh came much more naturally. A pang of bittersweet pride swept through me at what his family did for him. They were able to heal him so he could laugh like a normal person. And by God, his laugh was beautiful. Hypnotizing and strong. My laugh was gargled and strange. Like a rush of soundless air that people tended to wince at. Or at least Carol did, anyway. And right now, all I wanted to do was tell him all of these things. Tell him with my voice and laugh as I spoke. Instead, I lay on my back and let him get on top of me again. His strength became more potent with every attempt. He called it "honest" strength. The likelihood that the Vex would be gentle was very low. He wanted me to feel the threat of a real fight. The very real risk of what might happen if I didn't get the maneuvers right.

"Alright, now let's try something else." He slapped the mat, the thick thud of his skin against the plastic somehow satisfying as it echoed against the wall. "Lay down again."

I rolled to my back, pulling my knees back up, and watched him. A bead of sweat trickled down his throat as he knelt in front of me, his knees at my feet.

"You've got excellent runner's legs, Claire." His throat bobbed with a swallow as he placed his palms on the tops of my knees. "They're going to come in handy for this next move."

I stiffened at the way he was looking at me, the way his hips were so close to mine.

"Now with this one, I'm going to be inside your guard...or your legs. May I?" His eyes lowered as he applied the gentlest of pressure on my knees to part them. I didn't remember trying to nod; I only felt the mindless way my head bobbed. I sucked in a quick breath as he pulled my knees apart and his hips drove into mine. I arched with the movement, desire throbbing deep inside me. He lowered himself on top of me, his mouth inches from mine.

"I need you to remember this move like the back of your hand. If anyone puts you in this position, and you don't want it, you'll be able to fight them off." His voice was low, his breath feathering across my face as he spoke. His hips remained still, but the way his face looked pained made me wonder if he was fighting not to rock against me. Like I wanted him to.

I froze as he brought his hands to my throat. The familiar grip Frank had on me once before. A rush of air roared in my ears as the hateful memory circled. The stench of alcohol and cigarettes as Frank clawed at me, tearing at my skin.

I've had it with you, you little bitch.

"Claire?"

My eyes snapped to his, but they weren't Frank's dragon eyes. They were *Jason's*. Nate's. I swallowed against his tight grip and nodded, fighting away the tears that stung at the backs of my eyes.

"You remember to tap me if it's too much?" His grip loosened, but his hand remained around my neck. I shook off the terror and nodded, forcing myself to stay present.

"Alright, while my hands are around your throat, you're going to grab my wrist with one arm and chop at my neck with the other." I followed his instructions, placing my hands where he guided them. "Now throw your foot here on my hip." He grabbed my ankle and placed it at the crook of his hip and hiked my other leg high over his shoulder.

"Alright, now you're going to throw your other leg around my neck and roll me over. Keep hold of my arm as you roll." I pushed off, keeping his arm tight to my chest. He let out a stiff moan as he landed on his back, his arm still clutched tight across my chest.

"Jesus, girl. You'd take me out with one of these, and I'm not just saying that." He laughed again, and with every melodic tone of his laugh, I loathed Frank more and more.

"You see the control you have right now? If you thrust your hips forward, you could break my elbow backward." I saw the line of his arm, his shoulder just visible in between my legs. His arm was thick and strong, but with one tiny movement, I'd break it. Like I wished I broke Frank's.

"If you threw this move on the Vex, they'd have no idea how to handle themselves." He tapped my leg, signaling me to let go.

"Do it again."

He didn't wait for me to answer. His hips thrust back into mine, his movements more precise and demanding than before. His hands found their way around my throat, and he walked me through the movements again slowly. Step by step. Touch by touch. Aching memory after aching memory.

"If you get the chance, Claire. I want you to break their arm, no hesitation. You think you can do that?" His eyes crisped with heat and anger as his body hovered over mine. I just stared at him, more tears stinging at the backs of my eyes. Fury and anger flooded through me at the fact that I was even having to learn this. I knew it was the only way. I needed to know how to protect myself. *I wanted this.* But I hated this.

I nodded, the thought of breaking Frank's arm flashing in my mind. He'd still be able to cry out in pain. Something else he took away from me.

His brows drew together as he watched me. "Claire, do you want to stop? Maybe we can—"

I pressed my fingers over his mouth and shook my head forcefully. I needed this, and I wasn't going to stop until I learned how to destroy Frank. Destroy the Vex.

His jaw set as if he could see right through me. But I wasn't going to have any of that. I stared up at him, determined to finish strong. I wasn't a quitter, and I needed him to know I could push through. Something in my expression convinced him, and he patted the mat next to him.

"Alright. Then let's take it a step further. This time, I'm coming at you with honest strength. I won't be holding back. Are you ready?" His hands lingered next to my throat, his body weight relieving the pressure. And in the moment, I was. I was ridiculously ready. And so I met his gaze and welcomed the assault. But as his hands closed around my neck, and his face morphed into Frank's, I became the scared little girl who'd just watched her prince fall at the hand of a dragon.

His claws dug deeper, the weight of them crushing as my life danced between two worlds. His breath coated with whiskey and hate. My hands pushed against him, forgetting the maneuver completely as gravity fought against me. I couldn't yell, couldn't scream. Instead, I slowly sank away into that damned eternal quiet.

His weight was off me in an instant, and I wheezed in a gutted inhale. Sweet gentle caresses soothed my face and neck. Soft, apologetic kisses trailed across my cheeks, my lips.

"Claire, are you okay?" He shook me, his hands gripping at my shoulders. I blinked up at him and flung myself at him, my arms wrapping around his neck. His arms quickly swept under me and hoisted me up. And suddenly he was running with me in tow toward the hallway.

He threw the office door open and practically busted inside, shutting the door behind him. He gently placed me on the cot, his hands carefully reaching for my throat again.

I was furious with myself. I'd allowed my mind to take me there while I was under my king, his powerful body pressed against mine. Nate had been so respectful and informative. His touches were loving and instructive. He'd made every effort to ensure I was comfortable. And I'd let my mind slip into the depths of our dark childhood even then.

"I should have listened to your body. You were so tense, your face...you've been through so much today." His shoulders sagged as he reached for my shoulders, pleading for forgiveness.

"*No. It wasn't you. It was* me." It was Frank.

His eyes darkened as realization settled over him. Guilt gripped every beautiful feature of his face.

"Jesus, Claire. I—"

He tensed as my fingers traced his lips, and I shook my head at him, my eyes wide and pleading. Before he could say anything else, I slowly leaned forward. I half expected for him to stop me as I pressed my lips against his. But he squeezed his eyes shut, his mouth dancing with mine as if he needed this as badly as I did. Just like our castle outside in the yard.

My hands slowly trailed across his shoulders and chest and reveled at the way goose bumps formed at all the places I touched. My tongue slid into his mouth, and he let out a low moan that sent me over the crumbling edge. I greedily pulled him closer, and he followed. I slowly lay back against the cot, his hand resting behind my head before it hit the soft surface. His hand slowly threaded through my hair and then grazed across my skin toward my breasts. I pulled away, and his face was pained as if he feared he'd gone too far again. I reached for the hem of my shirt and lifted it, pulling it over my head. He blew out a breath as his eyes dropped to my bra, his gaze hungry and desperate. And I was going to satisfy him.

I unlatched my bra, dropping it to the floor, and lay back to let him in. His eyes lowered, taking me in appreciatively, his tongue darting out to wet his lips.

"My God, you're beautiful," he whispered as he leaned over me, moving my legs apart and closing the void between us. His hands slid from my hip to my breast, his palm careful and reverent as he touched me. Explored me. Our breaths quickened as he pushed his weight between my legs again, rocking against me. The need for more was suddenly too much to handle, and I dug my fingers into his back and pulled him toward me, arching mine with his thrusts. His mouth worshipped my throat, still sensitive from his assault. I lifted my chin, allowing him every access.

"Claire, tap me," he demanded, his hips pressing into me as his fingers pulled at the hem of my pants. I dug my hands further into his back, refusing, needing. I never wanted this to end. I needed him to keep going, this scorching push and pull between us.

"*Claire,*" he uttered, his tone desperate as his fingers dipped lower, exactly where I needed him to go. "Claire, please ask me to stop." He wasn't asking. He was *pleading*.

I quickly tapped his arm, and he was off me instantly, our breathing fast and heavy as we cooled off. I quietly pulled a blanket over me until our breaths tapered off into the quiet.

"I can't hurt you again. Please understand that."

Our eyes met. And though I couldn't agree with what he wanted, I wouldn't push him tonight, just like he didn't want to push me.

"*Hold me?*" This time I was the one pleading.

He quickly wrapped his body behind mine, his heat blanketing me from every pain. My protector, shielding me in his kingdom.

CHAPTER FIFTEEN

I woke up, heavy-lidded from a mind-numbing sleep. Her body had been curled into mine, my arms wrapped around her all night. Her intoxicating scent flooded the sheets, the room. I started to stretch when a coldness surrounded me. Claire wasn't in bed anymore.

Sudden panic overtook me until I caught her small frame huddled on the office chair.

"Claire, you...okay?" I lifted my head, peering at the small rectangular object she was holding. I could have recognized its faded fold anywhere. It was the picture the foster care agency had sent my parents when they asked if they'd be interested in adopting me. They'd only sent one photo, and by the looks of it, I still have no idea why they'd wanted me. They had likely tried to fix me up for the shot, knowing prospective families would be seeing it. I had some strange-looking gel in my hair, and I was wearing a blue polo. They'd attempted to make me look like a *normal* kid, though that was the furthest thing from reality. I had dark black sutures above my brow from where Frank had sliced my face open. Dark bags were under my eyes, and I was scowling. They'd asked me to smile a hundred times, reminding me that families would be seeing the picture. Hence the scowl. Because I didn't give a single fuck who saw the picture. I just wanted my Maddie back.

My dad kept the photo in his desk, though I'd asked him to throw it away a million times. He always refused and threatened to end me if I ever got rid of it.

"You had the strongest fight in your eyes I'd ever seen," he'd explained after I found it in his drawer after training. "When I see that picture, I remind myself why I do what I do."

Claire's face was pained as she met my gaze.

"My adoption photo." It was all I could muster as she wiped away a silent tear.

"You look so sad."

That was an understatement. I was fucking *furious.*

Her eyes locked with mine, and something nervous and fleeting flickered behind them as she placed the photo back on the desk.

"I want to talk to him."

"You want to talk to Captain Marks?" I asked, my stomach sinking at the thought of her agreeing to his offer. She'd only put herself in more danger, taunting them the way he wanted her to.

She shook her head, biting her lower lip. *"I want to talk to Frank."*

I just stared at her, unable to form a coherent word. A single thought.

She stood, recognizing the fury behind my gaze. *"I think Captain Marks knows where he is."*

I stood up, and she flinched as the cot hit the wall behind me from the sudden movement. I tried to regulate my breathing, but the idea of her being in the same room with him again sent me spinning out of control. Better yet, *me* being in the same room with him. I could feel his throat under my grip, the wheeze of his last breath just like he'd tried to do to Maddie.

"If I see him, I'll kill him." My voice was barely a whisper, but Claire flinched again. her head shaking side to side urgently.

"I want answers, not revenge." She pointed to her throat. *"I can't ask him questions without you..."* A sense of hope and regret crossed her face.

"Why would you want to *talk* to him? After what he did to you? Jesus, Claire..." I threw a hand in my hair and faced away from her, not able to look her in the eye. She wanted to break bread with the man who'd sliced her throat open. Took her voice. Her innocence.

A gentle hand, cool against my heated skin, smoothed over my shoulder. Her golden-honey eyes lifted up toward me, her hair framing her beautiful tortured face.

"I thought you would have questions too."

I swallowed the ugly words down until they flooded back up, breaking open like a burst dam. "Like why he couldn't just leave us alone? Why he hurt us? Why he couldn't teach us things and love us like other foster parents might have." I couldn't stop the tears before they started flowing. My hand reached for her throat, and she winced, but she stilled as my fingers grazed the reminder of the kind of man Frank was. "Why he couldn't keep his hands to himself and take away everything from us?"

She nodded, her cheeks wet with tears as she tried to kiss mine away.

"Claire, I made you relive what he did to you last night. I forced you to feel the pain he brought, and I thought I broke you. How can seeing him help you? It would only bring up the hurt." My voice was hoarse and clipped, but at least I could speak. Claire was left silent forever because of his actions. He didn't deserve to talk to her, after he'd stolen her voice. Her childhood.

"*Closure.*" She brought her hands together as if she were closing a door. As if it were that easy. The moment that his fist first slammed into me, into Maddie, he'd torn down that door. The unrelenting never-ending portal that let the memories of what he did play over and over until you were left broken all over again. Every sight, every smell or sensation that seemed remotely similar to Frank or that goddamned house was just another monster coming through to take away the peace. There *wasn't* a fucking door to close anymore because he'd ripped it clean off its hinges.

Her eyes grew as she surveyed me, like she did last night as my hips were driving into hers. Her chest heaved with her quickened breaths as if she needed me to do this one thing for her. But if I did this for her, I'd be leading her back into the dragon's lair on *purpose*. Feeding her to the fire.

"*Please?*" Her mouth moved with the word, her plea clawing right through my chest and ripping my heart right out. It wasn't even a whisper, just a silent move from her perfect lips. I would do anything for this woman. I would walk through fire for her, and right now she wanted me to walk through the dragon's.

"Okay," I surrendered, hating myself and breaking for her. And I'd break for her a million times more.

Captain Marks's police escort was waiting for us near the curb next to the gym. He introduced himself as Officer Roberts, and his eyes were piercing like a hawk's. For that, I appreciated him, knowing he'd keep his eye out for anything suspicious with the Vex. That was until his gaze lingered on Claire's scar a little too long for my liking. The ride to the station was silent as I prepared myself for the hell we were about to walk through. Her hand curled into mine, and I squeezed it like it was the only thing keeping me together.

When we finally arrived, Captain Marks had an interview room waiting for us. His eyes glittered with hope as he waved us inside. *Just wait, buddy*, I thought as we sat across from him.

"I hear the community really came together for your gym, Nate." He shot me a wary look, taking in our less than happy expressions.

"Yeah, it's back in full operation now. But...that's not why we're here."

His brows furrowed as he glanced over at Claire. "Did you make a decision about speaking out?"

"*Yes*." Claire nodded, and I turned toward her, hurt that she hadn't discussed her decision with me yet.

"*But first, I want to talk to Frank.*"

Her eyes shifted to me expectantly, waiting for me to translate.

"She thinks you can tell us where our foster father is. Frank Stevenson." Saying his name out loud nearly burned my tongue, the bitter memories of what he did suddenly crashing around me all over again. And now more than ever I wished that door was closed, locked, and the key thrown right into the ocean.

He lifted his eyebrows in shock as his disbelieving gaze shot between us. His eyes narrowed at my scar, then moved back to Claire's.

"I thought I recognized you, Nate. At first I thought it was because I'd watched a few of your fights...but..."

I stole a look at Claire. She was shaking, her arms wrapped around herself in a desperate hug.

"The last time I saw you was..." He trailed off again. Unsettled rage began to bubble at the surface, though I wasn't sure why. I just knew Claire was scared or...hurting, and I wanted to shield her from the pain."

"The last time you saw me was when?" I demanded, my patience running its course.

"I'll remember that name for the rest of my days. Frank Stevenson. He'd nearly killed his foster children with his broken whiskey bottle, but a little fighter had beat him to it. A little boy who was so malnourished, he could hardly stand. But he'd found enough strength to fight a full-grown man." He leaned forward, and every hair on my body stood on end.

"Jason Ramirez." Every muscle in my body stiffened at the mention of my name. "The last time I saw you, you were in the back of an ambulance, shivering. I'll never forget the look on your face, boy." He shook his head, crossing his arms over his chest. "Just like the way you're looking at me now. So much *fight*."

"You were there that night?" I bit out, the foggy haze of Frank's blood splattered across my face invading my every thought. The flash of red and blue across the yard, illuminating our castle, now broken and crumbling as they carried Maddie's lifeless body out of the house, followed closely behind by the slain beast I prayed never woke back up.

His eyes regretfully shifted to Claire, who was now still as stone. Her pained gaze was locked on the table, as if she were far away from here.

"Then answer me this. Why did they tell her that I didn't survive? Why had they let me believe that she was dead?" His brows drew together, guilt swarming his features.

"By the time Frank came to, he was eligible for a probationary appeal. They were going to let him free." Every piece of me broke at his words, and I could hear Claire's shattered breath right beside me. "At the time, they believed that *you* were the one that attacked Maddie and Frank. They painted you to be the foster kid gone rogue. Frank put on a good face around people. He was a charmer." He shifted in his seat, clear discomfort etched across his face.

"That was until the clinical psychologist spoke with Frank. She saw right through his ploys. But she was only one reputable source, outnumbered by so many pieces of evidence against you. We were fearful that if he were set free, he'd try to finish what he started. And so the state agreed that in order to protect you, we needed to kill you so to speak. They had to separate you and erase you from each other's lives. To protect you from Frank and the trauma that came with it."

"You don't think that finding her bruised and broken in my gym after the Vex tried to rape her wasn't traumatic?" Captain Marks flinched at my question. But so did Claire, and guilt sliced right through me at my unfiltered carelessness.

"*Where is he now?*" Claire demanded, her face twisted with determination.

"She wants to know where he is." I glared at him as he shook his head.

"There's no way in hell you're going to go see him if that's what you want. I won't let you do something you'll regret."

"What do you think we're going to do. Kill him?" I finished with a sneer, my muscles rippling, welcoming the thought.

"Precisely," he replied, his attention turning to Claire as she started to sign again.

"I will agree to speak on television, if you tell us where he is."

Now I was glaring at her, but her eyes still stayed on Captain Marks, ignoring me.

I forced myself to look back at him, trying to form her request out loud.

"She says she'll agree to your...offer." *Death sentence.* "If you tell us where he's at."

The chess game had neared its end, the queen lined up, ready for the kill.

"Why? Why would you want to do that to yourselves?"

"Closure," I choked out, repeating Claire's disturbing term for it. He stared at us for several silent beats until he finally stood and headed for the door.

"Stay right here."

Checkmate.

He quickly disappeared, closing the door behind him.

"Claire, please don't do this just to see Frank. Please." I reached for her, her body tensing with my touch.

"Claire?" I whispered, begging her to turn and look at me. Finally, she did, her nervous eyes meeting mine.

"Is that what you really think of me? That I'm broken?" Her lip trembled as she broke her fists apart like she was snapping a twig in two.

"No, no!" My hands curled around her wrists, placing her fists back together, mending her break. "I promise that's not what I meant, Claire."

She pulled out of my grasp, shaking her head. *"I know I'm broken. But I wanted you to see the parts of me that were still intact."*

Before I could respond, Captain Marks returned carrying a yellowed manila folder. He dropped it on the table in front of us.

"Give this to the guard when you arrive. It's an official notice stating that your visit is permitted." He lifted his chin as he read me like a book. "You won't be able to do anything to him where he's at. The federal state prison is heavily guarded, and if you so much as make one wrong move, you won't be leaving it. They'll be ready for you when you get there. And Claire—" He shot her a look that made my blood boil all over again. "—don't make me regret this. I've got the media team on standby for when you return."

She nodded as she pulled the manila folder to her chest like a shield.

Claire looked out the window most of the ride there, the silence jostling between us. I'd fucked up. I couldn't believe I'd told her she was broken to her face, just to drive home a point. And it was the furthest thing from the truth. Claire was far more pieced together than me just like she'd always been. She'd been tossed in a house with an indifferent woman, voiceless and alone. She'd been kicked out of her home, and she'd nearly been raped twice. All of that, and yet she was coping far better than I ever could.

I was the broken one.

A uniformed guard met us at the gates upon our arrival and directed us through several more gates, armed guards stationed at every corner as we drove through. After what felt like a dozen different security checks, we stopped at the entrance.

"I'll be here when you're done." Officer Roberts eyed me as if in warning. *Don't do anything stupid. She's counting on you.*

Claire threw her hand over her eyes as she surveyed the tall, sinister-looking building. A fucking crow cawed in the distance.

"Follow me," a broad-shouldered guard instructed, turning on his heel without another word. He guided us through several halls stacked with empty-eyed men blocked off in tiny cells. I pulled Claire closer to me as they looked at her like I wasn't even there. Maniacal laughter bounced off the walls as they taunted her with the things they wanted to do to her. Disgusting, sick things as their arms reached through their cell railings toward her. Jesus, I wasn't going to make it long in here without busting someone's face open before I even got to Frank. I pulled her closer to me, blocking their view of her as we wound through the endless maze of cells.

Finally, we turned the corner, stopping at two large double doors, tall and sturdy like a fortress. A sense of satisfaction rolled through me at the thought of Frank rotting in here. *Good.* He was right where he belonged. Our escort flashed a badge at a camera, and the doors whooshed open, a cold and clinical smell emerging from within. The steady whir of machines echoed through the hall as we passed each room, a different, much more depressing energy filling the space. In the previous halls, the prisoners were unrestrained and hostile. But here as the stench of death surrounded us, there lay an eerie quiet that made me want to tear out of here with Claire in tow.

"What the hell is this place?"

The guard didn't bother to turn around as we strode through. "The hospice ward."

An unwarranted chill ran up my spine as we stopped at the door at the end of the hall. A fierce-looking nurse who looked like she'd seen everything under the sun emerged. Her deadened eyes swept over Claire and then me, her glower deepening.

"He's eating now. He usually naps after lunch, so you won't have long with him." A loud alarm rang out behind us, the sound somehow final and all consumed by death. Without another word, she shoved past me, rushing toward the source.

"Another one bites the dust," the guard muttered under his breath as he pulled the door open for us. "I'll just be outside if you need me." He pushed the door open and stepped to the side, waving us in. I held Claire back and moved in first, bracing myself as the smell of rot and decay assaulted my senses.

And there lay the dragon.

But he wasn't fierce and clawed like he used to be. I hardly recognized him as he stared at the wall, something empty and flat behind his gaze. His skin clung to his bones, his face carved and sallow against the stark light above. A tube roped from his nose down to a small pouch hanging near his bed, no tray of food in sight. He was being fed through the tube. Claire pushed past me before I could stop her but froze, unmoving next to me as she took him in. Her hand flew to her mouth, and her body convulsed slightly as if she were about to vomit. I reached for her, but she pulled away to steady herself.

"Come on, let's leave," I whispered, knowing that nothing good could come from this. Instead she moved toward him, the back of her hand still clamped against her lips.

"Claire, come on," I begged, taking a step closer.

His eyes weren't fiery yellow anymore. They had lost its heat. No more evil, just neutral and gray like his decrepit skin. My eyes fell to his hand, turned upward. The hand that had stolen everything from us. A large scar was etched across his palm into the fleshy skin between his thumb and forefinger. The place where he'd gripped a shard of his whiskey bottle and sliced away at Maddie's throat. At least his body was marred by scars from that night like we were. He didn't leave unscathed.

She slowly moved her hand in front of his face, but he remained vacant and still. She turned to me and pointed at him.

"Tell him who we are."

I clenched my teeth, hating the idea of saying a goddamned word to him. But Claire wanted to use her voice, and I was going to be her vessel.

"Frank," I clipped out, his name burning my mouth again. He remained unfazed. "Can you speak?"

Images of his contorted face towering over me as he slammed his fist into my body flooded my mind. I took another step closer, my voice growing louder, more demanding.

"I asked you if you can fucking speak."

Nothing.

"Good, a voice for a voice. Seems you got what was coming after what you did to her." The words felt so good as they came out, but Claire's hurt expression made them taste bitter in my mouth.

His eyes came to life, but only vaguely as they shifted to me and then slowly up to her. I moved closer, hating that he dared look at her. She was in arm's distance of him, and I wanted her far away from his claws.

"Don't fucking look at her, Frank. Look at me."

His eyes flashed with that same fiery yellow as they locked with mine.

Another brutal image of him slapping Maddie, sending her flying across the room, clouded every one of my senses. Her desperate whimpering as he stomped over toward her to finish her off. My mind a haze of rage and fury as he dove at her small innocent body shivering in the corner.

I was next to him in a second, my fist pulled back, ready to finally take him out like I'd fantasized for years. I moved to strike, but Claire was in front of me instantly, her eyes squeezed shut, preparing to take my blow. My fist hovered mere inches from her beautiful face. Her already bruised face, and she was going to take another painful one for *him*. I dropped my arm, the weight of what I almost did to my queen crushing me as I crumpled at her feet. She froze as my arms wrapped around her waist, my mouth pressed against her stomach, begging for her forgiveness. Her hands weaved through my hair, massaging my scalp, calming me in the dragon's lair.

Her hand found its way to my chin and lifted it.

"*Eyes up.*"

She stepped out of my grasp, turning back to Frank. A single tear left a blazing trail down his cheek as he watched her. She leaned forward, her face far too close to his, and brushed her thumb over his cheek, wiping it away.

"*I forgive you.*"

Her fingers brushed against her palm, as if she were dusting every ugly thing he'd done right off her hand. She was finally clean of him.

She turned to me, pleading I tell him.

"She forgives you." I didn't recognize my voice as I said the words. I could hardly process what was happening as she pulled his blanket over him, helping him settle into his pillow.

She forgives you.

CHAPTER SIXTEEN

There is a stillness in the quiet, as things and people settle in their calm. Just sitting and waiting, *dormant* in their resolve. Until a separate entity allows it to speak. A tree stands tall and silent in the backyard until the wind rustles through its leaves. A tin roof sits happily on top of a house, in the thick of a forest until the rain slams against its surface. And it *sings*.

The quiet is the product of cause and effect. A boy and a girl dance around a tree, and they laugh. A girl hasn't eaten anything in several days, and her stomach grumbles in protest. A man knocks his fists into the little girl, and she cries.

A volcano erupts after years of silence because the pressure and the heat take over, building and building until there's nothing left but to scream.

I shivered as Nate ran his hand through my hair, soothing me as the news crew set up in his gym.

"Claire, you don't have to do this." His voice was calming as he whispered into my hair. Nate's coaxing murmur was almost enough to relieve the building pressure below the surface. But the thought of the Vex hurting another person again cut through me, the heat rising again, just on the brink. And then it nearly spilled over my jagged edges at the thought of Frank.

Frank was dying of liver cancer. He'd nearly drank himself to death, and he was rotting in prison from the sins he committed. I had forgiven him, but I was still furious that I would never get the one answer I craved the most.

Did he regret what he did?

Nate had been right, though it hurt to hear it. In taking my voice, he also lost his. Both of us damned to our quiet on his behalf. But today, I was going to change that once and for all.

I clutched the speech I'd written in my hand, as if it would keep me from falling apart. But I *needed* to fall apart. I needed the cause and effect of the quiet so desperately so my voice could finally reach.

I was done being dormant.

Nate had agreed to speak my words as I signed. He'd gone through each individual line, showing me the specific movements of my hands so I said what I needed to perfectly. He helped me with the cadence, how to move my hands with conviction and purpose. To be loud in my silence. I practiced for hours before Captain Marks finally alerted the news team I was ready. *Ready to erupt.*

A smartly dressed woman introduced herself as Macy Hendricks. She surveyed me gently, her bright blue eyes wide and alert as she ran through the basics of how the interview was going to go. She would introduce me, and then I would speak. She asked if I wanted them to do my hair and makeup, her kind eyes sweeping across the mess I undoubtedly was. I shook my head as I combed my fingers through my hair nervously. If they wanted a raw fight, I was going to give it to them as I was. Surprisingly, she grinned at me.

"Speak your truth, Claire. Just let us know whenever you're ready." She clacked away, giving me one last moment to breathe.

"You really want to do this?" Nate's dark eyes were imploring and careful as he stroked my cheek.

"*Yes.*" I nodded, swallowing the lump in my throat.

"Okay. If you want to stop, you just tell me and I'll take you out of here, no questions asked."

I cringed at the thought. Nothing worse than a cannon shooting out at the enemy, only for the cannonball to get stuck in the barrel. He led me carefully to the pair of chairs they'd laid out, right in front of the cage. A centerpiece to the chaos I was about to unleash.

I winced as the cameraman flipped on a large canvas light, shining directly into my eyes.

I blinked, my eyes adjusting to the brightness. Nate's hand curled around mine, his strength somehow calm and steady. This wasn't his first fight. But it was mine.

Macy Hendricks lifted her chin in question as she looked directly at me. "Are you ready, Claire?"

I tucked a strand of hair behind my ear as my speech crinkled in my lap. I swallowed again, my mouth dry with unbecoming thirst.

I squeezed my eyes shut, allowing the quiet to consume me. Captain Marks had shown me the dozens of missing victims he assumed had fallen under the

Vex. Their beautiful vibrant faces. Their tired and weathered expressions. Most of them were women living on the fray. Women that wouldn't be missed, much like me. But they each had lives worth living. They had gifts to share with the world, and they had voices that needed to be heard. But not anymore. I was their voice now, and it was time to fight the quiet.

I nodded one final time, facing the camera.

The woman counted down slowly.

Three.

Unwanted images flashed across my mind. Arsen's hands wrapped around my throat as he pinned me to the wall, his fingers dipping below my waistline where no man had touched before.

Two.

His fist pounding into my cheek, knocking me to the floor as he pulled his zipper down and then ripped mine.

One.

The dozens of faces of their victims filtered through. Unsung futures, lives cut too short. The quiet they left behind.

Go.

"After we shed light this morning on the horrible and violent acts the local gang, the Vex, has committed against our community, we wanted to share a beacon a hope. A glimpse of strength in times of weakness." Macy reeled in, capturing her audience. "The police suspect there are countless victims, all meeting the same unspeakable end. Except one strong and very brave woman. Today, we hear from her, speaking out about the terrible things she'd experienced and how she's fighting back after breaking free from their grip not once, but *twice*." Macy's voice was calm and careful. I wondered if mine would have been like hers. Unwavering and steadfast.

"Today we welcome Claire Jennings from the heart of our hometown, coming to you live from our local UFC gym."

The cameras along with every pair of eyes in the gym turned to me. I froze, my hands and every muscle in my body forgetting how to function.

Move. Claire, move!

I lifted my hands, numb and cold from clamping onto my seat, and peered down at my speech. They needed to hear this. Speak, damnit! *Erupt!*

"*I'm tired of the quiet.*" I paused, allowing my mind and my hands to catch up to one another.

"The quiet that clamps over our mouths after we experience the unspeakable. Because no one wants to recount evil out loud."

Nate's voice was steady as he repeated my words, leading me through the night, my lighthouse in the middle of a storm.

"My voice was stolen once, from a man who was lost and full of hate." I pointed to my throat and sliced my finger along my neck, right along the scar Frank had branded on me.

"At first, I thought that the Vex tried to steal something that had already been stolen. But I was quickly reminded that even a broken songbird can still sing."

Nate's voice was fierce and deadly as he repeated the last part.

"The Vex has terrorized our community for far too long. Stealing women, hurting them, and forcing them into eternal quiet. A quiet I'm finally ready to fight."

I felt my lips pull back into a sneer, the muscles in my face fighting against the unusual expression. I never sneered. Not until today, as I cocked my head back at the cage.

"And now I speak directly to the man who hurt me. Who put his hands on me and tried to silence me again. I'm ready to fight, but on my own terms. You meet me here tomorrow at dusk. You can finally show the world just how strong you are, and please bring your friends. I'm sure they'd all love to hear just how loud a broken songbird like me can sing."

I waved around the gym at the freshly painted walls and new gym equipment. One of the cameras panned out to capture the renovations.

"You're in luck. We just recently remodeled all thanks to your subtle suggestion. Just in time for the fight of your life."

I leaned forward, my body shaking, my throat tight as if the unused muscles I used to scream were aching to free themselves.

"Unless you're scared you'll lose."

Silence settled across the gym as the cameras turned off. Dozens of people stood still, unwilling to break it, letting my words fill the void. And then the room erupted with cheers and whistles.

Nate's arms were around me, blanketing me as the world buzzed all around. My skin felt hot and heavy, but now it was molten lava in Nate's embrace.

"That was excellent, Claire. They heard you loud and clear, and I'm sure you pissed them off good and well." Captain Marks grinned as he clapped Nate on the back. My stomach sank at the thought, fear crumbling every part of me. I'd poked the beehive, and I was doused in honey.

"Claire, we'll have eyes all around here, okay? The gym, Nate's house—you just painted the illusion that we wanted them to see, remember? You're not actually going to fight them. Officer Roberts will be taking you to a hotel where you'll be staying until we capture these guys, okay? No need to worry."

Famous last words.

"Nate?" a gruff voice called out behind him. I peered over his shoulder, just enough to catch a glimpse of a man larger than life not just physically but in every possible way. His smile was wide and contagious as he approached. At first, I thought Samone was behind him, her movements soft and delicate like hers. Her hair was dark and brushed back into a loose braid that fell past her shoulder. But then the color drained from my face as I finally realized who they were. Nate's parents.

"Dad...you guys shouldn't be here. The Vex—"

"Fuck the Vex," he laughed with that stunning grin again. A smile that could heal, that *did* heal.

"And this must be Claire."

I raised my eyebrows at the way he signed my name like Nate and Samone did. His hand over his heart. Nate stepped away, allowing the true king to move toward me, his queen at his side.

He offered his hand, and I accepted. His palms were tough and gritty like a fighter's. His eyes flashed with admiration as he lifted his gaze back to Nate.

"My God," he muttered. "She's got that same fight in her that you do."

The woman placed a hand gently on his shoulder. *Step aside and let the queen through.*

He removed his hand, and hers replaced it. Soft and gentle. Loving. "Claire, it is truly an honor to meet you. We just couldn't stay away after everything that happened. We wanted to support you both. After what they did..."

Her eyes moved across my face. My scar. Her mouth pulled tight, her dark eyes flooded with a reign of fury I wouldn't wish on anyone.

"I'm glad to see you've found each other at last." She dropped her hand and looped her arm around Nate's proudly.

"The honor is mine." The fear and doubt that shook through me once slipped away as I looked at them. Two people who'd pulled my Jason up from the ashes and dusted him off, piecing him back together so he could become

new again. Unbroken. If they could heal Nate after everything he'd been through, then I could survive the Vex's threat.

"Nate, why don't you take her and get some rest. I'll be taking over here for now." He glanced at Captain Marks. "I'll discuss protection details with the police, but I think you've been through enough today."

If only he knew.

Nate nodded appreciatively as he wrapped his arm around my shoulder and kissed my hair.

"And Claire...keep those eyes up." I lifted my gaze to his father, his hulking form towering over me. His presence could have been just as terrifying as Nate's, if not more so if someone crossed him the wrong way. I silently wondered what Jason must have thought the first time he saw him. What that must have been like after living with Frank for so long. A man who used his fists instead of his words. I read once that it takes five good things to outweigh one bad thing. Frank had left us drowning in a pool of bad things; I had lost count after a while.

Once, Frank threatened to shoot us. He'd slurred it out after a particularly bad night as he swayed toward the liquor cabinet. A cabinet that somehow always remained fully stocked compared to the ever-empty pantry. We had no idea if he owned a gun or not, but the thought of him sneaking in and shooting us in the middle of the night plagued our tired minds. Did that moment equal one bad thing? Or did each worried, anxious thought that followed gather up to equal hundreds of bad things?

Had his parents proven that they didn't own a gun? That's one good thing. Had his father pledged to never shoot him in the middle of the night? I suppose the pure reassurance equals two. Had they let him cry and talk about what happened? Three.

And now I was calculating the power of grief. And math made my teeth hurt, even when it didn't have to do with Frank. I suppose there wasn't any possible way they would have been able to take away all of it. Those bad things scar you just as much as a broken whiskey bottle. And even after you've forgiven your evil dragon on his deathbed, they still haunt you in the middle of the night.

"*I will.*" I smile, silently thanking them both for trying to take away even a small part of the bad. Because in that way, I suppose the effort alone can sometimes outweigh all of it. That someone *tried.*

Officer Roberts was able to gather some of our things, and I was grateful he'd thrown my notebook in my bag. It had been lying on my pillow because I was writing Nate a poem last night. Officer Roberts had eyes like a hawk, and maybe he'd spotted it. Maybe he knew that it was important to me and he'd added it to my clothes and other toiletries.

The ride to the hotel was calm as my head nestled safely on Nate's shoulder. Officer Roberts carefully checked us in and led us up the elevator to our suite. I'd never been in a hotel in my life, but I loved the smell of travel. It smelled like sunscreen and ambition, whatever that meant. When the door closed behind me, a sudden sense of being alone with Nate filled me. Our room was dark and small. Captain Marks had gotten us a king suite. There was a chair in the corner next to a desk, but the bed filled the room. Nothing but me, Nate's very male presence, and a mattress made for a king and his queen.

And a shower.

I watched him load our bags onto a luggage rack, his muscles rippling with each movement. After the bags were settled, he turned to me. There was a distinct charge in the room as his dark eyes moved over me, his jaw popping with an intensity that scared me and delighted me. I wanted to feel him against me again. To let my body hum underneath him as he drove into me.

The Vex had nearly taken my virginity twice. I'd been hit before, but I'd never been touched by a man until Arsen's punishing hands took hold of me. His touches were forceful and painful. He was only interested in taking from me what he wanted, uncaring of how I felt. I'd never been kissed on the mouth until him either, if that's what you could call what he did. Even in his kiss, he took, never gave.

I lowered my gaze, taking in all of Nate. The power of his body. Nate had every capability of taking just like Arsen had. He was a fighter for God's sake. He was trained to steal his opponent's power. If he wanted to, he could take me now even if I fought him. But Nate wasn't Arsen. He wasn't Frank.

He was my king.

Nate *gave* when he touched. And God, he was generous. His body took care of mine, and he made sure I was present with every delicious ounce of contact between us. I winced at the thought of the Vex capturing me for the third time. I had somehow been lucky the first two, narrowly escaping their assault. But after the way I'd provoked them on live television, they would crush me. But not before they'd taken everything I had.

I couldn't have that.

I wanted Nate to have my firsts. All of them.

Nate's jaw popped as he recognized the hunger in my eyes. The same hunger that filled his own. I sucked in a breath as he took a step closer.

"Claire...I...need to talk to Officer Roberts. You just sit tight, okay?" He brushed past me, the soft contact of his shoulder against mine enough to throw my whole body into the fire. I watched as the door closed, leaving me alone in my own puddled mess.

But he wouldn't claim me the way I wanted him to. He was waiting for me to heal, though I wasn't sure if I ever truly would. My spirit and my body were permanently broken in a way, just as he'd mentioned to Captain Marks. Perhaps I was too broken for him. The boy that had been pieced together would never be able to love the girl still shattered across the floor. I quickly ran to my bag and pulled out my notebook, tearing my poem from the binding. If he wouldn't have my body as the gift I wanted to give him, then he'd at least have my words. My voice, soft and delicate on a piece of paper. I placed it gently on the bed and moved into the bathroom, closing the door behind me. I flipped on the water, letting the steam rise in clouds around me. I glared at the mirror, the less than flattering image that stared back.

Good *Lord*. I was a hot mess.

My hair was in disarray all around me, and my bruises were somehow even more highlighted against the vanity lights above. I cringed at the thought of the bright lights the camera crew shined on me earlier, my bruises likely plastered and shiny all over my face. I'd looked like I ran a marathon. And in many ways, I had.

Today, I'd seen the man who'd ripped my throat open and abused me and my prince for months. *And I tucked him in bed and forgave him.* I sat in front of a camera and provoked a ruthless gang who had tried to rape me twice before, on live freaking television. *Looking like a bag o' trash.* Oh, and I met Nate's parents. My *boyfriend's* parents for the first time.

Still looking like a bag o' trash.

If I had a voice right now, I would do that thing. That extra-dramatic thing that every teenage girl does when they want people to know they're pissed.

Ugggghhhhhh!

I tore off my clothes and threw myself in the shower, letting the hot water beat down on me. Washing away the grime and the hell from today. Rinsing off the grime and hell from my *life*.

And the Vex...

I shivered even though my skin was raw from the scalding hot water. I imagined Arsen's face as I called him out live, taunting him.

Unless you think you'll lose...

He was going to find me, I was certain of it. It was the consequence I agreed to internally when I agreed to speak out against him.

I wrapped my arms across my chest, hating how fighting the quiet also meant sheer terror that gripped you like the claw of death. I shut off the water, the heat consuming me to the point I couldn't breathe.

I couldn't have Arsen take my firsts before he killed me. I needed to give them to Nate. I flung the shower curtain back and barely toweled off before I threw the bathroom door open.

And there he was, staring back with those dark, crisped edges.

Wearing nothing but boxers.

CHAPTER SEVENTEEN

I didn't need to talk to Officer Roberts. I needed to get the hell out of that room before I took her right there on that king-sized bed. I mean honestly, Captain Marks couldn't have been a little more candid with his suite choices?

The day had torn through me, catapulted me through every possible pain imaginable, and now my body was hungry, starving to collapse into Claire, to slowly sink into her until we couldn't feel anything else but each other.

"Everything okay, Nate?" Officer Roberts asked as he watched me pace back and forth outside the room. I waved at him awkwardly and nodded.

"Yeah, everything's okay. I'm just...hungry."

Something behind his piercing gaze understood what I was truly hungry for.

"I'm going to need you to stay in your room, Nate. But I would suggest ordering whatever you want, as long as the kitchen is open."

Fuck.

"I'll check in with you in about a half hour, okay? And please remember, only answer the door if you hear six distinct knocks."

I thanked him and paused next to the door, my hand hovering over the handle. Jesus, why was I so nervous? I'd had sex before, but it meant nothing, and I never let it go anywhere after that. With Claire, it would mean *everything*. With her, I needed to be gentle and careful. She'd been through so much, and I wasn't even sure if she'd had sex before. Knowing her sheltered past with Carol, I imagined she was a virgin. But with the kind of lives we led, my heart hurt to consider what other things she might have experienced in the past.

Get a grip and get in your room so you can protect your queen.

So you can claim every inch of her.

I finally pulled the door open and let out a low breath. She was in the shower. I closed the door as the spray of shower water blasted in the bathroom. Claire was surely undressing right now, the soft rustle of fabric against skin muffled behind the closed door. All I could think about was what article of clothing she was removing first. The shower curtain swung back and then closed. And now water was splashing across that beautiful creamy skin.

I threw a hand through my hair, trying to shift my focus to something less intoxicating. *Captain Marks.* Yup, that was enough to refocus my attention. I strode past the bathroom door but froze as another splash of water hit the wall. God, what was she *doing* in there? My hand moved toward the doorknob. I wanted to find out. I wanted to charge in there and join her, to let the steam cloud around our tangled bodies.

No, Nate. Let the girl bathe in peace.

I dropped my hand and pulled at my shirt. I needed to get the hell out of these clothes. They smelled like federal prison and death from Frank. I shed off my shirt and pants and started to pull off my boxers when I noticed a sheet of paper laid delicately on the bed, its edges torn as if it had been ripped from a book. I slowly picked it up, the paper heavy in my hand like sketch paper. The handwriting was messy and clean all at once. Musings in the moment.

It read:

Their castle in the yard
He held her once, under the moon
And she sang once, to his captive tune
They danced around their fortress of hearts
Built stone, and tree and their most sacred parts
Prince and princess, hand and hand
reigning together over their land
He kissed her softly as the night drew in
He loved her fiercely, her heart he would win
She wished on a star that the dragon would sleep
But he woke with a vengeance, his claws digging deep
He tore at her skin and broke all his bones
The princess left mourning the love that she'd known
The prince still holds her as she drifts to sleep
But only in one place, a secret she'd keep

Out there stands a tree, shady and scarred
Like that of their bodies, their castle in the yard

I read it three times more, and then again, her words washing over me like the summer rain from her hair. Her voice was everything it used to be out loud, the written form of it sweet and mesmerizing with each verse.

Without warning, the bathroom door flung open. And there she stood in all her glory. My queen, her body still dripping wet, a towel barely covering her, stood shaking and beautiful. Her honey eyes skimmed my body, taking their time as they lowered until it landed on the paper in my hands. At her poem.

"Did you write this?" I choked out, my voice coming out sharp and gutted. I knew she had. I recognized her creative scrawl. Who else would have written about our personal past? But I wanted her to *say* it.

"*Yes. I wrote it last night before...*" Her hands fell to her sides. Before the Vex came and ruined everything.

Her golden eyes lifted up at me, desperate, her lip trembling as tears welled. "*Nate...*"

I stepped closer but kept my distance. Her body was so fucking beautiful. *Wet.* I was in my boxers...so little fabric between us...

"Claire," I whispered, fighting the urge to lunge forward and pull her against me.

"*I need you. Please.*"

I swallowed, knowing full well I wouldn't be able to fight this off much longer.

"*They...almost took my first.*"

I frowned at her signs. They were broken and pieced together like they were back in the gym after she'd been attacked by the Vex. Her signs had gotten so much more confident over the last few days. Especially after I'd trained her to sign for the live interview. But now, as she stood in front of me, dripping wet and shaking, her hands just couldn't relay the messages she wanted to tell me.

"They almost took your first?" I repeated, trying to confirm what she needed to say. She nodded, taking a step closer, the space between us dwindling, heavy and heated.

"*The Vex. They almost took my first.*"

And then her meaning was loud and clear. The Vex had almost taken her virginity. Her first.

"*I want to have my first with you.*" She took another step closer. I could feel her breath on my chest, her eyes pleading as they looked up at me. Faded bruises still marked her face and her neck. She wasn't healed yet, and I wanted so badly for her to be fully ready. I didn't want to hurt her anymore, and losing her virginity would just be another way I would break her.

"Claire, I don't want to hurt you. Please...I've already—"

"*The Vex would hurt me, Nate. But you would* love *me.*"

And I *would* love her. I loved her then, just like I loved her now, and I would love her for the rest of my life. But I didn't want her to want this just because of the Vex. I wouldn't let them take another piece of her like that.

"Don't do this because of them. Don't let them force you to do something you don't really want."

She moved to take another step forward but stayed planted where she was. "*Nate, I want this because I love you.*" She hugged herself, her eyes lowering to the floor. "*If they take me, then at least you'd have my first.*"

I was in front of her before she took her next breath. "Eyes up." I lifted her chin as rage coursed through me. The thought of them taking her after everything nearly pulled me apart.

"I'm not letting you out of my sight. Do you understand?"

She nodded, but her eyes were still begging me to follow through with what she was asking. And I was losing this fight faster than I'd ever lost before.

"Are you really sure you want this?" I asked gently, tucking a strand of hair behind her ear. She nodded, her breath quickening, her chest rising and falling underneath her towel. I dropped my heated gaze to her chest, following a trail of water dripping from her hair in between her breasts.

"Do you remember what I said about tapping?" I whispered, keeping my hands at my sides until she gave me the green light. Her teeth sunk into her bottom lip as she nodded. She gently reached for her poem, still pinched between my fingers, and pulled it from my grip. It slowly drifted to the ground, carefree and graceful.

And now my hands were free...

I took her hand and led her back toward the shower, the steam still fogging the room. If I was going to do this, I was going to make sure that I honored her and cherished her. I turned the water on as she stared. Her eyes were both nervous and hungry, like mine. She slowly dropped the towel at her feet, and my eyes wandered over her. Every feminine curve, every beautiful, radiant part of her. She was stunning, and she was going to let me have her. All of her. I quickly stepped out of my boxers and dropped them on the floor. Her eyes lowered, her lips parting as she took me in. When her eyes reached mine again, something darker was behind them. Fear perhaps?

"*I want you.*" No, not fear. It was need and desire.

I flipped on the water, letting the steam rise around us again. I moved the shower curtain back and stepped in, the hot water bouncing off me. But my eyes stayed trained on her with my every movement. Claire couldn't speak, but she said a lot with her body. Her eyes. I wanted to make sure that I heard her loud and clear if she wanted to change her mind.

"Join me?" I offered her my hand, a king requesting his queen.

She accepted it and stepped in with me. I closed the curtain and let the water fall over us, between us. Her body melded into mine as the water rolled over us in waves.

My lips met her skin, and I kissed across her shoulder, her neck, my hands careful as they roamed over her. I wanted to love her just like she'd asked, but soon our movements became desperate and needy, her mouth demanding as it crashed into mine, her fingers digging into my back, pulling me against her. I jerked as her hand grazed against my thigh, and I pulled back for a moment, allowing her to see all of me. Her fingertips gently moved from my chest down my stomach. I let out a low moan as her hand wrapped around my girth, her eyes meeting mine again.

"*Please.*" Her mouth moved with the word, her eyes desperately searching for my answer.

And I was going to give her one. I dug my hands into the backs of her thighs and lifted her legs around me.

"Hold on to me," I bit out as I turned off the water and stepped out of the shower with her in tow. My feet landed onto the towel, still pooled on the floor, as her mouth sucked and teased over my neck, her back arching as her legs tightened around me.

I threw the door open and strode over to the bed, her body pressing into me with each step. I lowered her onto the mattress and carefully hovered over her, my lower region pressed into her stomach.

"*Please*," she mouthed again, her legs opening further, inviting me in.

Fuck.

I breathed, stilling over her, imploring with my eyes that she was fully ready.

She nodded, her fingers clawing and digging. *Yes, yes, yes.* I shifted her up so her head was resting on the pillow and came back down, our mouths meeting again. I lined myself up with her, the pressure from her body nearly sending me over the edge.

"Look at me," I demanded, fighting the urge to push. I wanted to see her face to make sure she was present and willing. Our eyes locked, and time seemed to stand still. Her chest rose and fell with anticipation but froze as I pushed forward. I slowly sank into her, a soft exhale escaping those perfect lips. Her cheeks flushed as she moved closer to me, asking for all of me. I stilled as I reached her flesh deep within, bracing myself to hurt her and tear at her skin.

"I love you, Claire," I whispered and drove into her. Her hands dug into me, her eyes wide as I buried myself deep inside of her.

"Are you okay?" I hated myself that my pleasure was her pain, but those beautiful honey eyes met mine, and she pulled me back to her, my lips meeting hers again. She pushed against me, asking me to move, but I wanted to take my time and allow her body to adjust.

I slowly dipped my tongue in her mouth and began the subtle movement and rhythm that would follow down below. After several wild heartbeats, I began to shift my hips against hers, careful and slow just like my tongue. Her breaths were soft with each thrust, her body clinging to me as if I were the only thing keeping her together. Her body felt too good. I wasn't going to last long, each stroke of my hips, more potent than the last.

She was so beautiful as she peered up at me, her body wrapped around mine in every delicious way.

"*Claire*," I moaned, her breaths quickening as I picked up the pace. Her fingers sank into my hips, driving me harder into her. My kisses moved to her throat, my tongue sliding gently over her scar. I wanted to honor and cherish her. Every single part, especially the parts that were broken. Because two broken pieces coming together can sometimes become whole. She lifted her hips, allowing me to go deeper as I moved over her, my hands fisting through her hair.

"*Please*," she mouthed one last time, a request I was ready to fill.

"I'll pull out," I muttered, slowing my thrusts before I came undone. She quickly shook her head, her fingers digging into me again, demanding all of me. A piece of me I wanted to give to her, but only if she wanted it completely.

"You sure?" Ridiculous ecstasy filled my every thought as I pictured her belly round with our child. I...*wanted* to get her pregnant. I wanted to wait on her hand and foot as she carried a piece of me with her.

A weak smile lifted her cheeks as she nodded. And I started to crumble, my body driving into her one last time, her name on my lips as I spilled into her. Her body curled around mine, my mouth covering hers, as she clung to me. As our breathing slowed, I pulled away, searching her face, her eyes.

"Claire?" I whispered, my thumb grazing against her swollen lips. "Are you okay?" I gently pressed a hand to her stomach where I'd just spread my seed.

She nodded again as sweat beaded on her forehead, her satisfied gaze moving over me with approval. I slowly withdrew from her and kissed every part of her beautiful face.

She lifted her hand, slow and unsteady with the sign I so desperately craved.

"*I love you.*" She pressed the sign to my heart, as if she were trying to transfer all the love she had into it.

"I love you too."

Her stomach rumbled, groaning in protest. Her eyes widened, and the most adorable smile flashed across her sweet face, her already flushed cheeks growing deeper by the second. We had hardly eaten today, but by now we were ravenous.

"Let me feed my queen," I whispered, pulling the phone from the nightstand and dialing for room service.

"Room service, how may I help you?" a flat voice answered on the other end.

"Yes, I'll have three pizzas from the kitchen sent up, please." I peeked over at her, delicately sprawled across the bed before me.

"*And did you want anything?*" I signed. Claire's shoulders shook with silent laughter.

"Okay, yeah, three pizzas should do," I concluded, shooting her a wink.

A long pause followed until he finally responded. "Will that be *all?*" His tone was cool and heated with the question.

"Yes, that will be all for now." Claire laughed again as she pulled the covers over her modestly, despite the fact we'd just shared our bodies. Our everything.

"Your food will be up shortly." The line ended with a click.

Strange. Something about the tone of the man's voice on the other end didn't sit right with me. I mean, hell, I did just order *three* pizzas. His tone wasn't just annoyed though. It was *hateful.* He might have been having a bad day. People have bad days all the time. But it's not every day that your girlfriend just taunted a ruthless gang on live television.

I glanced at the clock. It had been almost an hour since Officer Roberts said he'd check in with us. I eyed the hotel door, every muscle in my body going rigid. Something didn't feel right. No, not just something. Everything didn't feel right.

I glanced at Claire, her shoulders tense as she read my expression.

"*Nate?*" She sat up, pulling the covers up to her neck.

I slowly lifted a finger to my mouth.

Quiet. Be quiet.

I slid out of bed and tiptoed to our bags, pulling out some fresh clothes for both of us. I tossed Claire hers and quickly threw on a hoodie and some sweats. I waited until Claire got dressed and pressed my lips to her forehead, quick and urgent.

"*I want you to get under the bed and stay there. No matter what, you stay hidden. Do you understand me?*" Her eyes were wide and terrified as she stood, refusing to follow my instructions, knowing what it meant. The Vex was here, in the hotel.

She jumped as a quick knock rapped on the door. Only one, definitely not six.

"Room service." My stomach sank. Officer Roberts would have never let anyone near our door, not even room service. I pointed to the bed again, pleading for her to listen.

"*Get under the bed and stay quiet.*"

I watched helplessly as my queen lowered to the ground and slowly shifted underneath. Hidden for now, until we got the police back. Once Claire was out of sight, I pulled my cell phone out and dialed 9-1-1.

Another knock rapped on the door. "Room service," the voice repeated.

"9-1-1, what is your emergency?" an annoyingly calm voice asked on the other end.

The knock was less patient this time, a fist pounding on the door.

"Send all you've got to the Jamestown Hotel. The Vex is here," I whispered.

I laid the phone down, letting the call continue before I walked toward the door, bracing myself for the fleet of dragons about to storm our castle.

The doorknob sparked as something small and lethal penetrated through it, like a bullet. Another spark and the door flew open, three masked men tearing through. A bullet flew past my ear, but this time I was ready. I grabbed his wrist and his shoulder, breaking his elbow as the gun flew to the floor. Another tried to throw me in a choke, but my elbow smashed across his face, another loud crunch ricocheting against the walls. Blood poured from his mouth, a welcome sight as I threw another knee into his gut. Cold metal pressed into my temple, the click just barely audible with the sounds of the other two's muffled cries.

"Where the fuck is she?" It was Arsen, his unmistakable raspiness grating against my ears. I laughed as the other two bastards clung to their injured face and arm, their bodies racked with their pathetic sobs.

White-hot pain sliced through my leg as the echo of a gunshot roared in the small room. The fucker just shot me. But I didn't make a sound.

"Believe me, we'll find her even if you don't tell us where she is."

"Fuck you." I lunged for him, but another loud bang of the gun sounded. I didn't feel it at first. I just saw it. The blood pouring from my chest. Right next to my heart, right where my birthmark sat. Where Claire's name sat. A hard shove at the backs of my legs sent me forward. I didn't make a sound as my knees hit the ground or when I fell face-first onto the floor. And I certainly didn't make a sound as I locked eyes with my queen. Her cheeks were wet as she held my gaze. Her beautiful, gorgeous face framed by her wild raven hair.

She started to reach for me, but all I could do was shoot daggers with my eyes.

No, Claire.

Quiet. Be quiet.

And then it was.

CHAPTER EIGHTEEN

My heart was numb as the fire behind Nate's eyes slowly dimmed.

Don't do this, Nate. Get up!

A flurry of footsteps ran all around as they searched for me, but all I could hear was the roar of the quiet Nate left. A deafening final silence.

Nate, please wake up!

Claws dug into my wrist and yanked, pulling me away from my fallen king. I reached out, my fingers grazing his one last time before they slipped away. Unyielding force pulled me up, but my body was limp, the fight in me lost somewhere in a faraway kingdom.

Forceful wanting hands dug into my jaw, his evil dragon eyes scorching me alive. I welcomed the flames as they engulfed me, praying he'd end me right here.

"I knew you wouldn't flutter away too far." Arsen's fingers traced my scar with a hateful gentleness before his eyes met mine again.

"I'm looking forward to *ruining* you, little songbird."

But he already had.

He drew back his gun, and it crashed against my skull. Pain burst across the side of my face, a heavy flow of red raining into my vision. But I could still see my king, and I *smiled*. The deafening roar grew louder, like a song that only broken songbirds sing. And then there was nothing but blackness. A familiar place I'd been before as I flew above our kingdom once upon a time. The beautiful freefall into the quiet until there was nothing else.

****

"Maddie, you can't show the dragon that you're scared. That's how you let him win." Jason smacked his sword stick against our tall oak tree castle, his heated gaze landing on me. Color rose across my cheeks as he watched me.

His eyes always seemed to tell me a million different stories that I wasn't sure if I was allowed to read.

"Jason, dragons are going to win no matter what we do. They're just too big and scary." I shrugged, forcing myself to look away from him down to the flower crowns I'd made. One for him, one for me, made out of grass and weeds from Frank's yard.

His footsteps were soft as they padded over to me, and then he was in front of me, so close I could see his sun-kissed freckles across his tan skin.

"Dragons aren't unbeatable. You just have to show them you're strong too." Those cryptic eyes darkened, like he was speaking another language again. The kind where his words had a different meaning, but I just couldn't tell what he was trying to say.

I dropped my eyes to the crowns again, unable to hold his blatant stare anymore.

"What are those?" he asked, his voice softening.

"They're crowns. I picked the yellow and white ones for yours, like sunshine for your head." But he didn't need that. The sun always hit his hair perfectly. There always seemed to be a permanent halo glinting around his head, just like there was now as it set, a soft angelic glow dancing against his dark hair.

"I'll wear your crown, princess." He smirked at me as he handed me a long stick. "But only if you dance with me." I felt my skin heat with his words under the summer sun. I glanced at the stick in my hand and back at him, confused.

"Why do you want to dance with sticks?" His perfect smile grew as he lifted his up, almost in a challenge.

"Not like a dance with music. The kind of dance where you *fight*." His feet moved quickly with skillful ease, his sword waving around like he was fighting an invisible swordsman. "See? I'm fighting, but I'm also dancing. It's easy if you know how to dance. Do you know how to dance?"

"Yes." I blinked up at him nervously.

"Then stand up and let's see it." He waved his sword like a wand, casting a spell on me I never wanted him to break. I carefully placed my flower crown on my head and rose, sword in hand. If he was going to make me dance, then I was going to at least do it in style.

"You can't fight with that thing on your head. It's just going to fall off."

His laugh caught me off guard. He never laughed, and the sound of it was beautiful and strong. Just like him.

"It's not a thing. It's a *crown*. And princesses always fight wearing their crowns. It's a rule that all princesses know," I shot back with a grin as I lifted my sword. "Now are we going to dance or what?"

His smile faded, his eyebrows raised as he positioned himself for the attack. "Let's dance, princess."

His attack was fast, but I was faster. I jumped back, our swords clashing, the metal clanking with each hit. Our villagers swooned and cheered as we danced around our kingdom. Even the stars came out to watch as the sun fell below the horizon. He lunged forward, his sword slicing far too close to my wrist.

"Be careful with your sword there, prince. These hands can't make any more crowns if you chop them off." His beautiful laugh bounced around in melodic waves again. God, how I loved that I could make him laugh like that.

"You'll find a way, princess. You have a way of doing things you're not supposed to." He leapt forward again, but I ducked, my foot snagging on some tall grass from the step back. I tried to regain my balance, but nothing could save me as I flew to the ground. Pain shot up my elbow, and I let out a pathetic whimper as Jason's sword met the underside of my chin.

But the moment he saw pain flicker behind my gaze, he tossed his sword to the side and fell to his knees next to me.

"Maddie, are you hurt?"

I shook my head but winced as I lifted my elbow. I hated being weak in front of my prince. He was always so strong, and I just wanted to be like him. I gasped when his hand fell on my elbow, but he removed it like he'd touched a hot stove.

"Just let me look at it, okay? I won't touch it." I slowly turned my arm so he could see, and his face smoothed over with relief.

"It's just a scratch." He reached behind me and pulled my crown from the rubble. He then gently placed it on top of my head and dusted me off. "See? Good as new." He grabbed my hand and pulled me up. And now all I could see were his sun-kissed freckles again, dotted all over his handsome face. He stepped back and leaned over, retrieving his own crown.

"Would you do me the honors?" He handed the crown to me, so careful as if it meant everything in the world to him. Or maybe he just knew that it meant everything in the world to me. He knelt down before me and lowered his head.

I held back a giggle at how easily he could steal my pain away. With Jason, all it took was a good dust-off and a simple request to be crowned as prince before his kingdom. I lifted the crown above my head for all to see.

"With this crown, I give to you, Prince Jason!" I announced, placing it gently on his head.

"Now rise and greet your kingdom!" I demanded, waving my hand at all of our eager villagers. He bowed, and the crowd roared in adoration. Flowers and gifts were thrown at his feet as he turned to me.

"Princess, they're chanting for us to dance for real now. Can't you hear it?" He offered his hand, a sweet but sad smile lifting his face. The kingdom faded, and now he was just a sad boy, wearing a crown made of weeds next to an old oak tree.

"Jason, what's wrong?" I started to pull my crown from my head, but his hand caught my wrist.

"Leave that on, Maddie. You've got to fight now, and princesses fight with their crowns on, remember? It's a whole thing." His eyes were darker than I'd ever seen them. They were like hot coals, burning into me.

"But I already fought, and I lost." I lifted my elbow to remind him of his victory. He shook his head, his shaggy hair getting in his eyes.

"No, Maddie." My heart broke at how sad he was. My beautiful broken prince. "You've got to fight the dragon now. And you've got to be strong. Remember what I said about being fearless?"

I nodded, my lip trembling, though I wasn't sure why. His thumb caught my tear as it escaped and lifted my chin. "Now eyes up, and *fight*."

My kingdom shook and crumbled as the roars from our villagers grew louder, more demanding. But they weren't chanting for us to dance anymore. Their voices were furious and unhinged as they cried out. Disgusting horrible things, rippled all around me.

"*Get up, slut!*"

"*Fight, you little bitch!*"

Pain sliced through my forehead as I looked for my prince. Blurry lights cast shadows all around me as the demands from our villagers grew louder, more impatient.

"*Jason?*" I croaked, desperately searching for my protector. But I couldn't speak. The failed attempt to call out fell into an angry sea of yells and screams. I sat up, waves of dizziness crashing over me. I held a hand over my eyes to block out the blinding lights, like nails pounding into my head. Faces were everywhere. Furious, livid faces that only wanted to see me hurt. Their eyes were soulless and filled with rage as they clung to a strange fencing.

"Get up, songbird," a voice barked at me from an unseen corner. I slowly turned to find its source, only to find a dragon, his wings expanded, his fiery grin twisted with evil and hate.

"It's time to dance."

His words cut deep as the impossible memories of what they did to my king resurfaced. I would have traded everything to go back and dance with my prince again.

Take me back to my kingdom.

Arsen's yellow eyes zeroed in on me from across the room. No. Across the *cage*. His arms spread wide as he circled me. A large dragon tattoo snaked down his back, his shoulders heaving as he beat his chest. And the crowd roared louder.

The Vex.

I was in the Vex's lair.

"I said get the fuck up." His claws tore at the back of my shirt and pulled me up, sending me flying toward the cage walls. The metal clattered and shook as the other men reached for me with their own sharp claws. I backed away, my legs shaky and off-balance.

"You said you wanted to fight, so let's fight. Am I right, boys?" A deafening roar followed, filling the room as Arsen squared his shoulders at me, pointing up at the corner of the cage. A small black globe with a beeping red light stared back.

"I suggest you smile for the camera, sweetheart. Thousands if not millions are viewing right now, just waiting for the show to begin. And just to warn you, I won't be fighting fair...so anything goes..." A disgusting laugh trickled out of his mouth like a puff of smoke.

He started to move, his thick legs so much slower than Jason's had been as he danced. His toothy grin widened with his predatory circle.

Dragons aren't unbeatable. You just have to show them you're strong too.

He lunged toward me, his powerful arms outstretched, ready for the taking.

But I moved before he could reach me, his body slamming against the metal cage with a satisfying grunt. The muscles in his shoulders rippled as he turned back to face me, the dragon tattoo heaving with his movements. His sneer was vicious as he met my gaze, but this time I smiled back and lifted my chin.

Let's dance, dragon.

We circled again, our eyes locked as we moved, fire and honey twisting and churning in the cage.

"Your boyfriend was an easy kill, you know. The easiest I've ever had. Guess he wasn't much of a fighter after all…"

I stopped dead in my tracks, Nate's lifeless body consuming me and tearing my heart out with it. His glower deepened as he lunged for me again. But this time I tripped him as I leapt out of his way, his arms flailing wildly as he plummeted to the ground. A comical boom followed, the floor shaking with his fall. An angry roar flooded through the dark room, and I couldn't help but scan the dozens of faces that stared back. Until I spotted a familiar face toward the back, skimming the back wall, away from the others. His finger met his lips, his eyes urgent as he moved toward a door.

Briggs. The piece of shit came to watch my ruin. And he—

Pain crashed into my cheek, the blow knocking me off my feet. I flew to the ground with a thud, the lights dancing above as happy cheers sounded all around me.

Take the bitch!

I tried to scoot away, but he was too fast, too powerful, his dragon claws closing in on me, tearing and taking. His hands clutched at my shirt and tore, ripping it, the fabric pulling against my skin. His hands squeezed my breasts, his hardened lower region pressing in between my legs.

No, no, no!

More fabric tore, his hands invading all the places I'd let Nate treasure. The places that Arsen now tortured and bruised. And then his claws were around my throat, his hips lined up with mine. The familiar position that Nate had me in on the mat, in his kingdom.

I locked eyes with the dragon, his mouth drawn back as if he already had his victory. I smiled back up at him, my eyes flashing with the pain I was about to unleash. The beasts that Nate told me about were inside me too. Very real and very strong, always ready for the fight. I grabbed his wrist, threw my other hand against his shoulder, and lifted my leg, using his body as a stepladder. One foot on his hip, one leg over his shoulder. I threw my thigh over his head and shoved him down using my legs, his hand still in my grip. I thrust my hips upward, a distinct crack of his elbow as I bent it backward, breaking it clean in half.

"*Aaarrgghhhh!*" he yelled, his voice strangled as my legs settled around his neck. I quickly lifted my legs and slid away, my tattered clothes barely hanging on for dear life.

"You fucking *bitch!*" he spat, pulling his arm to his side as it dangled awkwardly. "You fucking broke my arm!"

I was on my feet again as beads of sweat and blood poured into my eyes. I ripped a piece of my shirt off and rubbed it across my forehead, smearing my blood away.

"*And?*" I wanted to say. But instead, I threw the dirtied piece of fabric at him, landing square at his chest before it fell to the ground in a splattered thud.

"Oh, you're gonna fucking get it." He charged, his arm swinging loosely with each step before his hand gripped my throat again, slamming me against the cage. His strength was brutal, and the quiet threatened again as his claws closed in.

Find the weak link.

Nate's voice was loud against the Vex's shouts. *The weak link.* Arsen's thumb was the weak link, and I needed to break his grip. My hand smashed against his wrist, shoving his hand away, and I hooked my arm around his neck, pulling tight, just like Nate had shown me. Arsen fought back hard, smashing me into the cage with deadly force. But mine was deadlier.

I pulled tight, wrapping him in a guillotine choke, Arsen's strength waning under my grip. Nate's dimming eyes flashed across my mind, and I pulled tighter. His knees buckled, and I fell with him, unable to hold on anymore. My muscles screamed, my chest heaving as he fell on top of me, his body crushing me with his dead weight. I tried to push him off, but he was far too big, his weight stealing each breath as I fought to inhale, each breath a battle I didn't want to win anymore.

Bright lights swarmed all around as voices yelled and screamed. But the whispering stars above were louder as my prince knelt down next to me.

"Did you show the dragon you weren't scared?" He offered me his hand

and pulled me up with ease. The moon was bright overhead, casting light over our kingdom as the fireflies moved to their own waltz.

I nodded as he pulled me toward a dance floor, the orchestra striking up a playful melody that fell in harmony with the crickets and frogs. The music hummed, his strong hands pulling me into an innocent embrace.

"Let me lead you, okay?" And he did. He swirled me around as the music swelled and sang in rhythm with our steps. He knew exactly where to take me, and I followed happily, his hands never failing me.

"You look beautiful tonight," he whispered, his hand reaching up to adjust my flower crown.

"Thank you. And you look very handsome." I tried to fight the blush as he dipped me, making sure I never dropped my crown.

"You're almost as good a dancer as you are a fighter," he laughed, the sound harmonizing with the strings.

"I have a good partner," I replied and giggled with him, my dress fanning out from a twirl. His eyes burned again with a sadness that tore at me deeper than any dragon could.

"I wish I could keep you here longer." The music faded, only the chirping of the crickets remaining.

"What do you mean keep me here longer? I'm not leaving. This is my kingdom too." I pulled away from him, throwing my hands on my hips as he watched me in that knowing way. That patient knowing way he always did when he was right. But he wasn't right this time.

"I'm staying, Jason. You can't make me leave." I almost stomped my foot, but his saddened gaze made me forget how to do anything but cry. "*Please.*"

He shook his head, his hair getting in his eyes again. "You can't stay here, Maddie."

"No, *please*. I want to stay here, with *you*." I couldn't stop the flood of tears as they poured out. His hands were there to catch them, brushing them away as he kissed my forehead, so gentle and calm.

"I'll see you soon, princess. I promise."

Before I could respond, bright light tore me away from him, my beautiful boy left alone in his kingdom. Where the band only played one broken song that I could never share with him again.

I'll see you soon, princess.

The steady beep of a machine sounded above me, and the all-too-familiar cold and clinical smell of a hospital flooded the room. I slowly opened my eyes, the fluorescent lights above shooting right into me as a buzz roared in my ears.

"Claire?"

I tried to lift my head, but it felt like knives were stabbing into my head.

"Stay still. It's just me, Captain Marks." I blinked and shifted my head slightly to see him sitting quietly in the corner. The unfortunate flashback of his much younger self resting across from me flooded through me just like this many years ago. After I'd lost everything. And I prayed that I hadn't lost everything again.

"Claire, the doctors say you have severe head trauma and a concussion, but you'll be okay." He shifted in his seat, uncomfortably. "I can't begin to tell you how sorry I am that we couldn't get to you sooner. That any of this happened to you. The Vex unfortunately had an inside source within the department that led them to you. And believe me, they are being dealt with on every possible level."

Images of Briggs skittering around the back sliced through me. Briggs had betrayed me yet again.

As if Captain Marks could read my mind, he shook his head, a hearty laugh filling the room.

"Believe me, I couldn't believe it either, but in the end, Briggs saved the day. He was able to hack into the Vex's system and locate where you were through their camera." He crossed his arms across his chest, his face once again hopeful like it had been so many years ago.

"We took those fuckers down, Claire. Every last one of them. We have them in custody, and they are under some mighty heavy charges right now. They will be held accountable for everything they did. To you, to their victims, and to Nate."

My heart nearly burst at the sound of his name. My fallen king.

Captain Mark's face fell as he looked at me, understanding the question in my eyes. The fateful question I couldn't bear to ask, but I needed to know the truth.

Is he alive?

But all he could do was give me that same look he gave me many years ago. Because sometimes the answers are the loudest in the quiet. And I slowly fell back into it where I belonged. Where it was safe, and silent. Where no one could tell me that Nate was dead ever again.

CHAPTER NINETEEN

Seven months later...

Jesse pulled into the parking lot and shifted it into park.

"Claire, are you ready?" he asked, his eyes soft as he looked back at me. Samone turned around too, her hand reaching out and squeezing mine.

"*Yes.*" I nodded, returning her squeeze before pulling my hand from Samone's grasp. Jesse threw his door open and rounded the truck, opening Samone's door first and then pulling mine open. He offered his hand, and I scooted forward, my hand falling to my round belly. Nate's baby girl . *Our princess.*

Jesse slowly helped me out, one foot at a time until my feet hit the pavement below. The cold, brisk fall air hit my face, the trees rustling in the wind as gold and ruby leaves fell at our feet, swirling around us. Almost like they were dancing to their own waltz. The soft music from a dance I danced once upon a time echoed and faded back into the quiet of the fall. The soft smile of a beautiful boy lifted to the melody of the music as he waved goodbye one last time.

I peered around at the morbid rows of stone and flowers behind the wrought-iron gate. Cemeteries used to freak me out, but today, there's the distinct smell of calm and change in the air. And there's a peace in the quiet today that somehow made what we were about to do easier.

Samone's hand wrapped around mine again as Jesse pulled a small metal capsule from the back of the truck. *His ashes.* A stillness settled over us as I prepared myself to finally bury him and move on. But the wind picked up, the quiet fading with a steady roar. The steady roar of a motorcycle.

A soft kick nudged from within my belly. *She knows that Daddy's coming .* The roar of the engine grew louder until I saw him, majestic and royal in every way as he pulled in and parked next to us.

"About took you long enough," Jesse taunted as he lugged a wheelbarrow out of the truck along with a set of shovels.

"I know, I know. I'm sorry I'm late. Art was kicking my ass for the fight next week." His beautiful smile fell on me, his dark hair falling into his eyes just like the boy I'd danced with in a kingdom far, far away, that permanent halo dancing around his head like a crown made of sunshine. He hiked a leg off his bike and made a beeline right toward me, that hungry gaze setting me on fire like it always did. His hands found their way to my belly as more pressing kicks tugged inside me.

"Whoa, she's active today." His eyes locked with mine, and I nodded, lifting my hands to sign.

"*What'd you expect? She's a fighter, just like her daddy.*" I grinned up at him, running my hand across his chest next to his heart. Right where my name sat, next to the scar that Arsen gave him. Next to the bullet that had narrowly stolen his life if he hadn't been such a fighter.

"I've never seen someone fight so hard for their life," the surgeon finally told me after I'd recovered enough to visit him. "He had every possible thing going against him, but he fought hard and loud to live, and he did. He's...a miracle."

"*Maybe so,*" I'd agreed. "*But he's alive, because that's what he does. He fights, and he fights hard.*"

Nate laughed and leaned down to kiss the top of my stomach. "Just like her mommy."

His face sobered as he took me in, took in where we were, what we were about to do.

"Shall we?" He offered his hand, and I took it, his lips pressing against my knuckles, heating them against the frigid fall air.

Yes, let's.

Nate dropped my hand to help Jesse pull the small budding tree from the truck, still tied to its roots, fresh from the nursery. The oak tree Nate and I had picked out to honor the kingdom that sheltered us once upon a time from the man we were about to finally bury.

We walked through the cemetery, past hundreds of rows of stone and mortar until we arrived in a separate plot, isolated and peaceful. One plaque sat in front of a pile of mulch, the bronze name glittering against the golden sun.

Frank Stevenson.

Captain Marks informed us that Frank had died in the early morning hours last week. We requested his ashes after they told us he had no other known relatives, living or dead. And somehow, we both knew exactly what we wanted to do with them.

Samone and I watched as Nate and Jesse dug the hole, until it was finally deep enough to plant.

"You ready?" Nate asked, plunging his shovel into the pile of mulch. Yes. I was more than ready. I was ready to end this chapter and move on to the next. With Nate. With his family, with *my* family. *Our family.*

He gently handed me the capsule. I carefully pulled off the top and poured the ashes into the hole. The man who had torn us apart, but somehow had brought us together in his own way. He'd broken us, but we still found our way, under our tall oak tree. Nate and Jesse took turns shoveling dirt over his ashes, and then they planted the tree. A tree that would grow to be big and strong, despite the hurt that might lay beneath it. A tree that would shelter and give and change with the seasons just like all the other trees before it.

The wind rustled through its leaves as Nate wrapped his fingers around mine. His lips pressed into my temple, his love loud like the wind as it swirled around us. Loud like the heartbeat that thrummed in my belly, and loud like the noise of our lives, its moments filled with laughter and joy.

Because in that loud, one will always win against the quiet .

THE END

ACKNOWLEDGEMENTS

Thank you to my parents, for nurturing my imaginative spirit. I proudly waltz to my own melody while the rest of the world marches on, because of you. I am so grateful for my family and their encouraging praise as I pursued this strange writing ambition. It has been everything.

To my beta readers, my mom, Kelsey Morrison, and Curtis Borst. For being kind, gracious and allowing me to give my characters a voice, when all there was, was quiet.

To my editor, Sandra Dee from One Love Editing, and Pintado, my book cover designer, for capturing my work intuitively and gracefully.

I am beyond grateful for the passionate reading community that has given my work a chance. I owe it all to you.

To my husband, for supporting me and taking care of our son, our lives, and allowing me to sit in a room all day and daydream. I love you, and I am forever grateful for you.

And to this godforsaken year, 2020. You've pushed me to go darker, dig deeper into the places I was too scared to go. You've helped me to write without holding back. To remind me that each day is precious and it's important to use your voice before it's too late.

About the Author

Dana Hoff lives creatively and enthusiastically in Missouri with her husband and son. After a brush with death, she started writing to heal but soon began to find this daydreaming business more of a necessity. She has also written *The Pavers*, a paranormal romance set in the historic district of St. Charles, Missouri.

Dana can be found online at:
danahoffauthor.wixsite.com/books
Facebook @DanaHoffAuthor
Instagram @DanaHoffAuthor
Twitter @DanaHoffAuthor

THE PAVERS

Georgia Lee Scott has spent most of her adult life in the historic town of St. Charles, Missouri, following the safe, traditional path she thought she was always meant to pursue. After all, life was just a mindless game of checking off boxes, and then you die.

Until she did.

To her horror, she finds herself in the hospital with no memory of what happened to her or the last three years she spent at her alleged place of employment. Even more puzzling are the memories she does have...when she was supposed to be **dead**. Now, she's forced to break free from her past, but nothing could prepare her for the hidden network of people and powers she'll discover as she learns more about who...or *what* she's becoming.

With the help of a dangerous looking ex-Marine and a mysterious young boy, she will get to the bottom of what happened to her. Together, they are bound to find the paved path that ultimately leads to their destiny.

www.ingramcontent.com/pod-product-compliance
Lightning Source LLC
Chambersburg PA
CBHW030746110726
47900CB00008B/2469